# Trigon's View

A Christian Sci-Fi Novel

Evan Prickett / Rick Chambers

ARCHDEACON BOOKS
A Publishing Imprint of
WOODY NORMAN LLC

ISBN-13: 978-0-692-079393

Picture Image Artwork
Rick Chambers
*pixabay/prisma filter*
*photoartz/prisma filter*

# CONTENTS

## CHAPTER 1: CONVERSATIONS

"Don't talk to me like that!"

"Whattaya mean?"

"Like I'm stupid or something."

"You're not stupid but you're still not gettin' it. Parkour!"

"Huh?"

"Parkour!" Louder, Blake explained, "Ya know, Parkour!"

"Nope, not yet. Keep it comin', Blake."

"Parkour," Blake defined, "is basically overcoming obstacles in the quickest way possible by jumping, climbing, and running, typically in an urban setting. Everybody knows that!"

"Not exactly everybody," Dawson mumbled, shaking his head.

"All right. Here's an example, Blockhead."

"What did you call me?"

"Let me show you. Some *Blockheads* need visuals."

"BLOCKHEAD!?"

Blake hopped to his feet, sprinting forward to a nearby alley. Two massive buildings, brick and concrete, stretching upward, squeezed together almost touching, as Blake ascended, quickly grabbing available projections, fire escape bars, protruding items, finally lighting upon a welcomed ledge. He spun around. Straining forward, Blake pulled off a *cat leap* to an adjacent building's ledge. He followed the ledge at a brisk pace. Blake looked ahead at a dead-end drop back down to Dawson, but he wasn't finished. With rapid fire, he popped himself upwards off the ridge with his right foot and gave a more forceful kick with his left leg, pushing off the concrete building's wall, launching himself back over the alley. He lighted on the opposing building's rooftop edge, scraping its brick surface, which he grasped firmly before hoisting himself up over it. Dawson followed alongside Blake, stretching skywards as he squinted in the bright morning glare. Blake found his footing soon enough and was moving like a cheetah in familiar territory, vaulting over AC units and dodging other obstacles while Dawson could barely keep pace.

Blake quickly looked for a continual path that could sustain his momentum. A brilliant possibility, yes, an unpopular parkour maneuver came to mind! Blake deftly merged his gait onto a foot-wide ledge to gain better perspective, ignoring a twenty-foot plummet inches to his left. He scanned several buildings ahead, traversing each precariously, as he eyed an intersection of alleyways which formed a cross, dividing the two buildings into massive quadrants. Blake was closing in toward the edge of a three-story rooftop, and in his swift trek,

2

a blur of brick and concrete, several adjacent buildings towered higher than expected, which would abruptly conclude in dangerously jagged rooftop edges. But wait, there, diagonally across from an emergency escape ladder, lay a perfectly placed brick wall; it compelled him forward.

"Come on, make this look epic!" Blake thought, digging deep within himself to scavenge any remaining energy he had left, to pull off the stunt. Blake had been depleted before. Many times. Exhaustion, muscle-pulling, *out-of-breath endurance, a running ahead to achieve his goal* had become his way of life. Blake simply ran, endured, *parkoured* and achieved proficiency to delight his Lord. Parkour stunts, practiced alone, in secret, held for Blake an endurance run that had become a kind of prayer, compelling him forward, as he gained ability which encouraged Blake to pick up speed, with balance better than a cat, to become unafraid, to push, to get beyond ordinary limits to achieve whatever goal stood enticingly before him! Yes, all this had indeed become his way of life! Blake excelled in highly competitive weekend games, running up and down the soccer field in amazing melting speed, zigzagging his way to victory beyond exhaustion, to the dismay of opposing teams, and the pride of teammates! Blake was rumored to possess an *excessive* endurance, an *I'll never give up* endurance of body, heart and spirit! He had a good heart, a strong heart for the Lord, as he pressed into God for more. Now his breathing, far beyond drawing hard for the next intake of air, had become measured, quite measured, possessing a solid peace, a peace with texture, even now in his blurring rapid descent.

Fifty yards became thirty yards, ten yards, five yards. Bam! He leapt at the building's corner at full charging speed, leapt, soaring into the air at gravity's mercy. He rocked backwards, allowing a beautiful *backflip gainer*, spinning mid-air. Suddenly, a blur of clanging metal flooring and hard cement slapped Blake's whole body. He tucked so his roll would spread pain evenly on all sides. As his pain evaporated, Blake was back on his feet. He shot a quick glance at Dawson, below. Astonishment joined wonder on Dawson's face, as his mouth stood agape. Blake smirked as he jumped off to the right to conclude his parkour adventure, landing on a thick window sill. From there, he grabbed a conduit, swinging over to a fire ladder, which with his weight, slowly lowered him to a narrow alley floor inches from Dawson.

"Now that's parkour, Blockhead!!"

"Parkour? That's more like, I dunno, *death wish* to me! Don't get me wrong, what you just did straight up defies physics. But I mean, come on, HOW STUPID ARE YOU? There were at least half a dozen times you could have died."

Exhausted, Dawson bent over, shaking his head. There was a long pause. Blake, easily retrieving normal breathing, replied, "It's actually very therapeutic. Helps deal with stress, angst, anger, anything, really. It's such a freeing feeling being so close to death but never allowing it to take you in."

"Well, here's my take on things, Blake! You're *insane*. You're doing nothing more than playing with fire. Yep, yours is a business for idiots and idiots alone!" Dawson shouted.

"Dos, it's not that. It's more. You say *idiot business*! You're wrong!" countered Blake.

Dawson laughed, "Well, I couldn't keep up. Look at me, still wheezing like a fool. You were runnin' pretty fast, and those moves! Amazing, Bro!"

"It's not me, Dos. Well, it's me, I know, but it's more than me. It's Him, you know, the Lord. I dunno. It's like my running, *my parkour*, is a gift from Him and when I open it, well, it's crazy I guess and it's hard to explain. But when I parkour I want to become the best I can be, to go beyond myself, to somehow delight God who has given me this ability, to not give up, to run faster, to run better. You know, Dos, God wants to give all of us amazing gifts! All you have to do is to receive. But most have turned their backs on God. You see, God wants all of us to know that He's not on some distant planet because He doesn't give a flip. He's here right now because He does care!" said Blake.

"More God-stuff, Blake?" complained Dawson. "You get on a roll and..."

"I'll get back to that later." interrupted Blake, changing the subject, "Hey, take a look at our new inventory."

"Oskar's new gadgets! I completely forgot about that!" admitted Dawson. "Let's sit on the curb here; show 'em to me." Dawson took his seat as Blake removed his backpack.

"Sure, here are some brand-new items and two updates." Blake plunked down his unzipped bag.

"Supercharged 'mallow shooter, this is sweet, and what's this? It reads: chameleon ghillie suit, totally awesome for manhunt and, ah, yes, I have one, wait, no, two mini air converters. Basically, whatever you inhale, whether it be gas or water, these devices will filter out all harmful elements, providing life-giving, invigorating, pure oxygen. Roughly, it's the same air we're breathing right now."

Blake inhaled and exhaled deeply. He tossed the little mouth guard up in the air and caught it. "These babies are factory fresh, completed this week! Oskar's second model; his first one leaked and had other issues. Yep, he needed to upgrade them, that's for sure."

"This is so cool, right? Well since we're done here, let's go to your place and check out the rest! Maybe go for a swim afterwards?" suggested Dawson.

"Ha! Oh no, you're not getting out of it that easily." Blake pulled his friend back to his feet. Dawson knew he was catching on.

"I have no earthly clue what you're talkin' about." Dawson responded sheepishly, brushing off his jeans.

"It's now your turn!" Blake gestured to the open street. You still have to show me those wicked parkour skills, right? Go ahead, Bro."

Dawson, perplexed, embarrassed, choked, "Uh, um, who?" He spun around, hoping there was someone else his friend had in mind. Blake pointed at Dawson and poked him, a mild battering ram into Dawson's gut.

"You, dummy."

"Um. Naw. I'm good." Stepping away, Dawson laughed as he defensively raised his hands.

"It's cool that you've got your own thing, but it's definitely not for me, man! Not now. Not ever. Get me, Blake?"

"Oh, come on! You got the stuff. Just do it!" Dawson wouldn't budge.

"Oh, come on! I thought we came here to parkour. Well, this is it!"

"Yeah, but I thought we would have brought something like pads in case ya fall. And for the record, I never agreed to jump off some eighty-foot building. How about the playground next to the skatepark just down the street, do somersaults down the slide or something mild like that." Blake was growing impatient.

He yelled out in his best *drill sergeant* voice, "Increase your *manpoints*, Dos!! Parkour. PARKOUR NOW!!

"The day *fastfoods* become vegetarian. Crazy, not happenin', man." Dawson grumbled unfazed. There was a long pause until their silence broke at the sound of gunfire!

Dawson ducked as he felt pain splintering down his face as an enemy's sniper paintball whistled its insult at his temple. He slapped his hands to the wound, howling in reply. Blake instinctively dove behind a tree, grabbed Dawson, pulling his friend protectively to the ground!

"Dos! Dos! You okay?" barked Blake above the military shouts of teenage boys and their pellets whizzing through the air.

"Yeah. Yeah, I'm fine." Dawson's eyes were now red with pain.

"It's just a stupid paintball anyway!"

"Oh, man! Dos, you're bleeding!"

"No, stupid! Its red paint, for cryin' out loud!"

"Sorry. Let's...owww! Crud, I'm gonna beat the living..."

"BLAKE! LOOK OUT!" Another paintball whistled by Blake's ear.

"COME ON, LET'S GET OUTTA HERE!"

"All right, come on! Get in that trash can. It's empty." Dawson threw himself onto the sunbaked can, which clumsily extended over the curb. Dos was ready to jump in first. Blake slammed the can to its side, quickly removing its lid, allowing Dos to scramble in. Blake wielded its lid as a shield against an army of paintballs, backing up carefully into the occupied trash can. He fit himself inside, quickly pulling his shield shut.

"Hey, Dos! Rock forward! Now!" he yelled. The duo began to rock back and forth, back and forth. They could hear pellets pummel their metal can, growing stronger and louder by the second!

"Faster, Blake, faster! They're comin'." The two rocked with all their might. One, two...here we go!

The trash can groaned as it went from level ground to a steep decline, then, rapidly gaining momentum, achieved its noisy, bumpy, yet protective-metal-ride-on-cement-speed!

"AHHHHHHHH!" the boys screamed, skittering across a sidewalk. Painful bumps of curbs and potholes defined their *speedway.*

"WHAT ARE WE DOING? WE ARE GONNA DIE! AHHHHHH!" cried Dawson.

"NO! NOT YET!" yelled Blake. He knew that they were now far enough from the gang. Forcefully, he kicked the lid open, revealing the spinning city.

"DOS! HOLD ON TO ME!"

"OKAY!"

"Wait for it, wait for it..." Blake murmured to himself frantically, knowing what was coming up just down the sidewalk: The Skate Park. Beyond that, a steep drop to the lake. By the sounds of skateboard screeches and people falling off their boards trying not to hit the rocketing trashcan, Blake knew they were almost there.

"WAIT FOR IT, WAIT FOR IT..." Then came the big ramp. The can sped straight up, swiftly releasing high into the air, then careening over a low fence. Slow motion, an eye-closing, stomach-dropping moment of mid-air screaming. And then, a full plummet to the waters!

"KICK NOW!" Blake shouted. Both he and Dawson kicked the bottom of the can out from under them, and as they expected, a drop to open waters.

"SPLASH!"

The two boys hit the water hard. Dawson immediately scrambled for the surface, but Blake yanked him back down. Dawson screamed a gargled, "COME ON!"

Blake pulled his backpack in full swing across his shoulder, hurriedly searching its contents. He found the air converters and jabbed one into Dawson's mouth and one into his. He prayed Oskar's inventions would work, exhaled his remaining air, then for the moment of truth, breathed in, deeply. The water was sucked into the air converters, and miraculously the hydrogen atoms were caught in the filtration system and a near perfect ratio of needed atoms entered Blake's lungs. Relieved, he thanked God and turned to Dawson, who gave him a nod and a thumbs-up. The duo allowed themselves to sink to the bottom of the lake floor, ignoring the painful pressure in their ears. Blake looked up the wall that went high above the water's surface. On its top perched a rusted chain-link fence.

Both he and Dawson sat on the sandy floor as they looked up to see if their attackers would come searching for them. Blake well knew the gang led by Rodney Drooge, a fierce bully who delighted in targeting him. Blake had switched to a different high school but, even then, Rodney still went after him from time to time, intimidating anyone under 18, city-wide. Moments later, Blake and Dawson heard a muffled commotion and the clattering noise of a fence shaking above the water's surface. Ugly thugs now peered through the fence, searching for the two boys with focused scrutiny.

"I swear, that's what I saw! They jumped outta the can!" Rodney shouted. "We all agree, right? The two runts got into the dang can as a *getaway car*, and rolled ALL the way down here, even scaling that ramp, right? Now, I could be wrong about them jumpin' out, but there's the stupid can drifting over there, and it's empty! Am I missing somethin' or what? Where could they have gone?" He kicked his foot against the fence post, and pulled out a cigarette.

"Well, hey, wut if they are just really good at holdin' their breath?" a few deep voiced, boys asked.

"See that over there, where the tin can is? That could be them, where the water's kinda wavy." This seemed like a valid explanation to the clueless gang. Not too swift, Rodney agreed.

"If they're down there, then we can still get them. 600-feet per second should be enough to cut through the water and *bite* 'em. Okay, boys, fire at will! Mow 'em down!"

Five paintball barrels were stuck through the fence holes, pointing at Blake and Dawson, and five pellets shot out, followed by more rapid fire. Blake saw the trails of bullets *zing* through the water, slow down, and eventually sink, only feet above their heads. Not one bullet grazed Dawson or Blake, and in spite of the impending danger, somehow, they enjoyed watching the ripples above them and the gang getting more frustrated by the second. Suddenly, a looming shadow slowly blocked the sun! Blake and his buddy squinted through the water to watch the bottom of a motorboat push across the surface. Another voice rang out, a local yelling at Rodney and his gang for firing their messy paintballs into the water. They had never answered to authority before this, and now would not be their time to start.

"GET HIM!" Rodney cried. And soon they began speckling the boat with bright orange splotches, up and down its sleek twenty-foot deck. The local spewed out curses and threats and speedily cranked up his engine to escape Rodney's onslaught. Dawson, all the while, laughed at what he saw, but Blake, quick thinking, contrived an opportunity of escape. He pulled at Dawson's shirt, beckoning him to follow, no time to lose. As fast as he could, Blake soared to the water's bright surface. His plan: grab the boat's side ladder which protruded well below the surface, secretly board the boat, hitching a ride far away from the gang's assault. Blake latched onto its lower ladder bar right before the boat sped away and Dawson grabbed Blake's ankle. Dos climbed up his friend's body to grasp on to the ladder. Blake went up first, which required tenacious strength that defied the pull of the passing lake water. Dawson received help from Blake and made it aboard. They looked back and saw Rodney, who had seen them get up onto the boat, screeching and yelling, and firing his gun in the air. He threw his cigarette into the lake in frustration, concluded his tantrum, and left with his gang trailing behind. All Blake could do was smirk.

He and Dawson silently stayed at the back of the boat, behind its loaded crates. Blake then realized that he recognized the boat; it belonged to a neighbor just down the street! Mr. John Lynch lived less than a mile from Blake. He kept mostly to himself and barely ever spoke to his neighbors. Blake thought it best to have their presence remain a secret. Before the ship docked, both boys quickly slipped back into the water, quietly *treading* as they headed toward shore.

"Aw, man. We really owe it to Oskar."

"Yeah." agreed Dawson.

"If it were not for these *guys*," Blake explained, holding up his air converter, "We would be covered in paint!"

"And bruises." added Dawson. "Let's get to your house and tell everyone our adventure."

The boys, undetected, slipped out of the water. They shook their wet heads and laughed. They were stoked as they ran along a sandy beach, which led to Blake's house. Energized, they recounted what had just happened, and as they laughed and groaned, Blake suddenly grew serious and stopped.

"Hey, is your head okay, Dos? That was one heck of a shot. Bam! Bullseye!" Blake said, pointing his finger, gun-like, barely touching Dawson's head.

"Yeah, it's okay. Nothin' a bag of ice won't fix!" After wandering through thick woods and scrub for a while, the boys entered a clearing. Just beyond, Blake's house stood formally at attention, awaiting his return.

"Man, I never get tired of your place. Such a cool house you got, Blake!"

They moved toward the imposing grand entrance. Blake removed his shoes, as did Dawson. The boys slowly opened the massive oak door. The paintball-scarred duo quietly moved, each brandishing soggy shoes, and headed to the pool, sliding open a screen door, and quietly closing it shut They moved toward a gated pool and adjacent game room. Manicured lawns stretched to the woods and beach beyond.

"I thought we were going to *see* your parents?" Dawson whispered.

"It's best they don't know, I think. I really don't want to raise their *concern index*, know what I mean? So, let's shower, jump in the pool and get cooled off, O.K.?"

Blake's pool was almost as unique as his house. Olympic-sized, the Italian tiled pool stood bordered by intricate gate-work, boasting marble figures, desert aloes, and potted palms which led to a huge redwood-like tree right at the pool's corner. The middle of the tree trunk featured two huge holes which gushed forth massive streams of water, astride a ladder which led to a high platform near its canopy. From there, one could easily slide down, tilt slightly forward, and move along at great speed through a wide tube, swiftly entering the pool. On the sides of the pool ten-foot rock projectiles provided diving platforms. A small waterfall, which slowly cascaded into the pool at the far end, complemented a perfectly designed array of cabanas, lounge chairs, leather sectionals, glass-topped tables, a bevy of luxury seating, and with perfectly spaced elegant market umbrellas. Blake and Dawson showered, suited up, and hastily stepped up to a canopied platform.

"Ready?" Blake asked Dawson, sitting, about to begin his downward slide. "Set?" Dawson asked Blake with a grin. Together, pulling themselves into the tube, they yelled 'GO!'" A blurry maze slid by the boys, going around the tree, until they saw light in the tube's end; as it rapidly got closer, and closer, they braced for the inevitable entry, shooting like two bullets into the pool, flaying arms and legs, screaming as they hit the water's surface. Wham! Laughing, sucking in air and water, the boys began to float. Blake and Dawson were good friends, you see. The best of friends, actually.

"Hey Dos, wanna check out KidzTurf for a while?"

"Yeah, sure." said Dawson, swimming towards the edge of the pool.

Dripping, Dawson moved quickly to a conveniently placed wall phone. "I better call my folks. Let 'em know where I am!"

"Oh, yeah, that's right. No need to get into trouble, right?"

Reaching for a towel, Dawson began to shiver.

"Ma? I'm over at Blake's. Back later, okay?"

11

Permission granted, Dawson smiled, turning back to Blake.

"One more time?" Dawson suggested, pointing to the wide-spread tree which sported massive tubes opening into the awaiting pool.

"Sure!" laughed Blake. "Let's go, Bro!"

For Blake and Dawson, the afternoon flew by in the *death throes* of conjured swimming battles and competitions.

*Cannonballing* to the center, Blake yelled, "Wanna go to KidzTurf now?"

Dawson answered, "Sure!" as he *cannonballed* Blake.

The boys, dripping, laughed heartily as they made their way toward the showers again. T-shirts and jeans sufficed as Blake and Dawson sauntered toward KidzTurf, a defunct parcel of decaying buildings, walkways and jumbles of discarded cable, lumber, and piles of trash. If only this place, now used only for occasional paintball battle and play, could be restored. This thought would weigh on Blake, more heavily than he could ever have imagined as weeks passed by. Invading his thoughts was a growing passion, a mission, a germinating vision. It was not fully defined. It came in rough sketches whenever Blake thought of *KidzTurf*. Others were unaware of what Blake wrestled with as each day passed. *KidzTurf* was more than met the eye. Of this Blake was sure, surer than life itself!

*KidzTurf* was close by, very close by. Running ahead, Dawson grabbed a rusted outer gate, which defined the outer edges of the abandoned land parcel as he pulled himself around, like a prisoner staring out from behind its grillwork.

Clutching two bars, Dawson smiled, "I wonder if Oskar has invented anything this week."

"Ha, I'll bet he has a cure for cancer under wraps. He's amazing. I'm glad the *Abanders* left stuff for him to tinker with." replied Blake.

"Abanders?"

"Yeah, *Abanders*." answered Blake. "You know, the people who left all the stuff behind in *KidzTurf*? A-band-ers. Get it?"

"Yeah, I get it. I'm not dumb," grouched Dawson.

Minutes passed. Heading deeper into *KidzTurf*, the boys stood before two massive oaks connected by a huge plank gate with a weary wooden sign faintly stenciled in black on its center timbers, a remnant left behind years ago. A sturdy wall stretched impressively in each direction away from the oaks and the illegible sign, away, far away, from the center gate where the boys stood.

"HEY, CHARLIE! OPEN UP!" Blake shouted, pounding the gate before him. In reply, the pull of a heavy interior crossbar revealed a *curious* security.

"Hey, man. How's it going?" asked Charlie, *high-fiving* Blake.

"Yeah! Goin' good. How 'bout you?"

"Oh, yep, things all good and dandy-like."

"Dandy-like? Really?" Blake snickered. "Where are you from? The '50s?"

"Yeah I guess. I got it on TV. Kinda stupid, huh? Actually, what I said wasn't really true, not true at all."

"Oh?" questioned Blake, suspicion crossing his face.

"Oh, don't worry. It's just a new kid we let in here a few days ago. Different, ya know? To begin with, his cell phone was weird, much smaller than normal, a circular device, obviously more complex. Now, where would he get a cell like that, anyway?" asked Charlie.

"Sounds suspicious. What's his name? What's he doing here? You say he just wandered in? Security breach I'd say."

"Well, his name is Geo. He didn't tell me where he was from exactly, but he did say that he wanted to be a member of *KidzTurf*. So, I let him in, ya know to look around. Then I called our *overseers* to escort him to *initiation*, ya know. So, we can be sure and..."

13

"Yes, yes, I know, Charlie. I made up that rule." interrupted Blake.

"Oh yeah. Sorry. Well, they questioned him and thought he was fine, I guess, that his credentials were OK and he qualified for membership. He was a little weird though."

"Oh? Weird?"

"Not only his cell. His eyes. Kinda scary. They kept darting, like a pinball machine ready to tilt. He couldn't look ya straight in the eyes. Know what I mean?"

"Yeah, I get the picture!"

"Good. But other than that, he checked out okay?"

"Okay, whatever. Where is he now? I wanna meet him."

"Sure. He's staying at the Clark house.

"That old dump?"

"Yeah. He said that he liked the *musty* smell. Yuck!"

"He's weird, that's for sure!"

"Yep. I recommended something newer, but he wouldn't even consider it."

"Okay, Charlie. Gotta go. Beef up your security, okay?"

"Okay, Blake! See you at closing time!"

"All right. Hey, DOS? You comin'?"

Dawson, turning away from Charlie, slowly looked back at Blake "Nah! I've got some stuff I gotta get to."

"Okay. Catchya later."

"Yeah. Ditto!" replied Dawson as he turned back to Charlie. Dawson had more to say, much more! "Anyways, Charlie, old Rodney shot me right here! Yeah, and Blake and I dove into this can and..."

Shaking his head, Blake strode away down the narrow street. He glanced at several boys maneuvering a soccer ball, as they vigorously scored multiple shots.

"Ah, *KidzTurf*! Ya gotta love it!" laughed Blake. He sauntered up a few steps to ring Geo's doorbell. Half a minute later, the door slowly unlocked, cracking open a few inches.

"Yes?" inquired a cold voice from the dark interior.

"Uh, yeah. Hi. Geo, right?"

"That's right. And who might you be?"

"The name's Blake Armstrong. I'm founder of *KidzTurf* and..."

"Oh? Founder, eh? Well then, come on in. Yes, do come in!"

"Oh, yeah. Thanks!" Blake stepped through the doorway. "Where is Geo?" he thought, as a powerful stench assaulted him. Blake pushed ahead into the dark room.

"Yes, yes! Do come in, Blake Armstrong. Come in!"

Blake felt uneasy, very uneasy. The door clicked shut, as Geo quickly pushed a metal bolt deep into its jam. Blake stood motionless, his eyes widening to overcome the dark.

"So, you're finally here!" said Geo. "I've been waiting for you!"

*He (God) speaks, and Lebanon leaps like a young calf.*

**Psalm 29:6 The Voice translation**

## CHAPTER 2: JAWDROPPER

BLAKE STOOD FROZEN, deciding whether he should take any action, or to play along with Geo's *dark game*. Then he heard him say,

"Wait! Right there."

And Blake did as he was told. Blake couldn't see what was going on in the room's enfolding dark, but he did hear Geo's shuffles across the floor. He heard him pick up an object across the room. It sounded like metal. Blake, just barely, heard Geo mutter under his breath,

"An axe will do."

Blake bolted back towards the door. This guy was insane. But wait! Where was the door? Panic rushed through him. Geo let his axe down, scratching it across the floor, making nails on chalkboard sound comforting. Blake would have yelled for help, but fear had removed his voice, completely. Blake jumped away, slamming into the kitchen, knocking over a stool as he fell to the floor.

"If you would like to do business in here," offered Geo, "that's fine with me. Anyways, the kitchen is always better, right?"

That sounded almost more terrifying than the unknown. Blake scrambled up, needing to run, but his foot was stuck in an intricate maze of stool legs. He tried to pull, push, jimmy, jingle, and squirm his leg out of the tangle. But Blake could already tell it was too late. The sound of an axe lifting and Geo's exhaled grunt of pulling it high into the air indicated what was next. Chop time.

"AHHH!" Blake screamed. Geo's axe sliced the air, and then it was done, but Blake was still alive, in one piece! He pushed up from the floor, facing the damage. Geo had sliced three planks of wood, which had covered the kitchen's sole window, barely missing Blake. Light gushed in past the sullen panes, now making it hard for Blake to see. As the dark whimpered away, Blake grabbed a bearing on where he was, precisely. Not only were the rapid *dartings* of Geo's flickering eyes distressing, but also the dirty light now filling the kitchen. It held within itself a foreboding, a musty odor, which assaulted Blake's nostrils. Quivers shot up his spine.

He was sure that all the tiny rooms, adjacent to where he lay, comprised a *cursed* house, a place, a history where *vagrants* in the not too distant past had died violently upstairs, people still there lurking in the cavernous *memories* of the house. Here among the tiled kitchen walls and floor, the old Clark house *nursed* its cursedness in the presence of Geo, its strange occupant! Geo now raised his arm into the air for a final chop, sending the axe's sharp edge into a stool's thick

18

crossbar. Warily, Blake accepted the help, pulling himself stiffly to his feet. He could now see that Geo was not very mysterious at all. He was, at least for now, on the surface, a *normal* kid, not a robotic anomaly, though every now and then it seemed the *dartings* would strangely contort his face. Or was Blake imagining things?

"Everything seems normal." Blake pondered. "Perhaps too normal, an *orchestrated* normal!"

The strange boy interrupted, sticking out his hand, "My name is Geo. What's yours?"

"B-B-Blake. Blake Armstrong."

"Nice to meet you, Blake." Geo's demeanor had done a *180*. "Come, sit down. I will fix us both something to eat."

"Yeah. Sure. Um, thanks." Blake stuttered. Geo was normal; he wasn't an axe-wielding murderer after all. He just wanted a little light on the subject, and to help his clumsy, tangled friend.

Blake sat down on the remaining stool as Geo took out some bacon, wrapped it in a paper towel and stuck it into the microwave."

"Sooo, how do you like it here at *KidzTurf*, Geo?" Blake asked, despising his awkward question!

"It's really cool. I was just wandering around when I found this place. I came across a guy named Oskar, and..."

"Oskar? You met Oskar?"

"Yeah. You know him?"

"Well, yeah. We've been friends for years. How did you meet him?"

"Like, I said, I was just wandering around and... Oh, do you want any soda? I've got bottles of whatever, anything really."

"Cream soda. Thanks. Oh, and is that a BLT you're making?"

"Uh huh. It's all I got. Want any chips?"

"Sure. Whatever you got."

"Comin' right up. Anyways, like I was saying, we met when I was given the town tour by Mike and we spotted Oskar standing across the street, checking out Tony's Repair Shop."

"Right." agreed Blake, his wheels turning.

Meanwhile, across town, as Blake and Geo continued to ramble, their conversation casual yet awkward, they had no idea what was happening, or what new horizons were opening for *KidzTurf.*

Oskar's phone screen, barely legible in the bright sunlight, waited for its next instruction, as Oskar maneuvered an uneven sidewalk just past the *KidzTurf* entrance. A blinking GPS icon and map danced about to get Oskar, genius inventor, to his next location.

Annoyed, Oskar shook his phone, a special *iteration* he had created which exceeded any smartphone currently on the market, for he had hacked, designed, programmed, carved, and soldered his way to an impressive invention, decades ahead of what ordinary people routinely held in their hands. Yet, before him was a simple task: *Where is the defunct car repair shop located?* Months ago, he had passed the repair shop in the jumble which was now *KidzTurf* and its location registered, sort of. It looked like it might be a perfect facility for a lab where the sky would be the limit; he could invent, far away from prying eyes.

"Blast! Where is it?" he murmured, adjusting his glasses.

The phone shot back, "Oskar, the address you are seeking is no longer valid. The construction of the former auto repair shop has been compromised greatly. It is not a valid address, but if you must, walk west for another 100 yards, turn left and there on your right you will find the former Tony's Auto Repair."

"Great!" he smiled. "Looks like everything's gonna be okay, at least for today."

Oskar slowly scuffled along the crumbling sidewalk as he scanned the debris before him. Construction sites always energized him, for his curiosity and inventive spirit sought to give purpose and possibility to whatever he might find. A discarded radio. A spring-loaded gun. A box within a box. Whatever. His mind would categorize, detail, analyze and create. It was a rush. Always. And here he was, about to turn the corner to what he imagined could be a fully outfitted lab, a transformation of a defunct auto repair shop, complete with a powerful lift and workbench, into a fully functioning inventor's workshop. The possibilities of Oskar's envisioned lab were many and in his imagination, he went beyond, far beyond, the limited listings and offerings others could ever provide.

He moved across the street as he further examined possibilities, scanning an immense garage door, a steel lift within, a power grid of supplementary electromotive and electrostatic potential, a workbench extending across the entire structure, an array of sinks, full plumbing facilities, and workshop lighting throughout. Yes, this could work! This definitely would work!

Entering a side door, Oskar pushed his way across a small room, which opened into the main workshop. Auto repair tools were strewn everywhere. What a mess, but the constructions were solid. Yes, the workbench would serve well. He was convinced that the hundreds of repair tools on the floor and hung upon several worn pegboard walls and other various equipment could easily be sold. Simply, Oskar conjectured, these items would provide needed funds to bring what surrounded him into alignment with his vision. Yes, this must work, and it wouldn't take that long either. His fired-up neurons connected more rapidly now. Ideas like sparks flashed across his inventor's mind, coupling with new possibilities for objects and combinations thereof. He was transported. The rapidity of these thoughts raced through him, over him, up to the shop's ceiling, quickly down to its floor and across its walls, to the lift, the sinks, and the vast array of industrial lights. He envisioned needed equipment, computers, monitors, cages, microscopes, freezers, goggles, Bunsen burners, piper bulbs, beaker tongs, glass cylinders and volumetric flasks, rubber stoppers, meter sticks, charts, thermometers, ring stands, funnels, evaporating dishes, outlets, network infrastructure, hardware, software, data projectors, cables and power strips. All of this merged into a series of waxing and waning dynamic collages, logically arranged according to purpose, function and application. It was heady stuff, to say the least. Oskar spun in a 360 to further draw in the massive possibilities.

Raising both hands, Oskar laughed, "Man, this is it. Finally, something that'll fly, really fly. Can't wait to get this baby started!"

He was rebooted, alive, challenged and fully pumped. He ran toward the gated entry. The walkway, though uneven and twisted, provided no obstacle for him whatsoever! Nothing, no, absolutely nothing would or ever could stand in his way now! Oskar was naturally clumsy, but now he flew like the wind! He was invincible! But for how long?

He jumped, then suddenly stopped, and looked back at the defunct repair shop, recalling encouraging words he had read a few days before from Isaiah, a prophecy, somehow thrusting him into his energizing vision:

*From this time forth I announce to you new things, hidden things, that you have not known. They are created now, not long ago.*

Now back where we were: Geo's! The microwave continued to beep its shrill signal into the air. Geo took out and set down hot bacon on top of the open BLT, joining fresh lettuce, tomato, mayonnaise, setting the BLT's top slice in place along with some wavy chips. He grabbed a cream soda for Blake from the fridge and walked over to the table, as if nothing had prefaced their lunch, no axe, no combat, certainly no enemy.

"Now get this. I had just met him and Oskar was overflowing with ideas! Guess he's kinda hyper, right, plans for *KidzTurf*, what his lab could be like and his latest inventions. Then he launched ahead, revealing YOUR future plans for *KidzTurf*. Anyway, he showed me around and I decided, then and there, that becoming a *KidzTurf* citizen could actually be a good thing. So, a few days later, as you know, I was screened, stating who I am, my past, what I wanted, and what job I would be doing."

"And that would be?"

"I am interested in doing something exciting, you know, adventurous. You know, like your security staff?"

"Just like that?" Blake laughed.

"They considered you as security guard. No offense, but you don't look like... um... you couldn't... um..." Blake laughed again.

"I know. I agree that I don't seem to have that ability yet, but I'm a fast learner and I can do just about anything, I guess. And I have always wanted to become a secret agent!"

Blake's heart stopped for a moment. He decided to be coy.

"There is no secret agency or need for secret agents here in *KidzTurf*, Geo. Nice thought, though."

Blake tried to terminate the conversation, but Geo wasn't giving up.

"Come on, Blake. You know that there is a covert agency here!" Geo's eyes began to dart! "And, Blake, are you not its leader?"

"Correct. I am." He popped a chip into his mouth, nonchalantly.

"Blake, you need to know, I'm on your team already. There is no point in keeping this a secret anymore. Summerlin told me that you, she, Dawson, and Nick are keeping this town safe from intruders."

"Great job keeping the agency a secret, Summer." muttered Blake.

"What did you say, Blake?"

"Oh nothin'. So, that's why you wanted to talk to me, huh?"

"Yes. She told me to get settled in first, then find you. But I guess you found me first!"

"Yeah. Obviously, you haven't settled in yet."

"No. No, I haven't. This place has a lot of potential though, right? Just needs to be picked up."

"Yeah. Your place is cheery, like a funeral! Sorry."

"Yeah. But I like it." said Geo.

"Well, hey, I gotta go."

"Wait!" demanded Geo. "I'm just gonna be honest here. You see, I'm really sort of a *treasure hunter*! I've scavenged the west coast here

23

completely. Actually, I am looking for a particular artifact called the Trigon. Ever heard of it?"

"Nuh-uh. Is that another invention of Oskar's?" asked Blake.

"No, no, no. It's very special. It stands alone! Incomparable one might say. More than anything Oskar could cook up in his shop! Seems like it might be from another world. A relic from the latest sci-fi flick! Here, take a look."

Geo flashed his photo at Blake. Its live 3-D image was impressive. It featured a blue triangle, about the size of one's hand and its rounded clear edges were brightly lit, with strange pulsing veins which moved across its screen. It had to be alive! Moving toward the Trigon's center, light swirled, shooting out penetrating rays. Blake froze as his eyes widened.

"No, it couldn't be." Blake thought. "Was Geo the one who was trying to... yes! It had to be. He knows. He already knows! The Trigon told me this would happen."

"Uh, no. Never!" Blake quickly denied. Maybe too quickly in fact. Geo noticed the strange expression plastered on Blake's *draining* face.

"Are you sure?" Geo asked. He took another bite of his sandwich, wiping his mouth as he stared at Blake. "Blake, no really, is there something you're not telling me?"

Geo's malevolent stare *creeped out* Blake.

"Now tell the truth, there's nothing to be afraid of."

"No. Really. I've never seen it." Blake answered, quickly standing as he moved back from his stool.

Ominously, Geo advanced towards Blake, around the counter, rubbing the handle of what could be a knife in his pocket. Blake kept his distance, until his back hit the wall. Plaster particles seemed to spray from his vibrating thud. Terrified once again, Blake knew that what was to follow would not be good. He frantically searched for a distraction, a defense, a way out. Then Blake saw it. A dirty fringed rug had two end strings tied together. He slowly slipped his foot

24

through its loop. Geo didn't notice as he moved closer, pulling out what Blake thought could be a knife. As Geo's foot stepped onto the rug, Blake lightly tugged his fringe-loop, causing Geo to lose balance. Blake won the moment, as Geo toppled to the floor!

"Oh, sorry about that! Nice meeting you!" said Blake, quickly slamming the door behind him. He rushed down Geo's steps away from impending danger. Geo stood up easily as he opened his door a crack. He grinned as he watched Blake run down the street.

"His story doesn't fool me. I know he's involved Trigon, somehow. Right in the center of all this business; he must be!" Geo mused. "Until next time, Blake Armstrong."

Down the street, across the field, finally hitting the sidewalk hard, over and over Blake's steps pounded toward safety, as he, now escaped, headed home.

"How's it going, Dos?" Blake breathlessly asked, as he ran toward Dawson who was making his way across the street.

"Good. Hey, Blake, what's the rush?"

"Come with me! Now!" demanded Blake. Side by side, as the boys ran across the lawn, then leaping up, up, up, both boys defied Blake's somber brownstone steps. Blake slammed the door behind them before he could answer Dawson. He locked the door, wiping sweat from his brow, as he grabbed Dawson's shoulders.

"I've found the enemy, Dos. I mean, THE enemy!"

That night, although Blake's thoughts swam laps through his head, sleep finally overtook him: what had happened, Geo's *dartings*, and how Blake and Dos had discovered the Trigon; all this mastered his dreams. In counterpoint ran the tune: "I've found the enemy, Dos. I mean, THE enemy!"

*Here is the bottom line: do not worry about your life.*

**Matthew 6:25 The Voice translation**

## CHAPTER 3: REDWOODS

BLAKE, LIKE UNWANTED DEADWEIGHT, pushed hard into his bed, as in his dream he now returns, heavy and sluggish, to the blurred passing of trees, giant, 350' tall redwoods, majestic, stately, unlike the rumble of Cliff's Ford *Raptor*.

"Hey, Dad, you're workin' pretty hard on these roads."

"Yeah, Blake, that's for sure," Cliff says. "Almost there!"

Blake's dream then quickens. Cliff, swiping his long black hair, turns quickly to the left; his truck rumbles happily to a stop, teasing a pile of dirt.

"We're here, son! Finally. Quite a trip, huh?"

Blake answers, "Yeah, but it was definitely worth it. Just look at these trees! How old did you say these *monsters* are?

"'Bout 2,000 years old or, maybe, more, I guess!" "Redwoods, huh?"

"Yep!"

A playful wind and blurred multicolored redwoods collide and burst apart as Blake's dream ever sweeps him deeper, back to his life-changing discovery. He knows inside that his life will never be the same. Blake's vision wanders about, separated, yet looking at himself and his father.

Cliff, grabbing a huge pile of empty *Slim Jim* wrappers, laughs, "Better throw these babies away! Got everything, Blake?" Cliff asks, gathering his backpack and jacket.

Blake, slamming the door, replies, "Yeah, Dad, at least my backpack and cooler."

Dad smiles, "Great! And, hey, put the cooler next to the picnic table over there, not on it. Needs to be clear for this other stuff, okay?

Blake obeys, lugging the heavy cooler toward the worn camping table. He clears off a thick layer of crisp leaves and dirt, and plops down to capture the moment. In his dream he is now tired, but exhilarated. He is totally amazed by the redwoods, especially here in the fall. A 40-degree morning shimmers in a descending sunlight, which quickly, and quietly, filters through the canopy, high up, heaven's loft on massive redwood trunks, reaching for the sky. You see, redwoods live in a damp, moist world. Their life depends upon an ever-present fog covering which abundantly waters the redwood canopy.

28

Needed water for redwoods comes not through its roots but through its leaves and skin. Cliff knows this. Blake is learning this. But Blake's dad, an established nature magazine photographer, who knows a lot about redwoods, found this particular spot. Not damp or wet, nor stale, nor extremely dry. This was just right. Then a small breeze floats by, adding an agreeable touch to the moment. Blake's body tingles. Camping, fall, Redwoods, and the raw wilderness adds up to equal a memorable time. Cliff works hard for *Nat Geo* and is a champion photographer. He knows everything about redwoods and he has led his son to this very spot where he made his first climb!

Cliff throws an order to his son: "Blake, start unloading, will ya?"

Blake snaps out of his daze yet continues his *dream.* "Sure, Dad!"

Slowly returning to Cliff's shiny, black, muscular-looking truck, Blake unloads a heavy tent and sleeping bags, unfurling them upon the tabletop. Cliff carefully adds piles of cameras, climbing equipment and assorted gear. Cliff and Blake silently go to work, busily setting up camp, (they've done this before) erecting their wilderness tent, setting a grill and scurrying about gathering firewood, splitting it, preparing the campfire and other tasks. Thirty minutes later, they are finished in precision time.

"Whew! We're done. Blake, go ahead and fix you a sandwich. We have all the provisions. The works! I'm gonna get some extra firewood at the lodge for tonight."

"Okay, Dad! You want me to make you one?"

"Um... nah. The woods are filled with animals and critters that would just love to take a bite out of an extra sandwich. Better make it myself when I get back."

"All right, see ya!"

"Okay, and if you wander, don't go too far. We don't want our stuff stolen or for you to get lost, do we?"

"No, sir."

"Okay, I'm gone."

Cliff hops into his truck, turning the ignition, as he makes the vehicle rumble obediently.

"Be good!" orders Cliff.

Blake watches the truck pull out, carefully maneuvering through hundreds of bulbous redwood roots, as his father vanishes slowly into a distant neighborhood of trees. Blake hears a strange rumble. And it is loud! Yes, it's his stomach chanting:

"Food! Food! Food! Food!"

And Blake agrees, looking at the cooler, slowly opening its lid.

"Food!!!" he laughs, noisily lifting, discovering and scanning different containers, bags and bottles. Exactly like his dad had promised: there set before him deli-meats, toppings, dressings, pickles, spicy *Slim Jims*, chips, and a dozen *chocolate chips*. Blake eyes the feast before him, as he muses, "Yep, definitely MANFOOD mania!"

It wasn't long before he takes his first bite of his original *whopper*, an overloaded, untoasted, cheese-steak sandwich. This satisfies Blake beyond his expectation. His stomach now smiles.

"Ahhhhh, now that's more like it!"

His feast continues. Blake chomps happily along, gazing deeply into the silent redwoods! The fog has now lifted from the morning and the sun has pushed its way inside, piercing the thick canopy above. Blake is inspired, motivated, lifted, as he decides to explore, just a little bit. He is curious, delighted, and obedient to the redwoods' call, enveloping him, just around that next tree, then a little beyond that one. Just a little further. Now over here. Over there. What fun! The beautiful sights before him infuse Blake with new energy. He must explore now. Far from his campsite, Blake is lured further into the lush wilderness. Blake, still clutching his tempting Philly, abandons it, and proceeding deeper into the forest, is suddenly overtaken by a pungent scent of redwood, mystical silence, and the ever-present heavenly canopy. He is drugged by all the surrounding natural beauty, completely forgetting his father's instructions,

*"And if you wander, don't go too far!"*

30

Blake climbs a fallen redwood, slanted upward, perched midway, locked onto another tree. The light now grows dim, like a stage spotlight withdrawing its power. Music in his head commands attention. Melodies Blake has never heard before, a primordial music now plays to the moment.

*"And if you wander..."*

Hundreds of redwoods now blur and spin about him. The tent, Dad's Ford *Raptor* moving swiftly away. Blake's dream is taking a new direction. Hundreds, thousands, millions of redwoods, ahead, behind, surrounding Blake, take authority over him. They spin. They lift. Reaching down, the ancient trees speak to Blake, and he screams back,

"Whooooooooo!!!!"

His voice bounces through the forest. Blake has never been closer to nature then at this moment. ⌐⌐⌐

He walks closer, closer, upward, to the edge of a fallen tree, a tree larger, taller than the rest. But then he slips forward, tumbling, flipping downward upon a dirt ledge, which instantly crumbles under his weight and momentum. Blake is a feather in the wind. He is out of control, and yet the dirt ledge saves him as he tumbles and rolls to the ground, instantly coming to a halt, slamming into the massive redwood trunk of a neighboring tree.

"Aaargghh," Blake moans. He slowly picks himself up, straining to a seated position as he leans against the offending tree. He wipes his dirt-caked eyes, and finds his body wrapped in dirt and redwood bark. Shaking the mixture free from his hair, Blake now stands up. The bottom roots of the slanted ancient redwood taunt him to try again! And in the silence and settling of redwood dirt, Blake brushes off his jeans and jacket, and is nearly jerked awake; yet still dreaming, he continues, remembering, *"And if you wander, don't go too far..."*

He is reliving what has happened, what had happened, what changed his life forever, charged fully in life and death consequences! He walks now with purpose. He must get back to his campsite. He goes deeper and deeper, as he brushes off the remaining dirt from his jeans.

"Gotta get back to camp, A.S.A.P. Man, I could be in deep trouble." Suddenly, there's a tug on his right foot. Powerful, like an enemy's wrestling move.

"Grab that foot, twist it, and it's over!" With lightning speed, Blake is ensnared, pulled forty feet into the air. He screams, hanging upside down as his body hits the tree's side; he dangles helplessly. Painful splinters make their presence known. Hands, legs and jaw begin to bleed. He stops swinging and in the silence of an overwhelming tangle of ancient redwoods Blake knows that he has just experienced *death's stroke.*

"HELLLLLLP!!!!" Blake screams.

Nobody comes, of course. Nobody's there.

"I can see it now," he thinks, "Twelve-year-old Boy Killed in the Redwoods! Falls to His Doom!"

More echoes. He screams louder as fear *grabs hard*! Blake helplessly dangles.

"Anyone! Please!" Suddenly, as if a miracle, a miracle in this dream of dreams, his pocket begins to buzz, to ring and buzz again. Slowly, carefully, Blake slips his hand into his left pocket, pulling out his cell phone.

"Can't believe this," he breathlessly says to himself: "*Facetime* from Oskar!!" Blake swings to a branch, jutting out at his side. He takes hold of it, and then grabs more branches, finding a temporary safe-spot, as the cell phone continues to ring. He climbs into a branch's crotch while gripping yet another adjoining branch, as the snare's rope continues to deftly bind his ankles.

"Man, I can't believe I'm getting reception all the way up here!" Blake exalts, tapping his answer button.

Instantly Oskar's grinning face fills the screen. Oskar is about one of the *nerdiest* guys on the planet, but somehow not weird. Oh, he talks a little bit like a nerd, definitely thinks like one, but somehow doesn't act like one. He's like any normal guy but has a major obsession with science. And although he doesn't exactly fit the usual profile of a nerd, he does wear thick glasses, looks kinda scrawny and is pale most of the time. Yep. He's a stereotype of sorts and he solves problems which could baffle Einstein! Other than that, I guess, he's just your *average* kid!

"Dude, are you okay?" Oskar's voice rings through the receptor, as Blake's dream continues.

"How would you know?" Blake retorts.

"I just got notification that my trap was set off. It identified you as human, not animal. I was 536 feet north of your current location, so I came here as quickly as I could, and I can clearly see with my zoom-in glasses that it's you, yeah, it's really you! Greetings from down below!"

"Hello to you, too. NOW GET ME DOWN FROM HERE!" Blake screams.

"Okeedokee! Don't panic; this is completely safe."

"What is?" Blake asks, concerned with a mad scientist's intentions. Oskar shifts his *communique* image to fit half-screen and pulls up his new innovation: an app he calls, "Trap Controls." Oskar finds the REDWOODS TRAPS onscreen, locating a flashing circle. "RETRACT" glows green and next Oskar's bony thumb presses down. Blake feels the snare on his ankle tug a bit, then paying out, a boat losing its mooring, except here he falls quickly.

Forty feet rapidly becomes thirty, then twenty, but at ten feet from the forest floor Blake abruptly stops. Eyes still squeezed shut, Blake collapses on the ground at the redwood's base. Oskar is standing only feet away.

"Hey, Blake, are you okay? Anything broken?"

"Yes. You have shattered my *standard* of insanity. What the heck, man? That was my life on the line!

"Correct me if I'm wrong, but I believe it was YOU who stumbled into MY trap."

"And it was YOU who set your dang trap up in a PUBLIC area in the first place."

"I have thirteen strong points that can demolish any justification you might have. Do you really want to continue this discussion?"

"Actually, man, I just want to get back to camp." Blake grumbles. Oskar was always the superior debater.

"O.K., then. Where are you set up?"

"Not too far east of here, I think. Come on. Hang out awhile?"

"That depends. Do you have any food?" Oskar laughed.

"You have no idea."

"It's a deal, Bro. Let's Go!" Blake leads the way back, eventually finding his campsite.

"Hey, Dad, guess what?" Blake announces, emerging from the dense foliage surrounding the campsite; the truck was back.

"What?" Cliff replies, lifting his head from his truck bed.

"I was wandering through the forest, sort of, when I run into Oskar. Kinda weird, huh?" Blake's eyes move from Oskar over to the truck bed.

They hear Cliff lift something heavy, straining, and watch him slowly walk towards them with an oversized bundle of wood, cradled in his arms.

"Oh really? Hey, Oskar. Good to see ya."

"You, too, Mr. Armstrong."

"It's good that both of you are here." Cliff heaves down some split wood next to the fire pit, wiping his hands on the back of his pants.

"Many hands make light work. Right, guys? Go grab some firewood from the truck and pile it right where I set mine."

34

"Okay." they say in unison. The two friends do as they are told, hoisting the remaining wood to the pile, emptying Cliff's truck bed.

"Great! Thanks, boys. Now, on to project number two."

"Uh oh. You need us to do more work?" groaned Oskar.

"Work is good for ya, Bud! Plus, I can't set this tent up on my own, right?"

"All right, Dad! Hand us the poles." Together, they now reconstruct an unwieldy tent, big enough for a family of six.

"Whew! I need something to drink. Oskar, want some water?" Blake asks, pulling out two bottles.

"Got soda?"

"Yep. Here, catch." Blake trades water for cola, tossing it to Oskar. They immediately gulp it down. Then after having a can free-throw, Oskar's pocket buzzes. A text from his dad: "Time to leave." Oskar's face drops.

"Oskar, what's wrong?"

"My dad just texted. Gotta go, Bro."

"Aw, man! Too bad. How long did you stay?"

"Approximately two hours and seventeen minutes." Oskar calculates.

"What! Two hours?"

"Uh huh. My dad didn't reserve a spot and all of the other ones are filled up! He thought there'd be plenty of room. Guess not."

"Too bad. That sucks." But then, Blake has an idea. "Wait. We have room in our tent for at least two more people. Why don't you two stay with us? *Whaduyathink*? Huh? Good idea? Anyways, Oskar, the two of us would have to come back here anyway, right, to take pictures for our language arts project?"

Hmmm. Okay. But see if it's all right with your dad."

"And what would that be?" Cliff asks, stepping out of his tent.

"Oh, Dad. Oskar and his dad can't go camping tonight. They didn't reserve a campsite and all spots are taken. Can they stay with us? We've got lots of room, right?"

"Um. Yeah, sure...but..." Blake's dad scratches his head. "I'm gonna be out photographing the canopy, um..."

"Are you taking pictures for *Nat. Geo.* with those fancy cameras?" Oskar asks."

"Yeah. I am. Why?"

"Oh nothin'." Oskar says innocently, always planning.

"But now that I think about it," offers Cliff, "It sounds okay. Go ask your dad, or tweet him, or text him, or whatever your generation does these days."

"I'll voice mail him."

"Oh brother!" Cliff mutters.

Suddenly, light shatters, piercing the immense canopy overhead. Redwoods, looming into the heights, quickly stretch upward, further and further upward, like hot taffy only then to break apart, infusing its tiny pieces into the air, raining debris far below upon Blake. All begins to swirl, turn, twisting within the particles, despite the particles, because of the painful particles pushing, impaling. "What's going on?" Blake yells. His shoulder is pinned. He is being shaken. "What?" he asks. "Is this a dream, or what?"

Blake shook his head away from his damp pillow. He had stretched across the wooden table for just a minute. Incredibly, the tabletop had looked quite comfortable thirty minutes ago after he had cleared it, and, well, with his pillow, it was a perfect spot for a little nap. He was sweating as he pushed off the tabletop, sitting on its bench. Just then, Oskar's dad pulled up in his truck. Another vehicle pulled in behind. "Look who I found a few minutes ago, Blake!" Oskar and his dad, jumped from their Jeep, laughing.

"Strangest thing," laughed Oskar, "we saw your dad just as we were losing hope. Seems all of the sites are full, and we were about to return home. Thought there would be plenty of room here, but *nada!* So, your dad invites us. Cool. Right?" smiled Oskar.

Oskar withdrew an old tent from his Jeep, inviting Blake to help. After all, this was going to be the boys' tent; the dads could share their own! After a few minutes the tent was up and ready. Blake and Oskar threw in their bags and other equipment and quickly began planning their photo adventure. Where and what to photograph. When? Secretly or not? Finally, they made up their minds.

"Are you sure, Blake?" Oskar asked. "This is risky."

"We need an A+, right, to win those tickets to the ballgame? Our pictures and videos have to be amazing," explained Blake.

"Yeah, sure, risk your life to watch a football game."

"It's the playoffs, man! Show some appreciation. Sports! Awesome! Right?"

"Right, but I suspect that the game is not your only motivation, is it?"

"What else is there?" asked Blake.

"Summerlin?"

"Get outta here! No way!"

"Then what's this?" Oskar clicked a couple of buttons and then spun his laptop over to Blake. His eyes widened at the photo of his third-period class notes. Summerlin was written all over, sketches of her and a 10-step process to win her heart.

"Oh, uh, that old thing... um..."

"Most people don't consider a note that is only two days old to be an 'old thing'. Butch found it and I photographed it in class." Blake's face turned full red.

"Who did he show it to?" Blake gulped.

"Oh, nobody really. Just me, Monica, Jessica, Dawson, Rodney, Courtney, Summerlin..."

"Say what?"

"Nothin'."

"Good grief. Never mind, let's get back to our work, okay?"

"Indeed, yes. Let's get to the task at hand."

The boys quickly finished their secret meeting, grabbing a football to toss for a while. The setting sun began to slip out of sight, replaced by massive dark clouds in the early evening sky. It seemed somehow like a prophetic darkening was quickly overtaking everything. All campers now sat by their fires as quiet spread throughout the campground. Only the sparks of very dry split wood and the sizzling of assorted meats could be heard among camp-wide hushed conversations. A lone dog barked in the distance. Crickets provided a persistent chorus. The boys deftly cooked a heap of chili dogs, baked beans and toasted corn on the cob, topping it off with a dessert of 's'mores. Delicious for sure. Outdoors. Fresh air. Umm, fire smoke and lightening bugs. And a secret plan ready to unfold when the dads had hopefully fallen asleep. Eventually, the four crawled into respective tents and sleeping bags, two out of four actually falling asleep! Blake and Oskar quietly laughed and *high-fived*. They had photos to take. Night stops on ready cameras.

A half hour later, by the time they could hear their old men snoring, Blake did a very quiet, "Woo Hoo! Whoo Hoo!" nice and soft, like an owl. Outside the tent came a response, "Whoo Hoo! Whoo Hoo!" This was Blake and Oskar's signal that everything was ready and it was time to leave. They crept slowly away from the tent and made no noise at all. Both boys quietly, very quietly, planted their feet firmly into their hiking shoes.

"Last one there is definitely a BLOCKHEAD!" teased Blake, running to his motorbike, pushing it quietly away from the campsite. He started his engine, steering away as he watched Oskar scramble behind. When Blake was far enough away from the campsite, he gunned his throttle and sped down a one-lane road. He knew this area intimately from other campouts and nothing came as a surprise. It was a map he would never forget. At the end of the road, a sharp curve poked into the night. But Blake did not take its turn. Instead, he purposely veered off into the woods. While maneuvering around hundreds of thick redwoods, he could hear Oskar's engine *huffing* in the distance. After several sharp turns on the dirt-way, both boys finished their shortcut into a wide clearing, a level area usually reserved for festivals, celebrations and other merry-making. Five hundred yards ahead, a hill rose quickly upward, abruptly ending at a steep edge, a sheer one hundred foot drop to a valley of hundreds more redwoods. Blake looked over his shoulder to see Oskar closing in, though it was obvious to see who was the winner. And, yes, you guessed it, it was Blake who made it up the steep hill to the top and stopped precariously at a tree, overhanging the cliff's edge. Then, followed Oskar, carefully slowing to a stop.

"Beat ya!" Blake laughed.

"Yeah, I noticed." Oskar grumbled. "Didn't have enough time to get ready. You took off, like, unexpectedly. Of course, you won!"

"Well, here we are, what is it, oh yeah, here we are, BLOCKHEAD! Got the equipment?"

"Yep. Here it is." Oskar winced at his new title, lifting a panier from the back of his bike, handing it to Blake. He looked inside as he removed heavy camera equipment, ropes, harnesses, tripods and long telephoto lenses, along with the ever present and needed *beef jerky*. It helps, somehow it helps. Anyway, Blake walked to the precarious edge, then over to a young tree. It was a sapling, an ancient sapling, tall, gangly, yet hitting the canopy. It poked into the layer of mist ever-resting in the canopy. The sapling's base and roots were strongly planted at the edge, yet the tree's top slanted dangerously far off the edge.

"We're in luck, Oskar! These photos are gonna be awesome. I know it. I just know it, man! Come on, harness yourself and let's climb! Just keep attaching your harness ropes to the trunk in case you slip." Blake and Oskar quickly harnessed to the massive trunk, starting their climb, Blake in the lead, of course, which meant that poor Oskar crawled slowly with a *panier* tied to his back. Usually climbers secured themselves to these redwoods in daylight, not foolishly in the dark. But the boys didn't care and were oblivious to danger. It was an adventure and that in itself would very much suffice.

"Careful with those cameras, Oskar! They're fragile!"

"I am." Oskar grunted, much annoyed. Higher and higher they ascended, not looking down. Eventually, Blake made it into the mist and the lower edge of the redwood's majestic canopy. He climbed the rest of the way and stretched, looking over the outward spindle branches. But there was nothing much to see other than dense, yet diminishing clouds and mist.

"Dang it! Too misty to see anything." Blake kicked a branch. Just making it up the climb, Oskar heaved himself onto a branch, as he struggled, breathing heavy.

"You... you mean... we have to climb... all the way... back down now... so soon?" he managed.

"Yeah, I guess... wait a minute. Look!" Blake scrambled towards the front. The mist was breaking apart and they were now getting a better view of things. Blake got his camera ready, aiming it straight forward, waiting for the rapidly disappearing mist to entirely dissipate. And when it did, it took their breath away. Blake lowered his camera in awe, shaking his head, taking a good look at it all. This was truly the REDWOODS in all its glory. There before them stood a vast, tall, green valley stretching beyond in the distance. Sitting above it all was a gigantic moon shining brightly, and the stars...well, they saturated the sky, flooding miles and miles in all directions, twinkling like rare and brilliant diamonds, reflected in the wet treetops as well. It was overwhelming. The awestruck boys started snapping away, trying to capture all possible angles of this majestic and, yes, holy sight.

Things were precarious, and as the limbs thinned out, Blake continued to climb.

"Not any further!" warned Oskar. "You're gonna fall."

"Nah. All is safe, Bro." replied Blake as a loud crack exploded into the canopy! A major branch suddenly broke, pushing Blake down swiftly into the night. What saved him was a river below. Like a bullet, Blake pierced the water, followed by the offending redwood branch. Lower and lower he went, and then, still alive, up, up, up. Blake burst from the water gulping for air, and screaming, as he began to paddle to the river's edge. Struggling, he slapped his hands on to several projecting bank roots, then up over the edge, to his knees, belching water, gasping for air.

"AHHHHH!!!!" he yelled in pain.

Meanwhile, Oskar, pannier and all, quickly descended the tree. Oskar to the rescue? Not yet, anyway.

"Where are you, Bro?" he shouted, pointing his flashlight at each turn. He stopped abruptly at the cliff's edge. "Whoa!" he thought. "Not down there. Nah. Too far down. Blake's gotta be nearer than that. Anyway, he couldn't make it back up here alive, so my Bro's gotta be near here somewhere!"

Oskar began to run about, not knowing where to go or what to do, when a brilliant light compelled him further ahead. He had been turned around in search of his friend; now he was returning to ground zero.

Having fallen hundreds of feet, a glowing triangular *instrument*, now wedged in a massive crack, where Blake's heavy branch had been ripped from its socket. It hummed and vibrated, compelling Oskar to reach for it. The tree had almost fallen to its knees. The redwood, rotted to the core, had easily split when encouraged, and now, what had been carefully placed inside was now REVEALED! Who had placed it there, and when? Oskar could only speculate. But on to more important things. Blake. For a moment Oskar pondered, as he inspected the triangle, searching for clues. Was it electronic? Was it a toy? Was it a weird flashlight of sorts? He had no clue. But then, ironically, its screen, like the dissipating canopy, cleared, exposing a glowing screen, which featured a small moving figure! And a background, a river, a tree, a boy walking to water and punching it. A *replay* of sorts! And wait, the imaged boy falls into something! The triangle quickly zooms into the hole and looks down upon the boy, lying prostrate, mouth open. His two front teeth are chipped badly, and he's chewing through his lip. As Oskar viewed closeups of the injuries one by one, the screen zoomed back out to reveal a face, a tormented face. A boy. Oskar dropped his jaw as he stared at Blake! Yes, it was Blake! He studied the image closely, wiping his eyes to be sure that

41

he wasn't seeing things. But this was real. Then the triangle's screen zoomed further out and backtracked all the way back, until he could see himself, looking into the triangle. Weird. Odd. Oskar was astonished. He looked behind himself and there were no cameras. He then turned back to the triangle to view his image and was surprised to find a map featuring a highlighted track.

"I wonder," Oskar thought. "I wonder if this triangle has revealed a path to Blake! He needs me!"

So, Oskar agreed to take the indicated path. He struggled along where he was prompted to go. He came across a small river, but, thankfully, he was led to a tree bridge spanning the swiftly moving currents.

"Good thing I don't have to jump into that. Brrrrrrr!" Blake shivered.

In the triangle, Oskar remembered, that Blake had crawled out of the river, which gave him hope that Blake was still alive, urging him on to keep looking for his friend. The path called Oskar to the beach to where there were deep struggling, dragging footprints, which were pushed hard into the moist ground.

"These must be Blake's," whispered Oskar.

Up ahead, yards from the strand and into the river grass, was a hole in one of the smaller redwood trees. Oskar poked his head in, yelling, "Blake! Blake! Are you there?"

A long low moan replied. Oskar reached for his flashlight, pointing its beam down the tree hole. There, motionless, lay Blake.

"BLAKE!" Oskar shouted.

"Osssar... helpth me."

"Comin' down, Blake. Don't worry!" Oskar spotted a ladder pushed against a wall leading down, so he jumped over and descended to his friend.

"Blake, Blake, are you okay?"

"I don'th thinc stho. My lipth hurths, my teeth hurths, my ankle hurths, and my arm hurths."

"It's okay, Blake. I will be right back!" Oskar ran back up the ladder and jumped out.

"Osssar! Don'th go!"

"I'll be right back!" Oskar yelled over his shoulder. He burst into the night, eyes wide-open, to where he had been at the river's edge, as he frantically searched for Blake's pannier, containing cameras and other equipment, including a desperately needed first first-aid kit!

"Where are ya, come on, where are ya?" Oskar looked and looked, but the bag was not there. He was ready to give up, when there, caught in a branch by its strap, *help* dangled. Oskar jumped and knocked it off. Quickly, he opened the case and dug through Blake's mangled cameras to his first-aid kit.

"Perfect." Oskar whispered, then raced to Blake's assistance.

"Blake, Blake, I just found your first aid kit. Here, let me fix you up." Oskar propped Blake straight against the wall and cleaned his wounds. Time flew. A very sore Blake finally wobbled to stand. A splint fortified his left ankle. His bloody lips were covered in *Neosporin* and a bulky splint swathed his right forearm. "Wow, man, you're pretty banged up." Oskar managed. It was hard to see his friend in such pain.

"Yo tellin' me. Ith pwetty painful."

"I can imagine. Come on. Let's go and see if we can make it back to camp."

Oskar began to climb, then noticed Blake wasn't following.

"Oh, yeah, you can't. Sorry, Bud, but you'll just have to. Unless you want to stay here tonight."

"Dudeth, there isth another way outh." "Where?" "Through that door."

"What door? Oh wait, that door. Yeah, let's see where it goes." Oskar jumped back down and jiggled the door knob. It was locked, and unusually icy. It was colder than a normal door knob should ever be, even in plummeting redwood temperatures like this.

"Give me a sec, man."

Oskar backed up, pressed his hands against the walls, and kicked at the door. His foot shot right through, creating a giant hole. A blast of cold air breezed past them. He pulled out his foot and crawled through. Once on the other side, he stood and unlocked the door, swinging it open as it creaked ominously. Before the boys lay a tunnel of crumbling roots and soil. Oskar quickly grabbed a flashlight from his backpack; its light was bright.

"Come on, Blake, let's go."

As they entered the tunnel, the temperature began to drop fast, although they hadn't descended at all. A rich odor of dirt walls and floor accosted them, as temperatures continued to plummet. Suddenly the tunnel walls, which now stretched further into the darkness, had become solid ice, not mere blocks of ice piled atop one another, but strange deeply textured ice walls which had been frozen for many years. Diseased roots, razor-sharp and twisted, now protruded like daggers through the ice above and below into the tunnel as if by some gruesome intent.

"What is this place...?" Oskar whispered.

The boys continued down the narrowing subterranean tunnel, slip-sliding along its icy floor. They kept on, moment by moment, not knowing where they would end up. The tunnel squeezed them, turned and twisted, an undulating serpent, which finally led to several wide stone steps into an ante-chamber. One room after another carefully, intentionally led the boys along the tunnel which now widened, propelling them toward an awaiting dark body of water, a lake of sorts.

"Hey, Blake. Look here." "Uh huh. Yepth Osssar."

"But, but is that even water?"

Oskar boldly stepped towards the liquid. Beyond wisps of hovering mist above the water, he could see dark currents swirling below. Oskar blew into the mist to get a better visual. Should they cross or not? This was no ordinary water. Yes, it was blue, but a very dark blue. It was as if someone had added too many drops of ink. The water seemed to have a life of its own. Was it alive? Oskar withdrew his pocket knife, unfolded its blade, and stabbed the water. When he removed it from the swirling liquid, his knife was frozen, pure ice. His eyes widened. Blake moved closer to get a better look. As he gently touched Oskar's knife it shattered, igniting a small disturbance of sparks. Surprised, Blake accidentally backed a few paces into the murky water.

"BLAKE!!" Oskar yelled.

He ran to the edge, repeatedly instructing his wounded friend who continued to back away. Blake suddenly fell backwards, entirely sucked under, then quickly bobbed up, splashing and gasping for air.

"Blake! Oh, Blake, grab me. Come on!" Oskar strained, pulling his friend from the frigid water.

"Buddy, are you all right?"

 "Yeah. I'm fine." Blake replied, shivering. "It's cold, man, but really not too bad."

"Okay, good. Hey, what happened to your slurring?"

"I, I don't know. Check my lip, will ya'?"

Oscar stared, amazed.

"Blake... you're not gonna believe this..." Oskar murmured, dumbfounded.

"What? What?"

"Your lip, its fine. No hole in it."

"You sure? What's goin' on? Like, no hole?"

"I don't know, but that's not your only healing. Your chipped tooth has grown back!"

"No way! Wait, give me a sec."

Blake stood up and walked over to a polished block of ice, which mirrored his condition.

"Oh, my gosh..." Blake silently mouthed his words, carefully examining his lip, as he pushed his fingers across his perfectly smooth teeth. He reached for his ankle, removing its splint. No pain. His arm had been restored as well!

"Whatever that water is, still, I don't think it's all that safe. Have you ever heard of murky water that could heal? Anyway, for now let's just stay away from it."

The boys stood deep in silence, scanning for a quick exit.

Blake whispered, "Well, there is always that boat over there."

"Hey, where did that come from? It wasn't there before!"

"Dunno." replied Blake

"Maybe there's an exit nearby, and the only way to it is by boat."

"Hmm, maybe so, but no. Doesn't look good, though."

"Yeah! Uh, why not?" asked Blake.

"Because, all of this is just too weird. First, it's this creepy place. Gives me the shivers. Second, we only came this far to look for any available exit. Well, we haven't found one, and now that you are able to, we can simply go back the way we came, right? We'll just climb back up the ladder, and, voila, return to camp, before dawn. And no one will be the wiser, right?"

"Good point. But I have a reason to keep on going, Oskar."

"Oh, and what might that be?"

"You know me. I have **a-d-v-e-n-t-u-r-e** in my DNA." Blake said smiling. Oskar rolled his eyes. Quickly, Blake then jumped onto the ice-sculpted boat now inches from the edge, momentum casting Blake further into the dark water.

46

"Oh, how do I get mixed up in these things? Geronimo!" Oskar complained.

Seconds later, Oskar leaped awkwardly yet successfully aboard, landing himself safely and sprawled atop the strange boat. Oskar grabbed two paddles and began to maneuver a network of massive columns rising from the water. Their ride was easy, too easy! Oskar withdrew his paddles from the water; the boys continued to move quickly, pulled by a demanding current. The boat listed leftward, facing the water's edge and an imposing iron gateway. Their ice-boat slid well on to a sandy edge, as the boys peered beyond the gate at a rivulet of the strange water, cutting under the gate, rushing, pushing out through several iron lattice holes, which flowed out and further below to a small circular pool. Were there rooms there? Such an odd place to have rooms of any sort.

"Come on. Let's go down and see what we can find. Remember, a-d-v-e-n-t-u-r-e!"

And so they scrambled to the lower pool, finding an ornate door on the cave's sidewall.

"Let's look around. Try to find a map of some sort, anything! This is high adventure!"

Blake searched, wandering about in circles as the waterfall called both boys forward, pulling them closer and closer. Peering through the icy cascading water, they could see an ornate door handle extending from the rocky wall, no sign of a door, just the handle. Odd, very odd. Yet Blake bravely stepped through the icy water to get a better look. Thoroughly soaked, he twisted the handle, initiating a sequence, a series of rectangular light-shafts which pulsed toward him, providing easy entrance behind the noisy waterfall.

A secret room! A massive library, leather everywhere, animal skins atop what appeared to be ornate furniture constructed of ice. Odd. Blake walked across the strange room to examine and explore. Oskar followed. Perched on a massive desk, lay a dagger, magnifying glass, and map. The map featured a clear blue land mass with white lines etched in all directions. And, somehow, it hovered, this map, above the desk about an inch. But what intrigued both boys even more was not the map but a strange triangular object, which didn't seem to fit in

47

the room's *old-world* context, this was a sleek, contemporary *futuristic* device. What was it, this shimmering triangle? An instrument of sorts? A measuring device? It seemed to be missing a piece, this clear dark green object which radiated bright light.

Blake turned to his friend, "Hey Oskar. Look at this!"

Oskar's jaw dropped as he managed, "Let me see that." Oskar fondled Blake's new-found treasure.

"I wonder, if this and... this..." he slowly said as he withdrew from his pocket his matching half of the triangle which he had found wedged in the redwood tree. "... could be put together like...this?"

Oskar carefully fitted the two pieces together, causing a "PINGPINGWOOOSH!" Light, like front-line warriors, pulsed toward the boys, spreading its *power* in all directions, across the room, up the walls, illuminating the arched ice ceiling and, like lightening, blue lasers shot down upon and through the overwhelmed duo.

"Wha... what is this?" Oskar stuttered.

"Look! Oskar! Look! It's.. it's a video *cam!*"

"I don't think so, Blake. It's much...much more! Hey, look, it's rising. Where's it going?"

Slowly, the glowing triangle, turning with purpose, agility, and other worldly *authority*, moved to absolute dead center of the room, pointing its full quiver of *light sabers*, hundreds of trembling lasers which remained at the ready to be thrust into the awaiting ice walls, bypassing the fearful boys below. Dead silence prevailed.

Later, in the not too-distant future, Blake and Oskar will be tested by this triangle, which is now suspended above them. And as it intensifies its fretful light, a shrill call to attention, can be heard, a humming *Johnny one-note* growing louder, from what they will later call *Trigon*, their lives are thus assaulted. Their wills are captured. Blake and Oskar, paralyzed, now staring at one another, eyes wide open, fear written across their very lives, now stare at each other in disbelief, both boys unaware of forthcoming battle and lurking danger just ahead.

*The dream ended, and Jacob woke up from his sleep. Jacob (to himself): There is no doubt in my mind that the Eternal One is in this place, and I didn't even know it!*

**Genesis 28:16 The Voice translation**

## CHAPTER 4: ARBOC

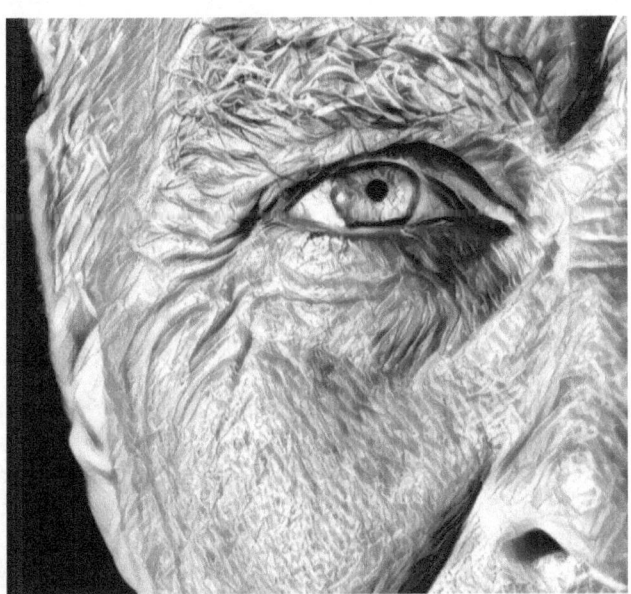

ARBOC AWOKE FROM DEEP SLEEP to the sound of Tridesicon's shrill ZRK, a daily early morning, cold crackling invasive noise, chilling to the bone. Every morning, at precisely the same time, Tridesicon walls become infected with an angry sound like a slap in the face. Generated by the confluence of DNA chemicals, Tridesicon citizens as well as walls become conduits for the ZRK and all awaken exactly at the same time! And this morning, again, right on time, the ZRK had done its job. Arboc sat up in his bed stuporous, way too groggy for his demanding day, ready to pound the walls in retribution. A thin outside light played with his face. His room, completely constructed of dark yet multi-colored ice, had been crafted by Queen Mordna herself. Ice windows, ice lamps, an ice door, ice bed, ice lights, all so very Tridesicon!

Ice furniture and accoutrements sound uncomfortable to the uninitiated! Sleeping or sitting on top of a block of frigid, solid ice might upset some, but here, on Tridesicon, it was rather routine! Emperor Micron and a group of researchers hundreds of years ago, had discovered chemicals and formulas, which made the ice somehow, how shall I say it, comfortable? Tridesicon's SKAFED ice feels exactly like most beds or cushions or reclining couches, almost fluffy, except still considered ice and still freezing cold, not exactly what you might choose if there were other options, but SKAFED ice was abundant, and really quite ordinary. Everyone seemed accustomed to its frigid ways. Tridesicon's morphed ice is called SKAFED ice, cushioned genetically, ice, cell by cell, alive! Very different, Arboc, his clothes and the many furry animal skins put about his room, were the only non-ice contents in the room. Arboc sat on his bed, dazed, turning slowly away from the light, pondering his day, his duties coming at him fast and furious, one by one, hard decisions from the heart of his Emperor Micron. Head in hands, Arboc mused.

Cycles that every living being goes through. Some have it good. Rich family, little responsibilities, awesome house, and the list go on. But others dream of these things, when reality is hard. Arboc felt part of the hard reality, and part of the soft and easy reality. He was fairly rich, had a family, and was a good man. He was adequately paid for his work. Assistant to Micron. There are people all over Tridesicon who would give their limbs just to work for Micron. But the ruler of Tridesicon was quite favorable toward Arboc and, when all was said and done, Arboc only. But Arboc didn't like it. It was wrong. Micron was a selfish, cruel leader who labored in cruel and selfish acts, in which Arboc, though quite reluctantly, assisted. Every night, Arboc went to bed with a heavy, guilty heart. And in that time, Arboc prayed for someone, perhaps Some One, to send a hero, someone to defeat the powerful Micron. One that would bring back the sun and radiant joy to the original land of Westron, Micron's empire which now lived out its fate, its cold destiny in an eternal land of winter.

Arboc stared at his mirror and thought, "Why, Lord, am I doing this? Why am I working such evil? Micron shouldn't have the Trigon, I know this with everything in me, for Micron and the Trigon are a sure recipe for the murder of millions and absolute Tridesiconian global annihilation. Lord, show me a way out." Life. He gave himself a long, drilling stare. His eyes were tired, very tired. His color radiated an ugly green-beige; he threw his hands up, hastily waving away his image from further scrutiny. Arboc quickly replaced his teeth with fresh ice ones; something quite routine in Tridesicon, and quickly changed into his transport uniform. Now, ready to go, he opened a small circular hatch to his main door and left.

Micron's palace, a rather gloomy affair, loomed upon a distant hill the size of a small mountain, no trees, only ice and snow. Behind the palace a sheer cliff cascaded two hundred feet to a sea of frozen water. Inside the hill a cave extended like the inner corridors of a sponge, searching every inner portion and level of the cavernous mountain, like an ant colony matrix. The cave's opening jutted through a mid-portion of the cliff wall. Tridesicons who lived there within the mountain were rich, very rich, and well adapted to serve Micron's every command. There were hundreds of family members who had throughout the years become enslaved, inch by inch, to Micron's evil ways.

A forest of colored, what we would call stalactites and stalagmites extended dangerously downward or stood teetering on the floor, all constructed of ice. Most Tridesicons called them *icelomes* for it is in these constructions that Micron's privileged individuals lived.

Arboc carefully opened his two-foot thick ice door, scanning a 360. This icelome had somehow become home, his formal address, but he was never was at home here. His tiny icelome comprised a sleek, minimal dwelling with walls that woke him each day and instantly obeyed his every need. All walls were alive, connected, networked, in a sense, and produced answers to many Tridesicon needs. However, Arboc in this moment, his hand scraping his chin, wondered if there ever could be more to his life, if he could somehow escape or be rescued. He squinted, staring through his main shuttered ice window at other dimly-lit icelomes beyond, as they stretched up and down, from the cave's ceiling and floor. Bridges connected the icelomes in a network of precision and purpose. Below, other constructions, scrambling about upon the cave floor, flowed between the abundance of rising ice structures, fighting for life like the small undergrowth beneath a redwood canopy. And still further down below the massive primary ice floor were bustling shops and markets. Yes, it was a busy place, but not home. He now felt empty. His heart ached. Wearily, Arboc ascended his icelome, traversing a spiral staircase. He finally reached an outer bridge: A-24-Zrk.

The walk was long for most people, but for any servant or soldier of Micron, transport suits enabled its wearers to lay upon any ice floor to slide forward with great speed without having to go downhill or be pushed, thanks to Tridesicon's *woything* leather, an invention of live skin which easily conveyed its wearer from point A to B in seconds! Arboc, attired in his best neon green transport suit, lay down on the ice in a luge-like pencil formation, just beyond A-24-Zrk. Pressing a triangle button at his throat, Arboc began to move. He slid down the spiral path that moved down to an outer icelome bridge. Dodging others also making their way downward, Arboc made it to the half-way point, a plateau of transparent ice, where a bridge extended straight forward. Arboc sped across the bridge like a fired bullet. After passing four icelome entrance bridges, he made it to a divided ramp, sliding down to the left, a path reserved only for Micron's privileged people. Service personnel knew to turn right here! All Arboc had to do from there was to take a massive loop around the center's metropolex to the cave's major opening. Arboc slowed himself by placing his magnetic glove tips upon the ice floor, gradually slowing to a comfortable stop. To the uninitiated this trek would appear to be awesome; to Arboc it was boring routine.

He turned off his protective invisible head bubble. Wearily, Arboc lugged to the left, trudging up a small slope to the edge of a huge transparent door. He stuck his tongue into a slit next to the elevator and then pulled it out. A mechanism immediately recognized Arboc's DNA, permitting entrance into the elevator. Arboc looked down at a furious fast-moving fan that whirled and whined below. He quickly jumped inside the elevator enabling a pressure shaft to grab him, shoving Arboc upward into the air, pushing his body through a transparent tunnel. It suddenly curved to the right, only to deposit Arboc onto a comfortable skafted-ice landing platform. He quickly walked beyond the skafted padding into the security entrance of Micron's palace.

"Good sun rises, Arboc! Today's job is in your office on your Zrk-24 tablet. Get busy!"

It was Micron speaking from his special room, a mixture of throne, leather, ice, animal skins, trophies, chemical ice inventions and evil.

"Yes sir!" Arboc obediently replied. Arboc shoved open a thick set of ice doors, pressing hard with his palms. They swung open and made a thud as they hit the inner wall. The room consisted of low-slung bookcases, leather books, animal skins, ice furniture and massive communication windows. His pentagonal desk boasted a top that lifted higher than its edges at its outer rim, slanting backward to reveal a bank of buttons, switches, throttles and levers, all *littered* about it seemed, each with its own purpose. But the section of the desk that stood in front of his chair was clean without any flashing mechanics. It was for writing on tablets, work that required his daily focused attentions.

Arboc scanned the room. Although luxurious with abundant radiant blue light, his room stood cold and menacing, for evil was at work and his workday normally included evil ways and decisions! All Micron-driven commands thrust Arboc like a rocket through his day. Arboc shook his head.

Massive columns proudly lined up outside in curious formations from the ceiling down, covered with carved Trigons and curious lifeless metal-plated alien and human body parts which were worked into an impressive complex design, looking more like raised foreign texts than what had once been alive. Arboc looked away in disgust, as he always did every morning. On the walls were many triangular doors leading to offices and supplies, but his room was at the very end of a triangular portal, opening to a grand staircase, of spirals and cuneiform triangles with small straight rods protruding, inviting all forward to their death if anyone should even touch its balustrade or step. A warning sign stood before the first step. Reserved only for Micron, Mordna, and for now Arboc, the staircase pointed upward to two offices, intimidating all.

Mordna's door sparkled, refracting Trisdesicon's ever-present blue light. Stairs extended above from her door to Micron's throne room. Slowly ascending the grand staircase, Arboc stepped upon a luminous yet transparent walkway to Micron's room. He quietly stood there for permission to enter.

"Enter!" Micron commanded.

"Sir, I was wondering...." began Arboc.

"You are not here to wonder. Obey is all you need do!" shouted Micron.

Turning his eyes away, Arboc said, "...but, but, sir, I...."

"Silence, Arboc! Do your work. Go!" Micron demanded.

"Yes, sir!" replied Arboc.

"One more thing. The instructions on your Zrk-24 tablet demand immediate action. Now, go!" Micron instructed.

Arboc backed toward the entrance and with a slight, yet hesitant bow, exited. Descending the staircase, his mind raced in defiance, "No, No, No, Micron. You need to stop your madness!"

Arboc entered his workspace. As Micron had informed him, a sleek tablet lay upon his desk with neon blue writing, glowing, and demanding his immediate attention.

Tridesicons speak English, however, their written language is different. Everything is written in triangles. Some with points, some with curves, and others with patterns in the middle, some with symbols and strange rods projecting from the curious shapes. All together the Tridesicon alphabet comprises several hundred letters, a language rich in meaning, emphasis and definition. Micron's message read,

"Arboc, my trusted ally, you must immediately check our main prison. Some of the new men there have just come back from earth. Inquire as to their purpose for leaving our galaxy without my permission. If they won't talk, make them talk. And after they do, kill them! This is their Imperial Punishment for the breaking of my law. – Micron, the one and only God."

Arboc slowly returned his Zrk-24 to its holder, musing upon what he would require of the Commander General Level 2. He picked up a heavy stylus, an instrument three times thicker than a pencil. Searing laser lava, an endless supply produced within, would now drain forth from the stylus at every word, freezing instantly upon the tablet as

56

soon as the solution touched the metallic slab, etching in Arboc's message:

"Iggip, this is your Commander...I have been instructed by Micron to interrogate a group of outlaws. I myself, though, have other business to attend to. You and a party of men shall take my place. My other business is also at the prison, so you will accompany me, therefore, for the long ride there. I will meet you at the docks at precisely AJ-D78 (8:00am earth time) – Arboc, Chief Commander."

Arboc walked across his room to a small slit in the wall next to the ice doorway. He slipped the tablet in, but it never came out, of course. You see, in the middle of the slot lay a portal specifically for sending tablet messages. The portal identified the addressee and sender. The tablet instantly made its way to Iggip's message portal, out a wall slot, and to his desktop. On Tridesicon one can actually feel time. Without having to see where its two suns' positions were or look upon the multiple shadows they cast, one just knows inside what time it is. It was YH-D78, which is 9:30am earth time. Quickly, Arboc pushed through half of his tablet work, leaving the rest for his return.

He lay upon the flat portal, sliding not back into the cave, but on to a roadway encompassing the palace front lawn. A snowy slope gradually led down to the bottom of the hill to a Shrine, where countless poor people lived, past the *Ghidmonga Land*, and finally to the docks. Along the jagged road, an artery from the heart of its Emperor, pushed its way downward upon his dark mountain. Barbed rocks bordered each side, rocks with points sharp as needles each boasting multi-faceted razor edges. Tridesicons feared every twisting and turn of the maelstrom roadway, trembling as they whispered their admonitions: *At all costs, avoid the ROGS!* (*Rocks of Offending Grievous Swords*). Without incident, Arboc shot down the path like a bullet, avoiding all jagged points!

He slid left onto an auxiliary path, passing by hundreds of travelers who laboriously traveled mostly uphill it always seemed, on foot step by step they labored without complaint. Arboc could then see the Shrine, a rickety old village constructed of stone and wood. It was a sorry sight, and Emperor Micron despised this place and its old and unstable inhabitants. He sent them there so they wouldn't get in his way, and Arboc found it terribly unjust. Every week, he went early in the morning when all were asleep, to set containers of food and other provisions, provided via Tridesicon magic. As Arboc slid by, he, a benevolent St. Nicholas, could see the massive poverty and lowliness they called life. He tried not to look too closely for his heart was heavy. As hard as this was, it was nothing compared to the danger that lay ahead!

He exited the village quickly and all that lay about him were open plains and a treacherous cliff, which abruptly concluded the path. An ice ramp suddenly and swiftly descended. Arboc's speed doubled. Down, below, *Ghidmonga Land* (translated "Kings of Death") lay vulnerable, open-faced.

Tridesicons are seasoned space travelers, you see, and never had they ever seen such savage, deadly, monstrous creatures in all of space and its planets. The entire land had ice creations in the shape of a cone with the point end up. It was as if a huge giant nailed in ice nails from underneath the surface. In these upside-down cones, which they called glaeforms, lived the Ghidmongas. They were disfigured velociraptors. Empress Mordna loved them. They had character and were fun to watch as they battled one another, like pups learning their way. Mordna could remember when, back during earth's Stone Age, they had visited, choosing only the ugliest, most ferocious ones, and when they proudly introduced them to Tridesicon.

There, the velociraptors adapted to Tridesicon quickly in a new atmosphere that mutated their reproductive systems. Micron shot most of them with poison-filled bullets to stop the rapidly growing Ghidmonga population. He tried to kill them all, but they grew stronger, immune to Micron's poison-filled bullets. With much effort and the passage of several years, Micron then relocated all Ghidmongas to Ghidmonga Land's massive clifftop and that is where they have remained ever since.

Arboc flew across the rugged way, which was now trampled and scarred with hundreds of ruts. He increased his power *two squared* by activating a triangular button at his throat. His *thrust power* made his way secure, potentially avoiding any foe. By now most of Micron's old soldiers had died, but a small remnant still lived. About ten miles beyond the *Ghidmonga Land*, Commander Arboc slid up a hill. A lonely beach lay just ahead. The water was darker blue than earth's seas. A shoreline literally sparkled pure diamonds, reminding one of the treasures of Uxtal, and its colony of escaped Tridesicons. Ten docks sprouted out, tethered to ten boats, which swayed upon the deep blue water.

Arboc could see some of his men already at their boats, ready to set off. Not more than a football field away, Arboc, smiling, suddenly thought of something that would add some levity. And, if there ever was a time for levity, it was now.

"Let's show them how cool and fit their Commander really is. Let's see if I can pull this off," schemed Arboc.

He stiffened, flailing his arms but with purpose. At the edge of a fast-approaching dock, Arboc continued to speed forward. His gloves held securely at his side; he then slapped at the dock which released him to rocket high into the air. The force of his increased speed had ripped off his gloves and as they lay upon the dock, Arboc, now in mid-air, flew into a front flip, landing on the tethered boat's deck. Everyone cheered and patted him on the back and said, "Awesome stunt, Commander! Totally cool! You should do it again, Bro!"

Some of them had already caught snippets of *earthy slang* in their maneuvers. Satisfied, Arboc bowed three times, shifting a little so he could bow to everyone as they continued to clap and cheer.

"Why thank you, men. We ready to go?"

"Yes, sir. We will push the button at your command." one of the sailors replied.

"Then, go ahead! Everyone, take your positions!"

All of the men ran to something, to railing, deck or door or to an array of belted seats. Grabbing his returned gloves, Arboc held tightly to a wood frame handle. The captain at the main wheel hurriedly payed out. The ship cut into the blue water.

"Captain, push it!" Arboc commanded.

Instantly the ship turned around, facing away from the dwindling dock. A huge *whooshing* sound accompanied a brilliant blast as the back of the ship's Tri-Rockets engaged. A miraculous upthrust slowly moved the ship up over the water and forward to its destination.

As there is absolutely no wind in the thin atmosphere of Tridesicon, it is a technical mastery, which moves heavy ships through its air. Flying above the partially frozen water wasteland, curious shapes had formed, piecing together random green, black and red ice floes. From time to time, ice projected hundreds of feet above the wasteland, arching to catch a fellow pillar. Most of them looked like stalagmites, larger than skyscrapers. Other pillars formed huge circular archways while others became transparent walls and icebergs, refracting Tridesicon's two suns, major and minor. Up ahead, the prison pierced into a flat sixty-foot black iceberg about a mile across. At its base ships could park in several of the iceberg's cavernous holes. Additional structures networked into the prison. It was a lonely, removed, miserable part of the Tridesicon Empire and Micron liked it that way.

Arboc looked below at the signs facing up at his ship, one by one as they flew by, zig-zagging between each prison point. The first 10 ten were Z10-Z1, the next 10, Y10-Y1, and then X10-X1. The fugitives that Arboc and his men now sought were held in prison point E-2. Intelligence had informed him of this. Thanks to his fire-powered ship, all made it to the right location point safely, and the ship slipped carefully under a parking archway of black ice to security check.

An invasion of twelve men boarded the ship, all armed. Four searched for any explosive devices or missiles. Two asked routine questions regarding Arboc's business and the remaining six trained their weapons on each of Arboc's men. Standard procedure required intense scrutiny and investigation; Micron was profoundly paranoid, and he never felt safe without taking the utmost precautions.

"Ah, good to see you again, Arboc. I see you have finally decided to visit my quaint prison point."

"Greetings, Elov. Business has brought me to many places, and I am glad that it has chosen to bring me here. I can see, though, that the past ten years have been unkind to you." Arboc inquired.

"No, my friend. Sooner or later Micron shall send me to the Shrine with the rest of the old, sick, and disabled."

Arboc winced at the thought, at the fate his old dear friend now faced. Arboc's heart ached. Suddenly, one of the prison guards, attired in standard uniform of silver and black, stepped forward to his commander, "They are cleared, sir. And their business checks out with Micron's message."

"Good. Gather your men, Arboc, and we will take you to our new guests."

Leaving the ship, the men stepped forward, one by one, on to a crude wooden platform. It made a small zig-zag which stretched to a somber grey wall displaying a massive iron door. No bars, just solid metal. Elov pulled out a short flat metal stick from his deep pocket, and plunged his entry key into a hole on the door's edge. Light shone from inside, as the door unlocked with a loud click. Elov jumped up to the rail on top of the door to pull it down. With difficulty the door slid downwards into a waiting crack in the floor. The party crossed over the lowered door, while Elov's foot kept the door down in place. Once everyone had moved ahead of the temporary barrier, Elov released his foot, allowing the door to spring noisily back in place. A loud metal clunk indicated a solid locking device was now in place.

He led them down a dark corridor. A mixture of moans and curses assailed their ears, filling the damp air. Prisoners banged on the walls and screamed for mercy. Arboc knew what each cell contained: a prisoner with no hope, only torment. Instantly, somehow, unexpectedly, an image popped into Arboc's head. Elsa, beautiful Elsa!

"Elov!" Arboc shouted. They all jumped at his sudden unexpected shout.

"What?" asked Elov, startled.

"Oh, sorry, I, um, we need to talk. You know, privately?"

Elov stared at him for a couple of seconds, then yelled, "Guard!"

His eyes remained fixed on Arboc, as he motioned to one of his underlings. A man instantly appeared, around a corner, saluting Elov.

"Yes, sir?" he said, breathless.

"Take the Commander's men to cell blocks QAR-QBC." He stiffened as if he suddenly had grown taller, more imposing, looking down at the guard. "Now!"

The guard beckoned for the group to follow his lead, and they marched down the hallway and then behind a wall out of sight.

"Well? What is it, Arboc?"

"I need to ask a favor of you, Elov. A girl who arrived not a month ago is a friend of mine. Please, just this once, bend the rules; let me see her."

Elov's eyes narrowed, as he considered Arboc's request. The room filled with awkward silence.

"Listen Arboc, it's none of my business knowing your passions, so I won't ask, as a friend. But you know the rules. You need permission."

"Forget the permission code, Elov! This is important! Just this once, please, my friend. Don't worry. I won't report you, I will..."

Arboc could see that Elov wasn't budging, frozen in refusal.

"Elov! Please! I'm begging you!"

"I will not let you do as you wish." Elov said sternly. "Unless you give something in return." he added.

Arboc was confused. "What do you want? My house, my job, my money?"

"No, friend, of course not! You do remember that I am not a Tridesiconian."

"I remember this fact completely. You are from the flat lands of Drow. But what does that have to do with..."

"Arboc, we need Borealis. If we do something against CODE, guilt will overcome us. We need Borealis to douse it out. If not, we will both die. The CODE is powerful; it knows. Borealis will win. I know this. But the enemy: It never gives up opportunity to divide and kill."

Arboc pondered this, quickly coming to a possible solution.

"What if... what if I gave it to you, after I see my friend?"

"Really, it just depends. If I have my mind focused on something that is distracting or that needs my immediate attention, then, yes. I can't let the guilt settle in or it will poison me. After an hour of guilt, I surely will die and so will you!" Arboc now knew that he was putting Elov's life on the line for this, but it was important enough to take the risk. He had to see Elsa; his own life without her would be death anyway.

"Elov, the woman I want to see...her name is Elsa. She was wrongly convicted of leaving the Galaxy. She was merely heading to Unigo for food and supplies, but was hit by an asteroid on her flight out. Her ship out of control, nearly crashed into Vulnus, just beyond Micron's galaxy. But then he saved her, only to bring her back to prison on the charge of exiting his Galaxy without permission. And do you know why she was even heading to Unigo in the first place?"

"No, this is the first I have heard about any of this."

"She was on her way to buy and collect food and find attendants for our... our... wedding."

Arboc leaned against the wall, slowly sliding down to the floor, hands covering his face. His tears fell slowly down his cheeks, summoning compassion from Elov. Arboc shook his head in defiance of his momentary weakness.

"She is secured up there, at the Tower AZ, Level 2, my poor friend." Elov turned away to remove his tears with his sleeve. Arboc could tell that Elov's compassion was enough to dissolve his CODE guilt. And if there was any left, guilt, Arboc intended for Elov to witness the wedding, which held the sentiment that could restore the guilt of the whole race of Drow.

"She has been here a while, Arboc, but let me ask. Why do you want to see her so badly, right now? Couldn't you wait until her time is up? It will be only a few more weeks."

"Because, I promised her that we would be married today." Elov then stopped.

"No, Arboc. I can manage your seeing her, but there is no way we can get her back to the mainland with you and..."

"I agree. So, we are going to have to get married the traditional way. We can return as a couple, she and I. It's the law. Couple's get a free pass, right?"

Elov's eyes bulged.

"So you're suggesting first we *loophole* Micron's law, letting you see a prisoner without his permission, then you want to remove the prisoner from her cell, and marry her here?" Why do you think this seems so possible, Arboc?"

"Anything Micron commands is unimportant to me, Elov, especially if his commands come between Elsa and me. I know that finding ways around Micron's laws is hard for you, and the power of CODE guilt will seek to kill you as you know, but I know also, for a fact, that witnessing a marriage can cure that instantly." Elov was startled at Arboc's logic.

"Me?"

"Of course, you! Who else? Every marriage needs a best man, don't you think? You are definitely my choice!"

"Me?"

"Oh, and I almost forgot, we need a *Sirman (priest)*! You were one once, right? You must still be! I bet you have the Book of Good and Evil somewhere around here? If you don't mind, would you marry us?"

"Me?"

"Elov, I'm not talking to the ice wall, am I? Yes, you!"

"Me, well, I um, this is so... um, thank you! Give me a second and I will be ready. First let's go through this door."

They merged into a tiny room, no bigger than a family size table. An iron spiral staircase to Elsa, thrust upward through multiple tower levels. Arboc looked up. The staircase reached high to the ceiling. Climbing in circles, they quickly reached the second level. Commander Arboc, emotionally spent, slammed himself into the epicenter pole and clung to it, his eyes sealed shut. This was his moment, to take her in his arms, to love her forever.

"Come on Arboc, we're almost there."

Twenty more steps. With one hand on the rail and the other on the epicenter, they continued to Level 2, Door Z. Elov reached Elsa's cell first, unlocking the heavy latch with his key stick. Arboc's feet froze. This was the moment, the one he had dreamed of for so long.

"On with the wedding," whispered Elov.

He formally extended his hand to Arboc, introducing entry to a cul-de-sac of cells. Each cell boasted a singular metal name plate: in Tridesicon fashion, names were simple. No family names, no middle names. Elov whispered: "Barkhad, Nimon, hmmm, over there, yes, there, Elsa!" This was all that mattered to Arboc. He was trembling. Elsa, only steps away.

"Elov, you go in first, okay?"

"Yes, Arboc, my good friend, she is here and has no idea...."

"Oh...oh...!" Arboc suddenly began to pace back and forth, around the apse in full circle. Elsa, stood inside her cell, waiting, questioning. There was only silence. Time seemed to stop.

Sitting in her cell, a beautiful brown-haired woman, slender, with sad eyes, looked at Elov, wondering why her captor had come once again to her cell. Perhaps there were more demands and questions. Her face was pale from prison life, a pallor that somehow remained graceful, enduring and elegant. Yet, her solitary life had taken its toll. She knew her chains were heavy and would remain so.

"Yes?" she softly inquired of Elov.

Another voice responded. It was not Elov.

"Elsa?"

The room began to spin. Could it be? Her hand covered her lips, questioning whether she was mistaken.

"Arboc?" she hesitated.

Arboc felt as if everything, all demands and questions and fears that had stood in his head, had suddenly disappeared. Elov stepped away as Elsa ran toward her cell entry. It WAS Arboc.

"Oh, Elsa!" Arboc embraced his true love. They hugged and kissed and cried. Elov stood in the doorway and looked away from Arboc and Elsa's private moment. Between sobs and tears that fell, smashing to the floor, and laughter, Elsa and Arboc could only speak broken sentences, remembrances, stories of where they had been and where they were headed. Their voices raised up to the ceiling only to float to the floor as they held hands, shook their heads and embraced and kissed again.

Elov, stepping forward into their *love dance*, removed Elsa's chains. "We need to hurry. My watch ends in two hours. I have a spot where you can marry. It's past all of the prison points on this god-forsaken iceberg, well beyond Micron's CODElimits."

"We can't do that, Elov. It's not Micron's way. He'll kill us!" Elsa warned.

"It doesn't really matter now. Already we have broken three major rules. But you will like it, I'm sure. This is something that you only see on earth or on Uxtal. Come, I have a secret passageway down to my ship." Quickly, the three exited the cell as Elov jumped up toward the ceiling, grabbing a chain, pulling down a ladder from above.

"How... how... did you...?"

"The roof is just a hologram, Elsa. It's not real. Pretty good fake, huh? All I have to do now is to secure this ladder, here, right here. Going up, anyone?"

They clambered up the vertical tunnel to its pinnacle where they discovered a commanding view of the black iceberg's Prison Points and surrounding deep waters.

"Now, Elsa, you understand that after this wedding you will need to return to your cell and I will have to lock you up again. Okay?"

"If you must, Elov."

"Now, here is another ladder. It will take us down to the dock below. We will use my ship." They made it to the cavernous underground dock and to Arboc's tethered ship. It was good to be safe, together, away from the terrors of prison.

"Now hold on to your hats," demanded Arboc. "I'm gonna push this button in 3... 2... 1... here we go!"

He slammed his fist on the red power button, propelling the ship's rocket to engage. Arboc steered past a few Prison Points until Elov took over. The wind whipped their faces. The sky was dark as it always was, and so were the boundaries. Up ahead, a wall of black ice rose from the sea. No one had ever been there before, ever, to Micron's knowledge. They shot through the wall, admitting bright light, which shone upon them from all directions.

Elov turned the engines off. The ship floated silently further into the light. They sat there for minutes as their eyes adjusted. The light was bright. Arboc looked up and gasped. The familiar Tridesicon dark night blue dome sparkled in the brilliant earthy, bright-blue sky. He could see all nine suns, in splendid formation: three triangles melting into each other. Three, yet one. The air was clear and clean. A breeze whispered its presence.

"Westron..." Arboc breathed.

"The last bit of it. You remember when life was like this, Arboc? When Micron tried to poison Tridesicon with Trigon's power; he poisoned the entire planet, except for this spot. This is where people like you fled. They sought any remaining light and worked to protect it, building a *protection orb* right here, so that this area would never be infected, remember? That is why other races say our planet is like an eye. They see mostly blackness, except for this dot of blue sky. I came here once, secretly, only to find that everyone had died from poisoned fish.

"You mean to say that Micron poisoned the fish just to kill the last bit of Westronians?"

"Yes, Arboc. His cruelty knows no limit. We cannot even eat fish because of Micron's evil."

"Curse the name of Micron forever." Arboc muttered.

"The tyrant though, cannot come here. As you know, he hates the light. Long ago, Micron sent the ZrkBOMB, infused with Trigon's power. Yes, it exploded on Micron's command, causing dark light to fall upon the entire planet, except here.

"Yes, yes, Elov, I was there when it happened. It is the source of my fiercest nightmares."

"And mine as well. Come, we need to hurry."

They stepped off the boat, all three dancing across the ice floes to a major floe, an island of multicolored ice. A massive archway littered with pink flowers, loomed over the *floe-island* to celebrate light and beauty of the Triangles which hovered and shimmered above. Below, an ice altar stood surrounded by an array of striped and furry animal skins and ice benches for a small gathering.

Arboc, embracing his true love, laughed, "And here we are. This is where I shall marry you, my forever Darling, Elsa!"

And in the passage of time Elsa returned to her prison quarters and Arboc to his. Micron remained unaware of the two lovers, now married, and best man Elov, and what had happened in the brilliance of Westron's remnant, and Micron's laws, which had been brilliantly transgressed. Arboc's heart remained heavy yet he knew that he and his beloved would be together one day, soon he hoped, beyond the oppressive life to which he had to reluctantly return.

Arboc's lab doors swung wide open with a loud thud against the wall, as he entered the room. He had been absent a few days and everybody knew it. Everyone stopped their work. Arboc looked about, checking everything. None were absent. Everyone stood in proper dress code attire. The laboratory was active with multi-colored swirls of smoke, bubbling liquids oozing over transparent beakers, funnels, and test tubes, just what Arboc wanted to see. Nothing had changed.

"Good, everything is in check, men. Now, *chop-chop*! We need to get a move on."

He walked to his lab desk when a short man, squat high, waddled to Arboc, grunting, "Good morning, Commander."

"Good morning, Mr. Tello. Give me good news."

"We have almost found the Trigon, sir!"

Arboc stopped dead in his tracks as Mr. Tello waddled up to him, face to face.

"Show me."Arboc demanded. He walked faster now to the main screen.

"Well, sir, we have found the galaxy. In fact, it is at Earth. Located in their United States, in the state of, how do they say it... Calficmacis?"

"California, you dimwit."

"Yes, well, there are still two sets of CODES we were unable to decipher. Oh, and, sir, did you just get married?"

"What makes you say that?"

"Oh, nothing. I just have never noticed the tattoo on your finger."

"My wife died years ago. End of story. Now go find the codes and I will decipher them."

In a flash, Mr. Tello breathlessly returned with a tablet filled with strange letters and writing.

"Someone found the Trigon and activated it, sir. The signal went off and our system sensed it and..."

"Yes, Mr. Tello, I know how it works. My question is WHO found it? I thought it was fully hidden."

"Excuse me, sir? You hid it?"

"It's unimportant now." Arboc explained.

"Oh, I see." Mr. Tello replied, confused.

Arboc slowly sat down in his chair to read his tablet. He attempted to decipher its Code.

"I'm sorry, Mr. Tello, but this makes absolutely no sense whatsoever. It is a language I have never seen before, though I don't think it's anything found on Earth. Your coordinates must be incorrect. It seems to me that it might be located on G2 or Proation."

At this, a worker at the back of the room stood up and yelled, "I found it! I know where it is. I found it!"

Arboc leapt from his chair. And sure enough, there it was boldly displayed on the hologram screen: a topographical map of Earth. On it appeared a tiny blue dot precisely where the Trigon coordinates intersected. The man, who made the discovery, Kale, zoomed in. It was in California, United States! Then it zoomed to its exact location. In the Redwoods under the big tree, right there! Arboc remembered and gasped that someone had broken into the hiding place, entering his tunnel where he had hidden Trigon centuries ago. The images of two boys scuttling out and walking away from the tree as they held Trigon in their hands, had Arboc's full attention. Every signal alarm went off inside him.

"I must inform Micron!" Kale taunted.

"No, wait!" Arboc countered.

Silence fell upon Arboc's echoed protest, as every head in the room turned towards him.

"Um... well... send it to me...instead. I will, of course, send it on to Emperor Micron personally. This would be the proper chain-of-command. Protocol, you know, right?"

"It's fine, Arboc, we will save you the trouble."

Before Arboc could intervene, Kale turned to the wall, and dropped his tablet into the receiving slot. Now it was too late, and everybody knew it.

*So, you, by the help of God, return, hold fast to love and justice, and wait continually for God.*

**Hosea 12:6 ESV translation**

## CHAPTER 5: MORDNA

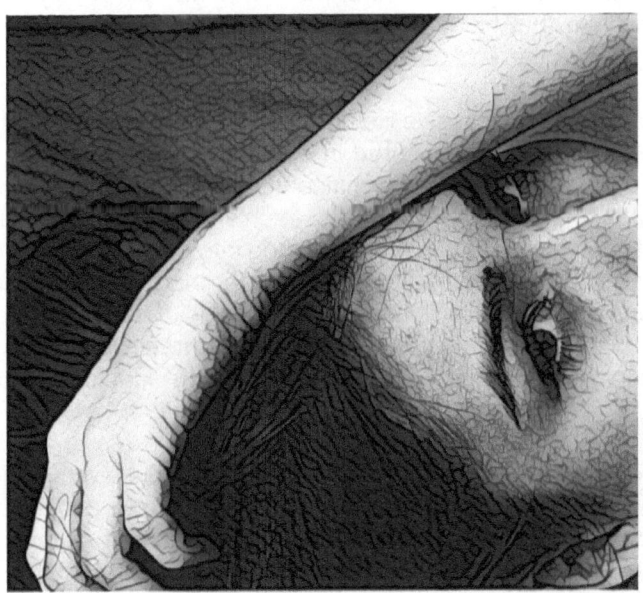

DOWN THE HALL, LITTLE SHUMBY scuffled past several of Her Majesty's ornate boudoir doorways, at her emphatic and royal request. Shumby, obedient and short, boasted sad and baggy eyes. His thick neck quickly led to a round torso, giving him a deceivingly friendly *Twiddle-Dum* look, yet without stripes! His blue skin glistened in the ambient light as he made his way down Her Majesty's Royal Hall, breathing heavily.

For many years, as Empress Mordna's assistant, Shumby had ably assisted Her Majesty in devilish tricks and evil doings. He had become accustomed to her ways and knew to expect the worst. He was there to serve and there was no way out! Royally tasked to clean up all of Mordna's Quarters and indeed any of Mordna's routine messes, in fact the entire palace, assisted only by a small team of robot workers. Cleaning had become his specialty.

It was early morning, too early, long before the Zrk would activate all walls, assaulting citizens to awaken to a new day. Why had she rung for him so early, Shumby wondered.

Mordna, steps away, grew impatient for Shumby. She desired him to immediately clean up yet another mess she had purposely made just to remind him that he was her servant, nothing more, nothing less. Simply, he was there to obey her every command!

Shumby swung two massive ice doors apart. He rushed past Mordna's Royal Guards, who were attired in standard purple with silver stripe. Mordna's Quarters were magnificent.  Her transparent ice walls featured an array of sharp icespikes, each spike radiating brilliant laser shafts of light, knife-like projections jutting into every room and corridor from her encasing transparent icewalls. Mordna's dangerous icespike formations and hate-filled patterns easily struck intended fear into the hearts of uninitiated visitors. Above it all, three skylights admitted Tridesicon's ever present cold and menacing light upon the room below.

Thin blue light fell upon her lush canopied bed, replete with huge Royal Crested silk pillows and animal skins of black, brown and silver. Over to Mordna's massive dressers and salon table the light flowed, revealing an ornate desk, its papers and leather appointment book neatly placed atop.

Shumby had been in Empress Mordna's quarters many times before, but it had never looked quite like this. Lying on the floor by her desk were two soldiers, obviously very dead. Blood had stained the icewall nearby. Mordna, seated on her bed, cradled the head of another dead soldier. She laughed, pointing to the lifeless bodies stretched upon her royal floor. A bloody knife slowly slipped from her hand. She remained unmoved.

"Oh, good, Shumby, pick up the place for me, if you will...NOW!"

She twisted her knife triumphantly into the air, then, grinning, began to playfully prick and slice the soldier's lifeless arm. Shumby winced; he couldn't stand the sight of blood.

"As you wish, Your Majesty." he whispered.

Shumby gathered the bodies like wheat shafts, tying feet, hands and limbs together. Now in a convenient bundle, Shumby dragged them across the floor, leaving a trail of blood. He made it to the hallway disposal shaft, and dumped the remains to the waiting incinerator below. He then returned to his Mistress' side.

"Shumby, get another set of men for me to practice on!" she demanded.

"Bu... but... but Your Majesty, the games will start at any moment. Do you think it wise to...?"

"I see," she admitted. After brief deliberation, Mordna instructed, "Let's just get along now. We must not waste any more time! Get my uniform ready and my weapons too."

Shumby hurriedly removed a black latex suit from the Royal Closet.

"Hurry, Shumby!" she said, yanking her uniform from his hands. Shumby shuffled back to the closet, retrieving a heavy battle axe, and two fearsome knives. In a flash, Mordna suited up, attaching her weapons to a leather vest which extended to mid-thigh. Lastly, she fit sleek red mesh goggles over her Royal Crested leather helmet. Now aloof and satisfied, Mordna, dispensing with her servant, shoved Shumby aside, as she strode from her room.

"Away, Cretin! You are of no further use. Remove yourself from my Royal Presence!" she commanded.

But Shumby quickly reappeared, breathless at her side. "Your Majesty, the games. I must accompany you, as you have instructed."

reminded Shumby.

"If you must, I suppose; follow along. The games, Shumby, await!" Mordna laughed gleefully, stroking her knives. "Well, get your helmet on. We're late!"

The guards, saluting, separated at the main door, admitting the two through the Royal Entrance, on to a perfectly straight five hundred-foot ice path, which led to a network of bridges spanning a moat of gelatinous yellow liquid. Carefully, the royal duo, luge-like, after pressing their respective triangular throat buttons, began to slide forward, beyond the castle, across a network of iceways, arches and citizens moving in formations, clearing a path for the two, as they slid further toward the Royal *Glaeform* to the Royal Games. Though Mordna never thought it was competing, because she always won, she still looked forward with great anticipation to the bloody event. You see, ever since she had started the Annual Royal Games for her sport to be sure, she had never lost. She was skilled in the art of death, of murder, of deception. She remained unafraid and determined to pursue murder-arts as far as they would take her. The Royal Games are a complicated survival game held in arenas called *glaeforms*, endless games which expected combatants to kill all opponents while simultaneously fending off Tridesicon's genetically enhanced and mutated Ghidmongas. No one ever would volunteer to play the Royal Games other than Mordna, for it meant sure death for all opponents. Fifteen men, shivered, forced to combat, outfitted with strange and sundry weapons of destruction, stood, awaiting their imminent death, as the bloodthirsty crowd cheered, banners flying.

The royal duo quickly maneuvered the last decline to the Royal Games entrance, as the cheering crowd stood, filling the arena with anticipation. Jubiliant shouts extended well beyond the game grounds, like daggers slicing into the surrounding city. Mordna whizzed by the loud crowd into the arena's center, then stood, Shumby by her side. The crowd erupted in thunderous glee.

"Good luck, Mordna!" Shumby said, mouthing his words carefully in case he could not be heard.

"I don't need it!" Mordna whispered back over the noise. Shumby brushed the snow from his uniform, then attended to Her Majesty.

"That's enough, Shumby!"

A noise rising in volume came from behind. "Make way! Make way!"

Shumby turned carefully about. Unwilling Tridesiconians with straps around their necks attached to thick wooden clubs and chains, were being pulled into the arena like dogs on leashes. They were shoved, forced into the Glaeform arena, much to the delight of the bloodthirsty crowd. Shumby closed his wide eyes; all this impending violence really didn't suit him. He did, however, love to watch Empress Mordna kick butt and slaughter Ghidmongas. He hated the fate of innocent Tridesicons. Suddenly trumpets erupted. The Royal Games had begun. Arboc, very much off to the side of the arena, yet with a commanding view, spoke into his cheat chest microphone. It went directly to Mordna's hidden receiver, cleverly worked into her helmet. Arboc announced that she was about to be attacked from her left, while others were approaching from behind. His warnings were clipped and emphatic, maneuvering Mordna away from impending death, an overview which otherwise would have been imposible. As the attacks increased, so did Arboc's warnings and martial counsel. His tactics were brilliant, bringing others to their death at the Empress' feet. Anything threatening in any way would immediately be warded off by Arboc's tactics via Mordna's secret helmet earpiece. It was devious. It was brilliant. She would thus remain victorious in her murder arts, all to the thunderous applause of her adoring crowd.

"Mordna, behind you."

Mordna spun around, slicing the flying animal in two with her battle axe. Two more jumped at her. She knocked one in the jaw with the club end of her axe, sending the Ghidmonga far from her presence, as where it lay on its side gathering needed air. The other twisted horror came at her with such speed that Mordna had to duck quickly, as it flew over her head, smashing into one of the protective wooden gallery walls. It stumbled to its feet, as Mordna withdrew a hidden phaser gun. One shot. Success. Another shot aimed at the other menace. Success.

"Good work, my Empress. Your fans are going crazy!" Arboc shouted.

"Shut up and help, Shumby!"

"Right. You will notice a team of ten behind the ice spike in front of you."

She laughed, easily ascending its side. Seeing that the team was surrounded by a ring of Ghidmongas, she fired five shots at five beasts, hurling her weighted battle axe at a remaining *unfortunate*, burying her instrument deep into the Tridesicon skull. Death was quick and complete. Her thrown knives spun deeply into two others. She leaped down with a loud *whoosh* and a mushroom cloud of snow. Mordna was ready for more directions from Shumby.

"Look out!" he warned.

Mordna spun around, but before she could see what was coming, she was pushed from behind by a massive Ghidmonga. She stood, only to be profoundly pushed into an icespike wall, narrowly escaping death at its numerous points. At the impact, she grunted at the thud, moving slowly then toward the arena's center to reply to her attacker. She reached for her knife, only to remember having thrust it in defense seconds before. Mordna leapt for her remaining instrument of death which was deeply imbedded in the savage's skull, its Ghidmonga blood oozing, staining the snow. She had nothing whatsoever.

Shumby, with all of his past martial art advice summoned, yelled, "Run!"

Brilliant. It was all that she could do now. "What?" she snarled. "He is twice as fast and undoubtedly twice as dangerous when I am unarmed."

"You have to." cried Shumby. There is an enemy hiding in an ice spike not far from you, yes, over there. If you get to him, you could steal his gun to kill the beast..."

"And then kill him too," she shrilled. "Good choice, Shumby. Maybe you are worth more than I thought. Instead of selling you for five centrons, I will bump it up now to six!"

Shumby lowered his big eyes. Mordna began her treacherous plan as she spun about, sprinting to another clutter of ice spikes. Very quickly, the blue monster smacked her in the back with its tail. She flew forward, crashing across an ice spike, removing its point with her shoulder. Mordna, recovering, hand to wound, ran to her new prey. Stealing his firearm, she leapt back to the approaching Ghidmonga, to shoot it straight to its heart. Then without looking, she fired two shots at the terrified man.

"Only four left, Mordna," cried Shumby.

"Four! A pittance! Only four?" Mordna whined, disappointed.

"Yes, four, my Empress."

"But I have killed eleven Tridesicons and four Ghidmongas."

"What happened to the other fifteen?"

"Assassinated by another. By one man. Over there at the arena's end. See? He is really kicking butt! Oh, there goes three."

"Stop him!" she screamed.

"Now you're talking crazy." Shumby said to himself. "You have to, my Empress. You have the skills. Go get him."

"Let me get my weapons back first."

In no time, she had regained her gun, axe, and throwing knives. Retracing her steps, she leapt to Shumby.

"Arboc, what is he armed with? You have looked over there, Arboc. Tell me, what are his weapons?"

"It's hard to tell from here but I think, I believe, yes, it's a diamond sword to be sure, and three grenades, and a... oh my gosh..."

"What is it? she implored. "What does he have?" Mordna shouted into her tiny speaker.

She heard Arboc gasp, as he said, "... A missile launcher." Mordna reviewed her tactics, scheming to kill the warrior.

"I will just need to take him out by surprise," she thought to herself. "Where is he?" she yelled into her mouthpiece.

"Directly to your left. Look out, he's just fired!"

Mordna dove to the right as a huge explosion hit directly where she had stood. Missile launcher. She shot a well-aimed knife into the air, severing his shoulder. He skillfully dodged the remaining knife. After twisting the knife from his shoulder, the competitor fired his gun at Mordna. She left from her cover and circled around to behind the man, as Shumby ran toward him, a minor but still annoying distraction.

"He is awfully good for a peasant." she thought to herself, catching her breath. Quietly, as the crowd grew silent, Mordna stood facing her opponent from behind, aimed and fired her gun. His hand grabbed at his chest as his chest wound erupted. All muscles tightened, and then loosened. He slumped to the floor. Fans resounded in a deafening cheer. It roared. It stomped. It swept around the arena, sweeping over all the Royal Glaeform. Mordna ripped off her goggles, throwing them aside and raised her hands in victory. She walked across the Glaeform, relishing her fans' worship.

"Soon..." she thought. "They will worship me unceasingly!"

She heard a Ghidmonga clambering towards her, and with her eyes closed, she killed the beast with a laser gun; the beast simply slid across her path and into an ice spike. If the laser had not killed it, the projecting icespike certainly did! Mordna jumped atop his stomach, raising her victorious arms. Again, the crowd erupted. She exited the arena, motioning to Shumby to follow. She was headed to her secret lair.

"Shumby, I will see you at our room."

"On my way, my Empress." He stumbled on to retrieve her royal weapons from across the arena.

Mordna, heading in the opposite direction, skimmed her way down from the arena, returning carefully to Her Majesty's Palace, hands stiffly by her side. Arrived, she paced through an elaborate and elegant entrance, one of several, through to her library. She curiously grabbed a book, head tilted back, laughing, then moved on to a hidden passage behind an immense *bookcase-wall* which slowly turned about at her touch, toward her dungeon below. She mused, turning back to scope the room, and smiled as she scanned her book: "How to Cook a

Ghidmonga." Her fingers tapped on the book's cover, as she stood there in victory. Again, head tilted back, she laughed and moved forward, slowly at first. The wall aside her suddenly made a low rumble, shifting, as the floor quivered. In a flash, as if a mist had unexpectedly dissipated, she faced what she had dreaded most, even on this, her Victory Day: a tiny, empty prison cell.

*Woe to those who call evil good and good evil, who put darkness for light, and light for darkness, who put bitter for sweet and sweet for bitter!*

**Isaiah 5:20 ESV translation**

## CHAPTER 6: MICRON

EMPEROR MICRON'S DARK CHAMBER lay under the castle, close to the world beneath him. Simply, it was a dark, gloomy cave with wet walls. Once one opened its heavy steel doors, one could see nothing except an island, situated in the middle of the blackness, illuminated only by a thin shaft of light; *Tridesicons* called it *dark light*. It was cleverly generated artificially via networked walls and canopies. You see, Micron hated the light and anything related to light. He sought what he called visible darkness.

Darkness was his friend, and with this ally Micron crafted a darkness which was alive, secretive and potent. In the middle of the island, it was mostly dark shadows, no rocks or trees, only a stepped platform surrounded by black gelatinous liquid which moved in angry turbulence as if to speak. On the platform, Micron's throne-chair faced a massive curved holographic screen. There was no way to reach the island unless you were Micron, Mordna, or Arboc. All they had to do was snap their fingers, the dark sensing their DNA, generating a response from the wall itself: ice stair blocks would obediently fly out from the darkness to the doorway leading to the strange island and the narrow path to Micron's island chamber and offices beyond.

The bald and bearded ruler had watched His Empress's game in the shadows, unknown and unseen. The match had peaked his interest for a while, but he had seen it all before, and quickly grew bored. So bloodthirsty was his wife. Could she not sing another tune?

Up he stood, slowly taking a back-path which led from his dark throne room. He strode alone, very alone, and suddenly stopping, as the familiar darkness stroked his face, imploring him to come intimately closer. Life had led him to this place of eternal dark, as The Emperor's Front Entry greeted him. He shook his head as yet another door swung open.

Micron's priest-like silver *scapular*, a simple narrow rectangular cloth-metal panel, stretched downward at his back and front, and swept the floor, as it gathered snow and scattered ice. Much to his chagrin, his scapular gathered as much light as possible, even in the darkness, a luminous lantern on his dark path. Micron was elegant, slow and purposeful, as his linen collar piece swayed in slow rhythm to his gait, turned up and away from a muscular, hairy neck. He walked upward, literally, effortlessly, crawling up, up, up a thick transparent icewall, then slipped like a spider through a hidden crevice toward the Royal Offices, to the Grand Staircase. He then moved to a circular platform from which he could view Arboc's room, then above, Mordna's, then onward to the very pinnacle, his. Avoiding Mordna and Arboc, he quickly took his place amidst an illuminated triangular entry, which when once he was through, would embrace him in his beloved visible darkness. He hated even momentary light, yet, as he was somehow standing at the two magnificent royal oak doors, he wondered if life would always be this way. He sighed deeply, pondering his fate.

Tridesicon walls everywhere continued to pump their ever-present music, even in the Royal Quarters. Simply, music was a way of life; it was engineered that way. Music which they could not exactly explain or manipulate. Whatever was happening, any event, any footstep, conversation, thought, the music, alive, flowed to it. Enveloped it, pierced it. Legend says that it's the stars that give such beautiful lullabies and melodies. But it emanated really from the walls inside and out. If a battle was engaged, there would automatically come dramatic music to accompany the bloody affair. Whenever Micron headed to his chambers, he would always hear his favorite melodies: low, dark sounds that sent shivers up his spine, which he loved, yet would scare the skin off one's bones if ever heard by underlings. The royal sound started soft and low, but then swept deep and loud, a terrifying sound, yet one of dark evil beauty. And it always increased in volume and drama, as Micron got closer and closer to his chambers. But once he snapped open the doors, it stopped. Completely. You see, inside his dark lighted chambers, music somehow ceased to exist. Complete, utter silence. The only sound that could be imagined at all in the Royal Office was the sound of distant and pleading Tridesicons, the one and only thing the stars respected, as the story goes.

Micron, looking up, his head reflecting ambient light from the entry, snapped his fingers, as an inner door obeyed. He moved to his ornate oak desk. Slowly he sat upon his ice chair. A holographic screen remained suspended before him as he began to orchestrate his day. He trashed most of his mail. After all, what can underlings really have to say for themselves.

"Useless information!" he thought. He scrolled down the screen, pointing to the missive. "Finally, something interesting, and from a lab worker indeed!"

The words appeared bright and clear: "Micron, Lord and Master, we have just discovered a faint signal from our missing Trigon and have located its galaxy, planet, and country. Please come quickly, sir, and we will fill you in on further details!"

Micron's mood now changed for the better, as impossible lost laughter made its way from his throat. For centuries, the Trigon had been lost. But now, after all this time, found? Could it be? This good news exhilarated Micron, a feeling he had not experienced in years. But before he stood to leave for the laboratory, a second message strode down the screen from the same source. It was from Kale, an old and well-respected lab worker.

"Sir, forgive me for not putting this in my previous message, but Arboc decoded the Trigon signal codes. We now have the exact location! In fact, we know who has it right now. Two teenage humans. Would you like me to initiate the ceremony?"

Micron thought for a moment, then responded, "No, not yet. Bring the *INFOCAPSULE* so I may see what you have indeed found. By royal permission, you may come and knock on my door. I will let you in."

"Time, sir?"

"Now, of course, you idio....!"

Micron threw his hands up, gesturing to the darkness. Right then, on the eve of the most important discovery in all of space, and this was happening? Micron didn't have the time or use for dimwits. The message box shifted as he looked to the left of his screen and blinked. Two security cameras obediently zoomed in, scanning all palace rooms. His commanding eye caught the lab camera icon. Blinking, it zoomed in, as he witnessed someone getting ready to leave. It was Kale, because, according to Royal Policy, if anyone left while on duty, they would be immediately executed. Just then an explosion boomed its way across the lab. Somehow chemicals and powders had been deviously prepared to explode at this precise moment. Micron bolted out of his chair and put his face to the screen.

"What's happening?" he roared, his rectangular beard emphasizing every word. Then, a sudden *ratt-a-tat-tat* on the door alerted Micron to turn back to his chair, as he snapped his fingers over his shoulder, quickly taking his seat. The entry opened wide, as light forced its way to his desk, assaulting Micron's eyes.

"Hello, Kale!" greeted Micron.

"Micron, sir. My Lord and ...." Kale bowed.

"Dispense with the formalities, man!" yelled Micron.

"Sir, I have urgent news! An explosion just went off in the lab. I was barely able to get out in time, but without the INFOCAPSULE or really much information...It... it was blown up. I'm sorry, sir, I meant to bring it."

Micron's narrow hands clenched his armrest.

"Who blew the lab up?" Words managed to come through Micron's gritted teeth.

"We don't know, sir. Since you have the security system and scan cameras, I was hoping that you would be able... er... that you would be able... to find out."

"Yes, well, thank you, Kale. That is all." He snapped his fingers again. The doors quickly shut, slamming Kale in the face. Micron pushed a button beneath his desk. Another set of ice blocks flew into formation, not to the door, but into the darkness behind him. Swiftly, cautiously he walked along its path, each used step falling back away into the darkness. Another island, of broken glass, smashed objects, punching bags, and more. This is where Micron would often dispense his heated anger. His rage escalated as he punched the wall. Tears streamed down his face, falling to the floor.

"Why now? When we were so close. Why, why?" he sobbed.

It was as if a new day had come. Micron felt much better as he sat before his familiar holographic screen. Messaging Arboc, he mouthed his words carefully as he spoke to the brightening screen, which would obey the Emperor's every command.

"Arboc, my dear friend, come and meet me in my chambers. I'm waiting, and somewhat impatient."

He sent it just as a pound on the royal door alerted him. It was Arboc revealed by his screen. Funny how things like this can happen! Micron smiled as he snapped his fingers, opening the door. There stood Arboc who had something of great importance to say.

"Arboc, how good of you to come." said Micron, deliberately.

"As if I wouldn't. What did you want, sir?"

"You, first, my good man! You, first." schemed Micron.

"The lab, sir...it is no more!

"I know this, for I have viewed the SCANNERS just a few moments ago!" laughed Micron.

"Well, I came here to tell you...by the way, what did you want with me, sir?" asked Arboc.

"Only the Trigon's location, that is all." He grinned devilishly.

"Sir, it must have been destroyed in the explosion." Arboc explained.

"Hmm, yes it was. Something that you know all too well, I am sure. Come, closer, Arboc. Don't be standing in the doorway like a wayward dog; come, stand here where I can see you." Micron suddenly snapped, and his obedient ice blocks reformed in precise position. Arboc hesitated, looking at the steps, yet slowly achieved a few ice blocks forward to his Master, and then one more, eventually striding the middle of the temporary pathway.

"Ah, stop right there." Micron commanded.

Arboc obeyed, freezing in place. Micron commanded all doors to shut. He and Arboc were now covered in thick darkness; only his screen glimmered.

"Give me the Trigon's INFOCAPSULE, Arboc, I know you have it. Did you forget that I have security cameras all over?

"You have no proof, my Lord." Arboc replied defensively.

"Ah, but I do, Arboc. I saw through the smoke of the lab explosion the information printed out on tablets sitting on the counter. A familiar hand then reached out and took the INFOCAPSULE. I saw it. The hand had your tattoo, Arboc, the one that reads LLM, Long Lives Micron!"

Arboc stretched out his collar away from his thick neck, enabling him to gulp. He slowly lowered his eyes. His treachery had been revealed.

"Guards," Micron yelled. "Arrest this man."

At this, the stone statues which had stood silently behind him, suddenly moved, advancing towards Arboc. He was about to turn and move to the entry door, but the ice blocks behind had fallen away into the darkness. He was trapped. The statues grabbed him and pulled out from his jacket pocket the INFOCAPSULE which contained the desperately needed Trigon coordinates.

"Thank you, my friend. Now, you may leave. Guards," he snapped, and several ice blocks fell into place, guiding the statues and Arboc to his doom. Micron spoke a passcode upon his screen. His chair suddenly lifted above the ice floor an inch or two. A second button on the armrest was engaged.

"WHOOSH!" Micron's chair, powered up suddenly, forcefully pushing down through the ice, through the dark island to a tiny prison below. There, Arboc lay dying at the very bottom of Tridesicon. Darkness had now somehow lifted. Micron winced at the light. He knelt next to Arboc, placing his assisting commander's hand in his.

"You've been a good servant, Arboc, through these many years, but nothing, absolutely no one, must or can stop what must happen now. The Trigon is the key, as you know, to ultimate domination. Yes, Arboc, I will be Lord of all, more than this miserable planet. As you know, I am the Destiny for all.

Arboc lay still, opened his eyes as if to speak, pleading, shaking his head. Words from Arboc's heart, slowly at first, then gushed forth: "No, Micron, only God Himself is Lord of all that is or ever will be. This is His time, not yours!" With this, Arboc closed his eyes forever.

Micron placed his servant's hand to his chest and wept. "If only I believed...if only I could once again *know*..."

He stood, looking down at his friend, now dead upon the floor. No more conversations. No more commands. No more brilliant ideas or ways or hopes. Only death, like the darkness Micron preferred. But here in this moment, death had triumphed, but at what cost? Micron turned away, shaking his head. Another door, on the opposite side of the room sealed the prison.

At Micron's loud command, tears still coming forth, cried, "Open, open you bast....!"

With this the door obeyed, calling Micron to a stiff commanding *stance* as he entered the massive space beyond. Thousands upon thousands of waiting robots stood saluting their robust Commander Micron the Emperor. He raised his gloved hand in triumph. Micron's army, all eyes lit red to full attention, waited for his words.

"Men of Micron, it is time! We have found the TRIGON!" They cheered in robotic reply, banging their metal together. "It is time to leave our life of silence. We will go, we will fight, and we will bring back our TRIGON and restore Tridesicon to its full glory!" The noise grew louder.

"Get ready, we are going to..." he paused for dramatic effect. "Earth!"

*The enemy spoke, "I'll pursue. I'll hunt them down. I'll divide up the plunder. I'll glut myself on them!*

**Exodus 15:9 ESV translation**

## CHAPTER 7: SURPRISE

DIRT FLEW IN THE AIR. Blake was tossed to the side by a *tsunami-like* shock wave that easily hurled him into a nearby trench. He was not wounded.

"Hey, are you okay?" a terrified soldier asked him.

"Yeah, it's all cool." Blake moaned. "One step closer and that *grenade* would have finished me. Come on up; maybe you WILL survive the war."

Clumsily, Blake wiped wet dirt from his eyes, and slowly crawled away, being careful not to get shot. Just then a *bullet* landed between his boots. He looked down, surprised at how perfectly the mark divided and separated his muddy footgear. Blake stumbled for cover, diving behind a dumpster. He looked around for his *killer* and found no one. But then, in his peripheral he peered through the morning fog at a sniper at the ready, who darted quickly behind a projecting elevator shaft on top of a nearby two-story building. He retrieved his pistol from its leather holster, rapidly shooting at his enemy.

"And now to save the hostages," he murmured, satisfied at his shooting ability.

He got up, making a run for it. He could feel *bullets* slicing by his body. He jumped and did a *Kong* over a lone backhoe, dropping a grenade into a window, landed and ran in the opposite direction.

"BOOM!"

At first, he thought he was home free. He could see a band of unguarded hostages bound to a tree. Before him lay a wide trench that he had to somehow traverse.

"There he is! GET HIM!!!"

A line of soldiers ran from behind a small brick building at Blake, all guns trained on him. Blake knew what to do. He dropped and slid across the wet grass into a trench while firing his gun at them. Blake took his last *grenade*, throwing it over the deep trench to where his pursuers were crouched. It splattered. Fog and smoke, curled together, lay low and menacing. Only the *rat-ta-tat-tat* return fire of guns told him where the enemy stood. He slowly climbed out of his muddy trench, his gun ready. Blake searched for enemy survivors. Nobody. The enemy had withdrawn. It was now safe. Cautiously, he made his way to the bound hostages lashed to a huge oak tree.

"Come on, guys, let's get outta here."

Obediently, quickly and silently, they followed Blake, able ninjas, now a swat team extraordinaire, scrambling up a nearby tree to where it extended above a platoon of brick buildings. A long thick branch extended out close to a huge fire escape, which led to the top. Every movement was precise, every step cautious, as they silently climbed a pair of rusted ladders, making a way to the top. Blake navigated his single file crew across the flat rooftop, a new battlefield, yes, a new opportunity to seize the *enemy*. His crew moved cautiously down a convenient shaft. They ducked under a low stand of rusted pipes, only to stare at a confusion of unexpected divergent passageways! Assailed by a terrifying distant roar of guns and voices, the young men twisted through the maze, which stretched before them. Blake's soldiers were spent. All seemed impossibly treacherous but everything considered, Blake really did have it covered. The wary soldiers squeezed, one by one, into an air vent, carefully maneuvering their vertical descent. Luckily, Blake was in the front and was expecting this. He let himself quickly fall to the awaiting air vent seal. As his feet securely reached their goal, the seal gave way, forcing Blake to solid ground below, surrounded by a cloud of dust. The hostages mimicked him, perfectly. All was silent, both the fall and the landing. No injuries occurred. They had dropped onto the fourth floor into a containment room, exactly where Blake needed to go. Easily, he ripped out rusted bars from a small window. He carefully crawled out, hooking his zip line system on to a thick sturdy wire. It extended from just below the gaping window hole, to a safe-haven.

"All right, everybody, listen to me! First, Amy goes, then Ranger, Clayton, and Jase. You have your orders! Now move it!"

Curious, Amy quickly saddled herself into a harness Blake had just handed her. Amy's eyes moved slowly, lifting to his, as she asked,

"What about you?"

"Oh, I'm comin'. But I have one last thing."

One by one, the hostages reached their sanctuary, plummeting down the zip line far out of *enemy* territory. As Blake withdrew a grenade remote from his backpack, he carefully scanned the area below.

He had one last thing to do. Blake had every reason to grin. Victory was almost in hand! He could feel it. You see, unnoticed hours before, he had cautiously placed *confetti-grenades* over an impressively wide area, in crates and boxes filled with other *grenades*. One press of a button, then WHAM! The whole enemy territory would be wiped out. He situated himself into his buckled harness, sat down upon the open window sill, leaned back, and went down the zip line. Woooshhh! Beyond the thick fog Blake could see soldiers running about, searching for their missing hostages. He smiled, then twisted himself, so he could face the buildings he had left, lifted his safety, his hand frozen in position as he silently mouthed: "Kaboom!"

The fog began to lift as sunlight sketched moving outlines, tracings, imperceptible at first, but growing more fearsome. What was the rhythmic noise now inserting its way into Blake's ears? It had authority, a penetrating attention-grabbing ability as Blake began to explore his expanding fear. The noise was shrill. Blake had never experienced such depths and fear before this, ever. Like a target's concentric circles slowly spinning, he was mesmerized in the moment. It was foreign, unlike his backyard world, something trying to break in, a beating at the door, a merging of dimensions, a thrust of sound, compelling him in further, into its grip, into a new reality. He shook his head, expelling his pulsating fear, as his finger quickly pressed the button. Hidden *grenades* went off. Blake could see everything now drawn up, thrown down, and scattered in the *explosion*. Some of it nearly got Blake, but his zip line had carried him out of harm's way. He descended further into the morning fog, crossing a huge gate to safety. His ride stopped abruptly when the pulley and Blake slammed into a padded receiving platform, all to the applause of his crew. He dropped from the line to the ground below, dusting off his protective jacket. His soldiers swarmed around him, congratulating him, patting him on the back, along with gleeful fist pounds. The rhythmic intruder was distant now and the fog had completely lifted! But he still wondered what had happened out there. Blake looked up, beyond his whooping tribe, to see someone very special.

"Oh, hey, mom. Is our *game time* over?"

"Yes." she laughed. Most definitely! Round up everybody. It's time to come in. Remember, breakfast?"

"Sure, mom."

Blake grabbed a bullhorn. "Game over, everyone! Let's get cleaned up and eat some breakfast. Gather up your ammo and paintball guns and set them in the bin by the gate. Meet you guys at the pool."

He turned off his bullhorn with a loud, resonating click, and headed for the outdoor showers, as he reflected on the boys' paintball game and the rhythmic pounding which had raised its clenched fists minutes ago, an unseen enemy, more fearsome than his buddies could ever be, ready to invade his life and conquer far beyond their paintball battlefield. But for now, in the moment of bravado's reign, you see, PAINTBALL was what it was all about, his favorite sport, and it seemed to be everyone else's around town as well! Today was Blake's 16th birthday, and the night before he and his *buds* had pulled an all-nighter, situated in the little village that had been abandoned for years, adjacent to his backyard. Literally, a tiny parcel of land, a nest of abandoned buildings, some tall, mostly two stories. Narrow sidewalks wove an intricate pattern through the overgrown lot. An overbearing clock tower proudly thrust into the sky as it mocked a small row of empty shops and a defunct auto repair shop. An assortment of tiny one-room buildings added intrigue and possibility. It was all magic and mystery, it seemed, to sixteen-year old wide-eyed Blake.

This space behind his back yard was an abandoned dream. The builders had simply discarded their project, a year before completion, literally, years ago; there was no money in it, so they moved on to something else, something better, to make a quick buck. Rumor has it, that there were ghosts perhaps monsters now that walked the abandoned walkways by night. Any people who had taken up residence there in the beginning, in the blush of the unfinished work, were evidently scared off, dispersing to places far away. They had run for the hills. The tiny *village* had been unoccupied for years. Blake's wealthy dad, David Armstrong, had built a nice manor adjacent to the village, planning that perhaps one day he would purchase the extra property. He thought: "What a sweet deal I can make here...someday!" Many afternoons David would trek over to the *village* alone, or so he thought, scheming and planning; Blake was forbidden to enter the mysterious *village* beyond the cedars. It could be unsafe! The mystery grew in Blake's mind whenever he followed his dad, undetected, to the gateway, wondering why his father took the exact same route, over and over, only to stand motionless, and peering into the abandoned mixture of overgrown patches and empty buildings.

But time can change things and what had been left as abandoned litter could possibly now become treasure, especially when seen by entrepreneurs like David Armstrong who was disposed to invent, plan, and scheme. He had a keen sense about such things. It just made good business sense, so, after several years of consideration and mulling over, he had purchased the mysterious parcel, ultimately giving permission to Blake and his friends, if they wanted, to explore his purchase first hand.

"Have fun, boys, but be careful," he instructed.

Immediately the abandoned land became Blake's playground where he and his friends, explored all buildings and walkways, which, in youth's imagination, morphed quickly to serious bouts of paintball and manhunt.

And so, as the passage of days would have it, Blake's sixteenth birthday arrived and more than anything, he wanted to celebrate with his friends an all-nighter in the clock tower, just beyond his backyard. From there they would play paintball and rescue hostages by mid-morning!

Blake, now gathered with his buddies at the poolside breakfast table, looked back at the village beyond the cedars. It shimmered in the morning light. Although the village was small, its collection of buildings, clock tower, houses, sidewalks, and meadows looked old, sad and abandoned, but this is what made it so special. One could relax there and not be worried about getting mud on the couch. You could be free here, yes, free to be!

Blake watched the sun rising over his clock tower to its pinnacle. He was stoked by winning the game, yet, perplexed by the rhythmic pounding he had endured while in battle.

Blake was a friendly guy, who felt sorry for a lot of the weird kids at school. He hung around them as much as the other guys, who admired Blake in his ability to sustain his coolness even while hanging around geeks and nerds. He was different, yet totally cool!

"Blake, we're needing some extra folding chairs from the storage room. Let's see, thirteen, fourteen...fifteen. Three more chairs, Blake. That should do it!" smiled Lillian Armstrong, a competent woman who loved to organize and plan, especially birthday celebrations for her sixteen-year-old son!

The Armstrong's massive pool was adorned with the usual jumble of tanning chaises, umbrellas, tightly woven outdoor wicker sofas and tables, plus a full assortment of floating devices, which were dancing in the pool. The Armstrong's backyard boasted a rolling lush cut lawn that featured a massive trampoline and basketball court to the left and right of the pool. Ahead, stood a beautiful oak tree, its width bigger than a car's length and its height taller than the Tudor house itself. David Armstrong had cleverly installed in the oak's trunk, tubes which chugged out water to fill the pool: massive rocks lined part of the pool, some with an array of waterfalls flowing down, including an impressive fifteen-foot waterfall and slide which jutted its way into the aqua water. There were hot tubs, diving boards perched fifteen feet above the pool over the sixteen-foot deep water. Here, water gushed from the oak. Up, beyond the tubes extending down from the tree, there sat a kitchen-size tree house. Hatches extended from its walls. When you went down one, you slid down a tube twirling through the oak tree and its branches, and then merged with powerful water jets that blasted you out of the tree waterslide into the pool, through the same huge holes that filled the pool with water. Most of the boys started tearing off their shirts, running to dive into the pool, but Blake stopped them.

"Guys, drop your stuff over there. Yeah, that's right. Sit here.

Time to eat!" Blake commanded, motioning the boys over to a massive poolside table.

Several servers with trays loaded with breakfast emerged from the poolside kitchen, happily placing a full array before each guest: waffles, bacon, fruit, scrambled eggs, grits, hash browns, sausage along with OJ and other beverages. It was a banquet, not just breakfast!

"Hey, mom, where's dad?" asked Blake.

Just then, there came a screech of brakes and running through the courtyard. Blake was already figuring things out! In minutes, David Armstrong, packages in hand, explained. "Last minute shopping."

David Armstrong, perfectly attired: khakis, pure white long-sleeved linen shirt, and brown leather jacket, complete with Armani shades and

*Docksiders*, no socks!

"Hey guys! Sorry I'm late. Just had to pull together some strings for one of Blake's presents." He removed his glasses, giving a thumbs-up to Blake's mom with a smile. This piqued Blake's interest. One by one, he ripped open gifts from his friends. But these didn't come close to what his parents had in store for him. Soon enough, it was time. Drum roll, please! Blake's parents presented a small box wrapped in ordinary gift paper. Billions of things came to mind in the birthday boy's head.

"Is it a watch? Maybe car keys to a Ferrari. Yeah, right...Hmm. Nope, It couldn't be that. Or maybe plane tickets for a world tour, or space! Ha!" Blake laughed. Excitedly, he opened the small box, a tiny puff of shreds of wrapping paper bounced out. Inside was just a piece of paper. Holding it closer, Blake read the boxed note to his friends.

*Dear Blake: Happy birthday! Your Mom and I have been throwing a few ideas around for months, wondering what you would like for your birthday. Well, we were just fresh out of ideas, when we remembered what you had said a while ago. In fact, you mentioned the perfect gift. I quote, 'Wouldn't it be cool if we created a barrier around the town in the backyard, fixed up the place, and remade the town the whole place? A town that would be run by me, and my friends and other kids nearby.' Well, Blake, you get your wish. I've already had construction teams scope things out and it's really going to happen! They will work hard to rebuild. Here you'll be safe, in a place where you can have fun, and deal with problems you will face in the future, and grapple with what it takes to run a town. Here you and your friends can grow up together. Anyway, congratulations, Son, you are now the owner and founder of the brand-new youth community: KidzTurf."*

Shocked, Blake dropped the note, looking at his parents for affirmation, silently asking, "Is this true? Do I now own a town?"

Smiling, his parents nodded intuitively. "Go ahead. See for yourself. But first, here's a yellow pad. Make a list of what changes, additions, or modifications you would like to your town. Don't worry about expenses. I will tell you if it's going too far."

Barely a second later, all of the boys crowded around Blake with animated suggestions and points-of-view. Blake's head raced with ideas. He laughed. The boys joined him. You see, there was much potential in the town, excuse me, *KidzTurf*. Minutes flew by as scattered blueprints, lists, and crude drawings replaced pushed-back breakfast plates.

David Armstrong, brandishing a pile of overview notebooks, raised his voice to the excited boys, "Here are some blueprint and overview notebooks of your new town, guys. Circle the buildings you want, and mark out the ones you don't. Right now, construction of the perimeter wall will begin in a few days. It will be sixteen feet high, made of cement blocks, stucco, and topped with security wire so that no unwanted strangers climb over. And that old rickety gate will be taken down and replaced with this!"

David laid a picture of it on the table. It was two big double doors that were the same height as the attached front walls. Two long planks crossed from one corner to the other diagonally, creating a big X. In the center of it, where a diamond shape was formed, were the intricate carvings of the city's initials: KT. The double doors featured a line that went from the top to bottom, cutting straight through the middle of the KT. Blake shook his head in disbelief: a town of his own! As his dad jabbered on, Blake thought to himself, "I have a town... I have a town," and smiled. "I have a town."

Lost in thought, it was only after Mr. Armstrong filled everybody in on more details that Blake came to his senses. Quickly, he and his friends scribbled down their ideas and ran out back to the town. Blake sped across the lawn, joined by his friend Dawson and right behind, everyone else followed, laughing. Blake always had good speed and stamina. He ran far ahead, easily kicking dirt into the sunlit air! All had grown quiet, his friends far behind. Blake suddenly stopped, his mouth agape. He could see it; he understood now: Construction workers with hard hats, bulldozers, planks of steel and metal, buckets of paint, and drills. Blake stood dazed, ten feet from the gate, as he scanned *reality*, which in all its possibility now came to life before him.

"Wow..." he gasped. "This IS...massive!"

Closing his eyes, he imagined his tiny town finished. Inside his mind a battle raged. Why had construction stopped so abruptly years ago? What was wrong? Images of smashed glass, crumbling pillars, lonely spaces, vents leading far underground, canopied areas, and timbered stucco walls pushing up in turreted splendor here and there. Weeds where manicured lawns once led to busy walkways in the small, yet fashionable, center. What had happened? Why all the weeds, broken glass, crumbling walls, twisted trusses? Blake felt his comfort ebb away as he heavily pondered. Yet, woven into this tapestry was an unbroken spirit, his, like a people set free, a thread woven which said: "All will be well. Yes, all will be well.

*"For I know the plans I have for you," says the Eternal, "plans for peace, not evil, to give you a future and hope.*
*Never forget that.*

**Jeremiah 29:11 The Voice translation**

## CHAPTER 8: BREAKING GROUND

THREE MONTHS HAD PASSED since Blake's sixteenth birthday. Reconstruction of his birthday gift, a defunct parcel of land, adjacent to his home, had finally begun. As Blake stood by his father, an energetic crowd of construction workers and engineers waited for upcoming instructions from Cliff's bullhorn. Blake winced at an intense high-pitched *screeching*, as his father tapped the bullhorn. Blake refused to cover his ears to maintain his *cool*, as his eyes swept over the crowd of eager workers. He began to count just how many were gathered before him; at 37 he grew bored and stopped. Minutes flew by and Blake began to fidget, shifting from one leg to the other. He hadn't planned on tuning out, but his mind wandered off. For Blake, early morning *zoning* was not unusual but in the moment, as his father glared at him, Blake knew he had better get his act together. A sudden applause snapped him to further attention, causing Blake to stand straighter. He cleared his throat. He quickly pushed his hair back. Now things seemed clearer. Much clearer! He was ready to move on.

Cliff smiled, encouraging Blake, as he clapped in unison with the crowd. Pulling back from his bullhorn, Cliff asked, "You got anything to say, son?"

"Sure!" replied Blake, *check-tapping* the bullhorn now firmly in his grip. "Good morning! Ah, thanks for coming. I mean thanks for working with my dad and me on this! Hope everything's gonna go great and nobody gets hurt, right? Well, that's about it! Oh, and thanks again!" Blake stood for a moment, scrambling for more to say, but with a shrug, he returned the bullhorn to his father as more applause broke into the morning.

"All right, crew!" shouted Cliff. "You have your assignments. Today we are wiring all units and installing initial plumbing systems. Have a good day."

Cliff, handing the bullhorn to Lars, whispered, "Take over now. Blake and I are heading off."

Lars eagerly grabbed the bullhorn, ready to call out further instructions to his workers, as Cliff instructed Blake, "Hop in the Jeep. This won't take long and the five-minute drive to school will give us just enough time to follow up on what you said, O.K.?"

Minutes later, Cliff's Jeep pushed away from the busy construction site, down an overgrown path, which followed a stretch of chain-link fencing, concluding with a tumble of cement barriers. Cliff got out to pull a metal gate aside, then quickly returned to his *wheel*. As neighborhood homes, massive oaks and manicured lawns swept into a blur, Cliff laughed, "Ah, well, Blake, this is really happening! Finally, huh? Day 1: *KidzTurf* construction! You excited?"

"Yeah, I'm stoked, Dad! Can't wait till it's all done. And thanks for everything! We're gonna have so much fun. We're..." Blake's words sleepily trailed off.

"I'm sure you guys are. Now listen, understand how much responsibility you have now. You are not alone, of course. I'm with you on this all the way. You need to know why I've given you *KidzTurf* to run. Listen, Blake. Here you will spread your wings, grow and mature, and perhaps become a good leader, know what I mean? I believe in you, Blake. You've got potential, son, to change the world. And you're going to have to be ready to face it one day, all its trials and hardships. You'll have plenty of those in the future. That's for sure. Just wait until college." Cliff chuckled. He glanced to his right, then sighed.

Perhaps it was the *drone* of the car or the early hour. Blake had fallen asleep, envisioning *KidzTurf* adventures, his head now bumping against the passenger window. The Jeep swayed in hypnotic rhythms. Suddenly, the car screeched to a jolting halt at Pacific High School.

Blake *slumped* out, slowly shifting his backpack into place. He waved and spun toward the school, lurching forward, tripping over a high curb in the way, dramatically spilling his books on the sidewalk, which called forward a curious assortment of peers standing at Pacific High's main stairway. Flustered, Blake got up, scrambling to collect his things, as Rodney, the school bully, *dirt-biked* over Blake's scattered books, ripping and destroying needed textbook material.

"Oops! Sorry, Blake, looks like ya better watch out; you're a walking catastrophe! Ha ha! See ya, klutz!"

Behind his red face, Blake figured it wasn't going to be a good day, at all. Later, during math class, Mrs. Taylor pulled a surprise open-book test. But Blake's pages were missing, torn from Rodney's bike assault. Blake thought he had flunked, pushing pages for any needed info. His textbook lay on his desk, helpless and war-torn. Everything was piling up; he couldn't remember a worse day. When it came time for gym, Blake got *pants-ed* by one of Rodney's friends as he took the basketball for a *layup*. More bad luck seemed to come Blake's way as his day played out, finally ending with an abrupt halt at the bell. Momentary relief. Blake, being not so popular with himself and others that day, slumped out of class without a word and headed for the parking lot. He could hear someone running down the hall. A sudden abrupt punch on his shoulder startled him. It was Oskar.

"Hey dude, how ya doin'?" Oskar inquired.

Blake didn't feel like talking.

"I can tell you're havin' a great day, man." Oskar noted.

"Rough day, Oskar!" complained Blake. "More than most!"

Oskar laughed in reply, "Trig's usually challenging, but I must admit it had elements of calculus today, which left even your friendly neighborhood nerd baffled!"

"That not what I meant!" Blake exclaimed.

More silence followed. Seeing that discussing his bad *I-guess-I'm-feeling-sorry-for-myself-day* any further would be fruitless, Blake decided to expound upon his *trig* fiasco.

"But yeah," mumbled Blake. "I hate it too. I gotta get better at that stuff. It goes in waves, man. Waves. It's up or it's waaay down. Waves. Some days trig makes all the sense in the world. And then there are those times when I haven't a clue."

"Well, I think I've got it most of the time, bro. But I admit it can be hard, really hard."

"Enough of this, Oskar! You got some time?" asked Blake.

"Not today, Blake. Gotta check some lab possibilities and don't have much time. Got chores piling up and I promised my folks I'd get to 'em today after school. Gotta go. Bye!" yelled Oskar as he ran ahead to accelerate his afternoon. He had lots to do!

Blake muttered, " Yeah, bro, do what you gotta do!"

Oskar flew ahead. His phone screen, barely legible in the bright sunlight, looked back at him, anxious for its next instruction, as Oskar now maneuvered an uneven sidewalk just past the *KidzTurf* entrance.

A blinking GPS icon and map danced about, to get Oskar, genius inventor, to his next location.

Annoyed, he shook his phone, a special *iteration with add-ons* he had recently created, which excelled any smartphone on the market, for he had hacked, designed, programmed, carved, and soldered his way to an impressive invention, decades ahead of what ordinary people routinely held in their hands. Yet, before him was a simple task: where is the defunct car repair shop located? Months ago he had passed a repair shop in the jumble which now was *KidzTurf* and its location registered, sort of. It looked like it might be the perfect facility for a lab where sky would be the limit; he could invent far removed from prying eyes.

"Blast! Where is it?" he murmured, adjusting his glasses.

The phone shot back, "Oskar, the address you are seeking is no longer valid. The construction of the former auto repair shop has been greatly compromised. It is not a valid address, but if you must, walk west for another 100 yards, turn left and there on your right you will find the former Tony's Auto Repair."

"Great!" he smiled. "Looks like everything's gonna be okay, at least today."

Oskar slowly scuffled along the crumbling sidewalk as he scanned the debris before him. Construction sites always energized him, for his curiosity and inventive spirit sought to give purpose and possibility to whatever he might find. A discarded radio. A spring-loaded gun. A box within a box. Whatever. His mind would categorize, detail, analyze and create. It was a rush. Always. And here he was, about to turn the corner to what he imagined could be a fully outfitted lab, the transformation of a defunct auto repair shop, complete with a powerful lift and workbench, into a fully functioning inventor's workshop. The possibilities of Oskar's envisioned lab were many and in his imagination, he went beyond, far beyond, the limited listings and offerings others could ever provide.

He moved across the street as he further examined possibilities, scanning an immense garage door, a steel lift within, a power grid of supplementary electromotive and electrostatic potential, a workbench extending across the entire structure, ; an array of sinks, full plumbing facilities, and workshop lighting throughout. Yes, this could work! This, definitely, would work!

Entering a side door, Oskar pushed his way across a small room which opened into the main workshop. Auto repair tools were strewn everywhere. What a mess, but the constructions were solid. Yes, the workbench would serve well. He was convinced that the hundreds of repair tools, which were on the floor and those, hung upon several worn pegboard walls, and other various equipment, could easily be sold. Simply, Oskar conjectured, these items would provide needed funds to bring what surrounded him into alignment with his vision. Yes, this must work, and it wouldn't take that long, either. His fired-up neurons connected more rapidly now. Ideas like sparks flashed across his inventor's mind, coupling with new possibilities for objects and combinations thereof. He was transported. The rapidity of these thoughts raced through him, over him, up to the shop's ceiling, quickly down to its floor and across its walls, to the lift, the sinks, and the vast array of industrial lights. He envisioned needed equipment, computers, monitors, cages, microscopes, freezers, goggles, Bunsen burners, piper bulbs, beaker tongs, glass cylinders and volumetric flasks, rubber stoppers, meter sticks, charts, thermometers, ring stands, funnels, evaporating dishes, outlets, network infrastructure, hardware, software, data projectors, cables and power strips. All of this merged into a series of waxing and waning dynamic collages, logically arranged according to purpose, function and application. It was heady stuff, to say the least. Oskar spun in a 360 to further draw in the massive possibilities.

Raising both hands, Oskar laughed, "Man, this is it. Finally, something that'll fly, really fly. Can't wait to get this baby started!"

He was rebooted, alive, challenged, and fully pumped. He ran toward the gated entry. The walkway, though uneven and twisted, provided no obstacle for him whatsoever! Nothing, no, absolutely nothing would or ever could stand in his way now! Oskar was naturally clumsy, but now he flew like the wind! He was invincible! But for how long?

He jumped, then suddenly stopped, and looked back at the defunct repair shop, recalling encouraging words he had read a few days before from Isaiah, prophetic words which thrust Oskar into an energizing vision: *From this time forth I announce to you new things, hidden things that you have not known.*

The afternoon wore on as Blake continued his slow shuffle along the sidewalk, pushing his sneakers into the pavement, rearranging his hefty backpack, which was year by year filled with more and more weighty *tomes*. He felt sorry for himself and a darkening gloom was having its way...again! It had become a familiar companion as the school year progressed; he felt an overwhelming burden each afternoon and Blake knew he'd have to do something about it soon. He had searched for diversion, any diversion, some other thing he could consider, something better than Trig and his daily heavy heart. He continued past his house for some reason. His steps proceeded toward the adjacent lot, his incredible gift, which for so long had remained a defunct tiny parcel of broken sidewalks, small towers, smashed windows and torn awnings, a playground of sorts which Blake and his friends had used for hanging out and paintball. His gloom still would not lift, yet his steps quickened toward the construction site. Maybe there was hope!

Stopping at the entry gate, Blake looked past the jumble of worn buildings amidst the day's new constructions, to a tall clock tower which for some reason had survived very much intact. He was grateful for his gift of land and thus began to carefully list upgrades he might suggest to his father who, after all, was *orchestrating* the renovation. Workers were now crawling everywhere, *ants* scurrying about. Blake smiled as his day's *gloom* lifted. "Now." he mused, "Yes, now is the time for renewal, not depressing thoughts, but restoration, high spirits and innovation!"

Days whipped by, merging into months, two years. Cliff's workers were constantly busy and happily open to *overtime* as cables were laid, finish work completed, sidewalks poured, and plumbing lines refitted. Years ago, Blake's gift had been a tiny *community* squeezed into a ten-acre parcel; now, unfurled before him, day after day, as buildings came to life and walkways networked his complex, Blake could admire each accomplishment one by one, and the final polishings and *refinings* of the massive work project. He could hardly believe two years had passed. Blessedly, school problems had *evened out* and now at 18, standing at the gleaming *KidzTurf* entrance, Blake surveyed his finished product. He smiled, raising his fist in victory, at long last ready to call friends forward into *KidzTurf,* a landmark self-governing community of teenagers: of the youth, by the youth, for the youth.

*Write down this vision. Write it clearly on tablets, so that anyone who reads it may run. For the vision points ahead to a time I have appointed; it testifies regarding the end, and it will not lie. Even if there is a delay, wait for it. It is coming.*

**Habbakuk 2:2-3 The Voice translation**

## CHAPTER 9: A NORMAL DAY

AT EXACTLY 9:00 A.M., A BEAM OF LIGHT shot through the window on Blake. He moved. Sunlight slowly had crept up his bed, over his covers, and finally into Blake's eyes, forcing a complaint. He shifted to avoid the penetrating rays, only to clumsily roll off of his bed with a thud and groan. He slowly made his bed, brushed his teeth, and changed clothes, wobbling down the stairs into the kitchen. His grogginess dissipated as a sweet aroma of sizzling bacon rebooted him. "I'm really late! Gotta get moving." he thought. Blake stood at the kitchen table, belting down an orange juice, as he stifled intermittent yawns. Turning to his mother, he whispered, "I really gotta go, mom!" Blake lightly kissed her cheek. He could smell her mother's love now filling the kitchen, a delicious mixture of bacon, eggs, toast and waffles, including the acrid scent of coffee!

"Gotta go! Really late." Blake explained as he rushed out the door. "Love you, mom!"

Blake stopped at the last step and turned. "Love ya, Ma!" he shouted.

"Have a good day, Blake. Love you too." came her reply through the screen door. "That boy needs to slow down!" she muttered, shaking her head.

The sun shone hot as Blake slid into his electric car, another Oskar invention, a handsome pile of scraps, leather, shining chrome and glass. A working car. And for it Blake was grateful for all its bits and pieces, designed by his good genius friend Oskar, yes, gatherings from scrap yards, junk dealers and those desperate to get rid of their *clunkers*. Blake pushed the engine button *on*, pulled out the charge cord, as his vehicle lurched quietly ahead. Ever since Oskar had rolled out his new invention, Blake had wanted to push its emergency button, the zero to 30 in 8 seconds, but he refrained.

The car sped past a laser beam, which activated an upgraded outer gate. On both sides, bordering woods passed by rapidly. The car traced a huge loop around the shady entirety of *KidzTurf*, then approached the main KT gate. It gleamed as it swung open, admitting morning light to pour upon his electric wonder, momentarily blinding him. Blake slowly moved across the entry's cobbled cul-de-sac, with the gate swiftly closing behind. Several friends waved as they stood close to his parking spot. Blake didn't feel like small talk, not now. He was late. All he really needed now was to park and get to business. He exited his car, briefcase in hand. Blake held up his remote key, pressed its button to lock his prize conveyance, as its bonnet slowly rose upward, then across to the windshield, locking in place. He waved to several friends, as he quickly scanned *KidzTurf, its* jumble of buildings and bunkers, all set in clean and tidy rows. The morning was hot. He casually wiped his brow with the back of his hand as he nodded "Good Morning!" to several workers finishing up their mowing. A few steps more and he would be inside. He unlocked his bunker and walked in, quickly closing his door. The bunker was a simple concrete construction with stucco façade, which perfectly matched the others, which closely nestled on each side of *KT's* clock tower. His bunker was definitely home away from home. He turned on solar power Oskar had installed. His wide-screen TV instantly stood at attention, announcing that the weather would remain sunny, 80 degrees, with no rain in sight, at least for a few days! Blake plopped into a comfortable leather chair, his favorite.

"Now after two years," he mused, *KidzTurf* had grown from a measly ten people to a gigantic fifty citizens, all screened for security. Blake and his council had decided one hundred was its limit and at one hundred it would stay. No exceptions. He checked his watch again as he removed a couch cushion, pressed a button on the seat, then slid open its base panel, exposing a full-size entry leading tunnel-like to a long ladder, which in turn descended to a small platform from which one could look up and see a mass of clockworks and gears. This comprised the *secret agency* HQ the leaders had envisioned.

One by one, they came, all five leaders. First Dawson, then Summerlin, then Oskar, Jared, and finally Dirk Romanov, a nineteen-year-old Russian immigrant obsessed with espionage, a *stereotypical* fellow.

"All right. *Guys*, now that we're here, let's look at a few *goals,* for openers, okay? Here is today's *task-sheet.*

"I got dibs on the guy who drives around in cool cars with tons of money, and gorgeous babes!" Blake rolled his eyes at Dawson.

"DOS, *Bond* is definitely not our role model here. After all, he's old and we're, well, let's just say we've got a lot more years ahead of us. Hopefully. Our *agency*, remember, is basically to keep *KidzTurf* safe, and make sure it stays that way, not anything glamorous, ya know what I mean? In time you'll all receive full assignments. I will coordinate this. Anything strange that happens, you inform me, okay? I will be on the first shift, patrolling. Oskar, your job is to make stuff and inventions to aid us in our mission! You will be a combo inventor-security guard! Ha! Think of it, man! Daily you will report here, HQ,

111

and carefully scan our security screen networks, notifying us, any of us, of anything suspicious."

"Looking forward to it, Boss."

"Summerlin, you will serve as our *primary* detective. You have a natural sense of finding and solving things, so I'm sure you can and will do this job well. You will also be our *source finder*. If we need information, it's up to you to *squeeze* the secret out from any suspicious source. You know what I mean? Yes, I can see, you know what I mean!" Blake's eyes locked onto hers.

"Fine. I can see that being a *detective* in *KidzTurf* will be a challenge, but not impossible," replied Summerlin.

"Now we need a pseudo SWAT team, so Jared, Dawson, would you like to work together in this?"

"Yeah!" they both chimed in.

"Oskar will design any *protective devices* if needed, nothing more, nothing less.

And last of all, Dirk. I have given you the best job of all; you can do whatever you want. You know the secret stuff way better than we do. You have great skills for any job I could *throw* at you, so do whatever you think is needed and let me know what's up."

"I will do my best, *comrade*." he responded with heavy accent as he grinned.

"I ask nothing more. These are your assignments, so let's get going!"

The five-member security patrol turned to leave the tower, planning their respective missions. Blake returned to his bunker, dragging along an assortment of *KidzTurf* HQ equipment. A scanner, one monitor, an assortment of folding tables and chairs, several paintball guns and equipment just to have on hand until Oskar could come up with something better. On the table he laid out a map of *KidzTurf* and surrounding areas.

In the days to follow, Blake pressed on with a passion he had never known before. He got to work designing a *pseudo*-SWAT team truck. Oskar rolled out an old vehicle, restored, having then spray-painted it a cool matte black. He had replaced all windows with dark *one-way* glass and loaded it with weapons and a couple of computers. Large yellow letters, announcing SWATKAR completed Oskar's project. It was all sort of *tongue-in-cheek* cool, but it would work. Perhaps all of this was *over the top*, but no one seemed to mind! It was just cool!

Blake then collected an assortment of cams, placing them in hidden and unexpected places throughout *KidzTurf*. After, days, of going secretly back and forth from home to *KidzTurf*, from *KidzTurf* to home, Blake was exhausted. Once again, he drove back along the short familiar route to his house, then, next day, once again, crept through his couch's secret passageway into *KidzTurf* HQ. He turned on his 5K flatscreen, which immediately captured multi mini screens, live recordings via his cams, and current updates across KidzTurf. Blake then called Dirk.

"Hey, man, how's it going?"

"It is going great. There's nothing suspicious whatsoever. It's fun, though, scrambling around town like a *secret agent*, Ha! I could get used to this sleuth stuff!"

"Well, you will be stuck with it for the rest of the summer anyway, according to plan."

"So, I will. Thank you for the assignment, Blake. Now I need to go and see if anybody's in our slammer; I will need to *interrogate* them."

"All right, Dirk, take it easy. I'll see you on my patrol. You can bet on it, Dirk!"

"Any time, my friend. Any time! Bye."

"Catch ya later, dude." Blake shut off his cell and strode back to his car and drove off. And, as Dirk said, there was nothing unusual. Nothing anyone could see, at least. Oh, yes, a lineup of kids entering the *parkour* training gym which had just opened its doors. Everything seemed to be running smoothly. Blake drove past a small soccer field and watched for a moment, then over to K.T.'s sole basketball court, and then, only then, did he call it a day! His team of five had excitedly met back at HQ at five, animated, eagerly and loudly, sharing what they had accomplished. Oskar had brilliantly begun creating innovative tracking codes. Summerlin had finished the uniforms and Dirk had thoroughly scoured *KidzTurf*. Nothing extraordinary. Nothing out of the ordinary! The day had passed fast, and it was almost time for everyone to go home. Soon enough all had vanished, one by one, and Blake was the last one to leave. He paused as he looked back at *KidzTurf*. Carefully, he remote-locked the main gate, securing *KidzTurf* for the night. He stood still, turning away from the door, in place, searching, looking down to the wide cobbled *cul-de-sac* entrance to *KidzTurf*, his dream gift.

"Something's off-target." he thought, shaking his head. "Something major!" For some reason, as crushing doubt squeezed hard, Blake knew that today would somehow be his last day of *normal*, and that the next would take a turn for the worse. Much worse!

*Provide security and protection for Your servant's welfare. My eyes are strained as I look for Your salvation and Your righteous promise to be fulfilled.*

**Psalm 119:122 The Voice translation**

## CHAPTER 10: RUMORS

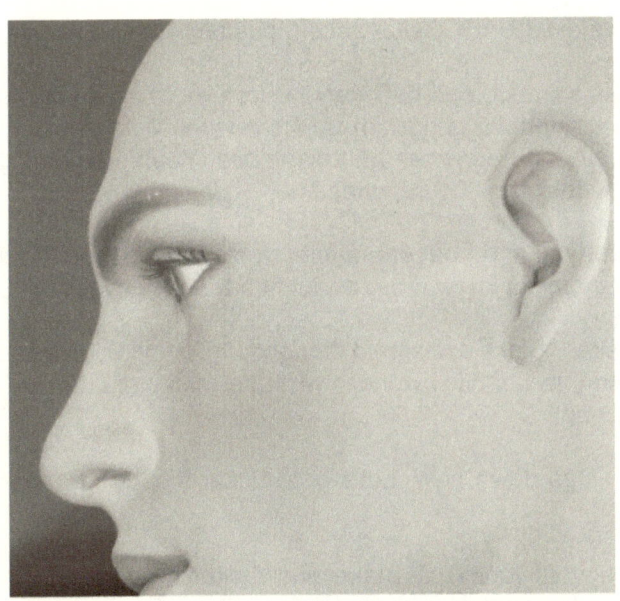

OSKAR SHOOK HIS HEAD, ENGROSSED IN HIS NEWEST invention, when Blake stepped through the door.

"Hey, Oskar, how's it goin'?"

"Well, actually, it's not going. I'm still trying to figure out the equation for its geometrics! It's puzzling, to be sure."

"Man, if you can't figure it out, nobody can. But I didn't mean how's your *work*; I meant how's the *agency* comin' along? Have you spotted anything unusual yet?"

"Well, as a matter of fact, Blake, Geo has been arousing my suspicions."

"I knew it, I knew it! Everybody's talking about him. Precisely why is he here? All he does is lock himself up in the old Clark house. Every once in a while, he actually comes out, I'm told, but he's always in a hurry. The guy is just creepy. He's a bomb about to explode. He's just strange, ya know what I mean? I don't know, there's something! Something's not right, if you ask me!"

"Should we *evict* him?" Oskar asked, pushing his spectacles back.

"Yes. He is suspect, and definitely far from *normal*. No one seems to want him around. I'll bring him up for *review*. If he doesn't state his business around here, then he's *vamoose*. Yeah, something's about to happen, but I can't figure what it is."

"How about you and I get some *intel* from his neighbors?" suggested Oskar. They might know more about him then we ever will!"

"Okay, Oskar!" Blake exclaimed thoughtfully. "Hey, Bill lives across the street from this weirdo! I wonder what he thinks of Geo; we can ask him what's up."

"I'll shut things down now. Let's go!" Oskar flipped the *open* sign to *closed*.

Rushing across *KidzTurf*, Blake and Oskar made their way to Bill Loring's, and parked way down the street from Geo's.

The boys ran toward Bill's house, up his front steps, both knocking on his door! The red door responded, opening wide.

"Hey, guys! What's up?" asked Bill.

116

"We have some questions, Bill, and we really need some answers in order to proceed forward."

"Then, by all means, come in, gentlemen!"

Oskar and Blake made a beeline to Bill's kitchen; he was the best chef in town, and maybe, just maybe there would be a snack or two!

Blake began, sitting on the barstool. "It's Geo. Something's going on and we're not sure..."

"Oh yeah, gottcha!" said Bill. "It's like this, man. The other day, it was raining, and I was inside fiddling with the TV, when I saw lightning. I looked out the window and it had hit Geo's house. The strangest thing was, instead of a quick flash, it just stayed there for several seconds, and then vanished. I grabbed my coat and ran over to see if everything was okay. I barged in and looked for Geo to make sure he was fine. I found him upstairs, and then I saw the strangest thing. Sparks flew from his skin! He was lying against the door frame, stunned. I then saw that he was working on some kind of techno-science project or something because there was a huge assortment of beakers, Bunsen burners, coils and colored liquids bubbling, all haphazardly set on a table. A huge hole in the ceiling, I guess from the lightning bolt, opened the room to the rain coming down. I was going to call emergency for help, when Geo started moving, slowly at first, then quickly sprung up, alive! He saw me, and a devilish look crossed his face.

He said in a quiet tone, "Get out. You are breaking and entering! Get, get out!"

"And so, I did."

Oskar then spoke up. "A boy of his age, our age, cannot withstand a lightning bolt, certainly not one that held for several seconds! This is weird. And did you say that sparks were flying off him?"

"Yep, some of 'em stung me. I'm sorry, guys, but he is trouble. He freaks me out. If he stays, then I'm outta here!"

"Well, thanks for telling us. This is maybe nothing, but this could get serious. But I think it's now out of our hands. I have two more people I want to talk to, and then Geo. Take care, Bill."

117

"Go easy on that TV," advised Oskar.

"Thanks. I will!" he called back, resuming his repair.

The two *detectives* crossed the street, passing Geo's house. For some reason, Blake felt as if *eyes* were peering out of numerous slits and cracks, watching their every move. He shuddered and walked faster. Oskar knocked on the door and Avery Myers opened it.

"Oh hey, Avery. Gosh, I almost forgot that you hung out here, with you always being at the journalism club and all that."

"Yep, this is where I *hang out,* she sighed. "...when I'm not home. So, what can I do for you guys?"

"We need for you to tell us about your neighbor. Geo. You know Geo?" Her eyes widened, and she slammed the door.

"Go away!" she protested. Oskar stepped back a few steps, wincing.

"Avery, Avery!" Blake replied, pounding the door. Avery wouldn't budge.

"Come on, Oskar. Let's' see if Geo's other neighbor cooperates." Blake didn't glance at Geo's house again, but the feeling struck him. He looked over his shoulder slowly.

"I'm being paranoid." he thought, trying to shrug it off, but couldn't. In seconds, they reached the next neighbor's house and banged on the door. A short fella opened the door. His mouse-brown hair fell forward over one eye, nearly hiding his crooked grin. He stepped forward to happily shake Blake's hand.

Surprised, and stepping back off the stoop, Blake managed to speak, "Uh, hey, I'm Blake Armstrong president of..."

"It's an honor, sir! Thank you for coming over. I'm Harry. Would you like to come in?"

"Sure, why not?" Blake and Oskar quickly exchanged glances and with raised eyebrows, walked in, and sat stiffly on the couch.

118

"So, Mr. President, what brings you here?"

"Blake, just Blake, and, well, we wanted to talk about your neighbor, Geo." Suddenly the man's face turned from bubbly-glad to frenzy.

"You mean that creep who sneaks out at night and climbs over the wall to the mine?"

"Wait, what?"

"Yeah, the creep lives over there, across the street, in the house right there, see? He does crazy stuff, experiments, never comes out in daylight. But every night, most nights anyway, I see him sneak out, climb over his back fence and ya know, I don't get it, there is security barbed wire all over there and he never gets cut up, but it is as if he doesn't care."

"Good observation," thought Blake, puzzled. "And where did you say he went off to?"

"The old mine. A few nights ago I followed Geo there. I don't know what he does, but I'm not ever going in there again. Creepsville!"

"Hey, Oskar, I think we need to pay Geo a visit," said Blake

"Now, Blake, do you really need me to come? I got lots of things to do, so..."

"You're coming, Oskar. Why don't you want to? Afraid?"

"No way, man! I'll come, but not for long. I need to get back to the shop."

"Okay, well thanks, Harry. Thanks for the info. We'll take care of Geo. You'll see. You never know, he might be leaving *KidzTurf* before ya know it." Blake smiled as he and Oskar made their way to the front door.

"Hey, are you sure you want to do this, Blake? You look kinda uneasy."

"I'm game if you are." Blake retorted.

Slowly they crept across the street, up Geo's steps. Blake's fist came up to the door then stopped. It hung, frozen, for a second, then managed a minor pound against the door. Instantly, they could hear a strange array of chain locks and bolts being undone. A main key twisted with a low thud, as the metal door swung open, only to forcefully slam against the wall, as if wind had pushed its way in. Geo stood there, his face pale, eyes wild. His hair was unkempt, perfectly matching his wrinkled attire.

"Geo! Uh, Hi! Remember me? Us? Blake, and, uh, this is Oskar." With a shove, Blake pushed Oskar toward Geo.

"Yeah. Sure." Geo shot back. "I'm very busy. Now is not the best time..." Before he could shut the door, Blake pushed in, ignoring Geo's excuses.

"Hey, Bud, some people are complaining about you. They're saying weird things about you. They're asking who you really are and what you're doin' in *KidzTurf*. Let's talk. How about a bite at Russo's? It's dinnertime and we can talk over some burgers, okay?

Geo hesitated, and then said, "Sure, that would be great." He turned to lock his door.

"And how about an after-dinner swim?" Blake taunted. He was on to something. Oskar didn't have a clue.

Geo nervously replied, "Oh, no. Oh, definitely no!!! No, no, no, not for me! Thank you, but, no, I hate water!"

*Place your trust in the Eternal; rely on Him completely; never depend upon your own ideas and inventions. Give Him the credit for everything you accomplish and He will smooth out and straighten the road that lies ahead.*

**Proverbs 3:5-6 The Voice translation**

## CHAPTER 11: ENEMY

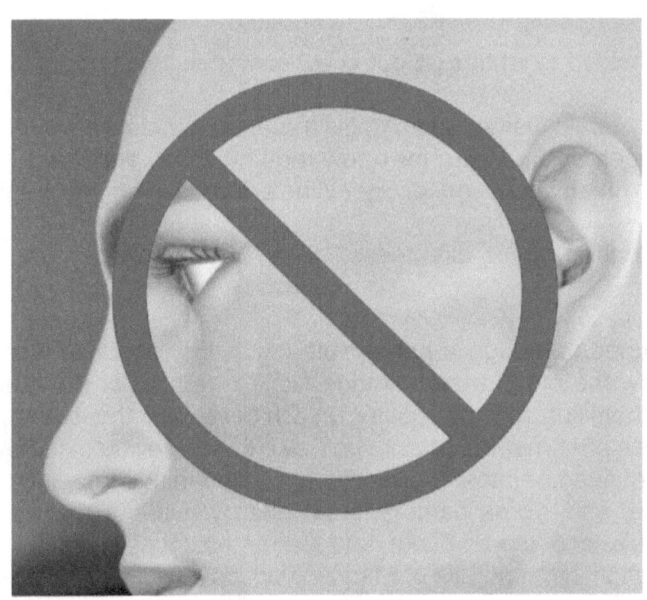

"Mario Burgers are the best, right, Geo?" inquired Blake.

"Yeah, sure, Blake, the best." replied Geo.

"Hey, Geo, what's you been up to? I, er, mean, all those nights

A.W.O.L. and stuff. Got any bruises or cuts?"

"What you talkin' about, man? Cuts? Bruises?"

"You been *mine snooping* recently?"

Geo clumsily pushed his water glass to the floor. His poorly maneuvered glass now lay in shards under the table, sprinkled across his feet, as he tapped a rhythm on Mario's restaurant floor. A buzzing came from under the table. Nobody seemed to notice. Somehow it escaped Geo that Oskar had a perfect view of everything. Geo remained calm, tapping his foot one more time as the shards reassembled into a perfectly clean and dry Mario water glass! Oskar raised an eyebrow.

Geo commented, "No prob, guys. Nothing's broken. Mario's floor must be rubberized!"

Oskar decided to let this go but knew something was up.

"All righty," said Oskar, clearing his throat, as he stared at Geo. "Geo, you've been around here for a few months, right, and man, we don't know too much about you, do we? Who are you? Who are you, really?"

Blake laughed at his directness, "Yeah, Geo, how did you end up here?

Geo grinned, although a perceptible lag in his response was noted. You know the old *Godzilla* vintage flicks where all of the characters speak, their lips quickly moving in Chinese, but the sound comes nano-secs after mouths are closed? Like this annoying cinematic flaw, Geo continued, almost perfectly, but something was off. Timing, response, and words came without energy, without feeling. It was perceptible and made Blake and Oskar anxious. How would their interrogation in the middle of Mario's develop? This was not the place. They could see that now. Why had they come here, anyway? The time, nightfall, seemed right, but now they keenly knew they would need to get Geo alone to continue questioning.

Geo pushed his plate away. "I'm done. Good burger, guys!" His eyes darted to the entrance. "Guess I'd better go. Got lots to do, you know."

"Not so fast! We've got a few more questions, but you're right, we do need to go. We'll go with you. Oh, and, by the way, where are you going, Geo?" queried Blake.

"Nowhere. Maybe home?" replied Geo.

"I don't think so!" said Oskar, quickly standing up.

"Yeah, Geo. You need to come with us." demanded Blake.

"With you two? Naah. Not tonight!" argued Geo, as he stood, walking toward Mario's front door.

Blake grabbed Geo's arm. "You're coming with us, whether you like it or not, bro!" He tightened his grip, opening the door for Geo. Oskar followed.

The night was still, unlike the three fellows, who were making their way down a sloping sidewalk, which quickly fell away from Mario's. The autumn trees hung low and menacing bordering the wet street, and pointed to a lonely part of town. The outskirts. A tract of land, little vegetation, some scruffy shrubs, and no trees. And there, a mine, all but a few had mostly forgotten.

"Let go of me!" demanded Geo.

"In your dreams!" laughed Blake. Oskar joined him.

A buzzing seemed to come from the trees, a new life suddenly rising like springtime sap ready to be harvested! An arc of blue light from two of the trees blazed forward, joining in one stream, and suddenly, instantly, circuiting its beam fully into Geo's hand. To Blake and Oskar the pain was excruciating; they immediately let their prisoner loose.

"Do you know who you're dealing with, punks? You have no idea do you? You are ridiculous! Weak. Stupid. You're like all humans. Totally inept!"

Geo's *assessment* pounded into Blake's and Oskar's ears.

"You go on your pathetic rounds, trying to figure things out. Slow. That's what you are, slow and stupid. Watch me, and learn!" instructed

123

Geo.

Though ear-piercing, his words came without passion. Geo remained calm, collected.

Blake and Oskar, *freaked*, quickly taking off into the woods, as far from Geo as possible. Out of breath, they came to a steep cliff, which pointed to the muted light of a half moon.

"Thought we were gonna die, Blake!" whispered Oskar.

"Nah. Just interference. Geo's not going to do anything major yet. Too many of us. Only one of him, get it?" said Blake.

"Yeah, I guess. We better *book* it home."

"Gotta rise, bro, at dawn. Geo's not goin' away!"

"You, waking up at the crack of dawn? Ha! I'd like to see you try. Just go, bro!" said Oskar, breathlessly. "No need to waste three hours of sleep; see ya at nine."

Blake held a finger up in the air to pause the convo, then opened his mouth. "Geo's on the loose. We'd better get home. six, dawn. O.K.?"

"Well, bro, do what you gotta do. And be careful, man. I'm not going to the mine. You never know what you'll find out there. Stay safe!" Oskar shuddered, ready to sprint home.

"Thanks, and I will!" whispered Blake, as he watched his friend move swiftly away.

"You never know what you might find out there..." Blake's imagination got away from him, as he envisioned horrific images of what might be found in the abandoned mine: a sea of dead bodies? Booby traps? Mutated monsters? His thoughts raced and loomed larger than life! Making his way home, Blake's pace rapidly grew more determined as he raced ahead in his *nightmare*. But this wouldn't last much longer. He could see that now. Reality has a way of its own, sometimes cruel, at other times sudden. Now it simply slapped him awake as he opened the door. Silently, he walked to his room, turned the covers down, grabbed his Bible with trembling hands: *Though I walk through the valley of the shadow of death, I shall fear no evil, for you are with me; your rod and your staff, they comfort me.* Blake prayed. His fervent words lifted him closer to God, upward, heavenward, above his encompassing *tangle*, what he was to do and how he would need to handle the days ahead. He turned off his light. It was going to be an interesting morning, in just a few hours.

Blake surprised himself as he stood alert at his bedside at 4:00 a.m., far beyond *awake*. He was ready! He quickly packed supplies, food, water, rock climbing gear, shovel, pickaxe, and, of course, Oskar's latest GPS device. He crept down the stairs, rattling with his gear, and, left a cryptic note to his parents:

**"I'll be back around mid-afternoon.**
**Going to KidzTurf - Blake"**

He slapped it on the fridge and walked out, pulling his motor bike to attention. Silently, he wheeled it beyond the gate, then gunned it full throttle. In less than twenty minutes, he had blown down the path, zoomed past *KidzTurf*, maneuvered through a jungle of trees, finally pulling near to his destination. A huge clearing and sudden upthrust in the narrow road, alerted Blake that he was almost there! To most the incline was unimpressive but to Blake it radiated danger as he carefully ascended the road leading to the abandoned mine. His bike slid about, avoiding rough patches and potholes. Suddenly, to his left, he spotted the mine's boarded entrance, a mismatch of wooden planks, one over the other, as if constructed in a hurry to avoid detection. Blake had arrived. The mine. A crunching noise alerted Blake, as he spun around. It was Dawson, *Oskar's replacement!*

"Hey, man, glad you're here! Let's go get 'em!" said Blake. Removing several planks from the gaping hole behind, Blake quickly thrust the timbers, one by one, behind him.

"Finally!" he muttered, ready, so ready, to find Geo and pull him to court.

Blake and Dawson lunged into the mine's entrance, gear clacking as they made their way into the darkness.

"Geo, old boy, where are you?" the boys yelled together.

Something out from the dark, a shovel-like weapon, came spinning toward Blake, barely missing his shoulder.

"What the....?" Blake yelled.

Geo stepped toward Blake and Dawson, lifting his weapon to strike once more! Blake lunged quickly forward, cracking Geo against the wall. This, along with a major punch to the head, disabled Geo's balance, as he slid downward. To further his cause, Blake grabbed his enemy, pushing Geo further to the mine's dirt floor. Geo squirmed, trying to free himself. Blake's grip tightened around Geo's neck, forcing him to relent. In astonishment Blake found Geo's flesh to be paper thin and beneath it, the hardest bone he had ever felt. Geo showed no sign of pain, although he continued to struggle. Dawson grabbed Geo by the shoulders with massive strength, lifting Geo with both arms, and threw him forward into the air, against the wall. Geo tumbled several times but quickly got up for more! Again, Dawson pounded his opponent to the floor. Blake yelled for Dawson to stop, but he didn't listen. He couldn't. He wouldn't. On and on he pounded Geo. No response. Geo stood up, totally cool, collected. Dawson spat.

"You'd better listen up, punk! If you don't comply, I will feed you to my uncle's dogs and then strap you to my fence for target practice! I will make it my personal goal to climb the tallest redwood with you on my back and chuck you down to your death! I swear on my life that your mother will cry when she sees what I've done with you!"

"Dawson! Stop!" Blake yelled.

The more menacing Dawson became, Geo matched his bully's anger with a curious calm. Red-faced, Dawson sweated in uncontrolled fury as he held Geo who had surprisingly quit struggling!

Grinning from ear to ear, Geo bared his teeth, whispering, "I will comply."

Dawson dropped Geo, kicking him forward, "Get moving!"

Blake staggered at what his friend had just accomplished. He stormed up to Dawson and harshly whispered, "That was uncalled for! You reminded me of Rodney, man! Snap out of it. This is just a weird kid! Nothing more. Nothing less, right? We gotta find out the truth about him, but not this way!"

"This is no *kid*, Blake. He's a bomb ready to explode. More than a bomb! And if we don't contain it, everything will be chaos. BOOM! You get me?"

Blake agreed with his friend's reasoning, and responded, "Yeah, he's dangerous. You can see that. But remember, the punishment always comes after the crime. And who are we to punish him? That matter should only concern the court, not us. So, get your act together, man!"

They pushed Geo forward into the mine's main tunnel, winding their way down its clammy corridor, as the air temp began to significantly decrease. Here it was winter, cold enough for snow to fall in the narrowing maze of tunnels.

"Wher.. wher... where are w..w..we?" Blake stammered through freezing lips.

"Buh..Buh..Blake....Let's get outta here."

Blake nodded, turning around, when Geo quietly started to laugh to himself. His musing morphed into a cackle, then hysteria, and his head tilted back, as he leaned against the wall. His face was radiant.

"Run!" Dawson yelled, freaking out.

Geo chanted with unstoppable laughter as Blake and Dawson ran, terrified, through the dark passageway, looking for an exit. They were surrounded in the cloying darkness. A loud rushing sound alerted them. It was dead ahead. The running boys instantly halted as a blast of water surged toward them, rising around their ankles, and moved up to their knees. They rolled in the water, losing their bearings, as the rushing torrent overtook them, plunging them, down, down, down in its winding contortions. For what seemed forever, Blake could see nothing. As he twisted and jerked about in the dark, searching for an answer, an escape, an exit, there it came: a pinpoint of light, growing brighter, fluorescent light, as the tunnel whimpered to its end, opening into a jumble of levels and steps. In the rushing water Blake and Dawson shot forward. Dawson's head hit a metal platform, and after that, unconscious, he fell to the floor.

Blake pounded into some platform rails, clinging on for life as the water rushed through a grate beneath him. He looked down to his left, several yards from the sucking grate. Below, Dawson lay sprawled upon a slowly lowering platform. Blake climbed over a railing and landed on his back, too weak for any *parkour maneuvers*, then stood himself straight up. Walls in the mine's lower levels had grown slick with ice. Blake slipped down a cascade of metal steps, and then waded to his unconscious friend. The remaining water, now dead still, as Blake stood within his watery enclosure, reflected a gathering of suspended light bulbs above, a perfect yet unsettling image of a summer starlit sky. It was surreal. Perhaps more Van Gogh than anything else! He dragged Dawson from the embracing water to a nearby platform. Blake, now fully spent, still persisted as he leaned over his friend, rhythmically pushing upon Dawson's gut, and turning the unconscious boy's head to one side. Dawson began to fiercely expel water, and soon gained consciousness. Blake was relieved, but his relief lasted for only a moment. There before him loomed a tall shadow cast upon the water. It was Geo. Cackling. Blake whipped around.

"Wha, what is this!?!? What are you!?!" Blake yelled in horror.

Geo continued to mock. His bony hand went to his smooth face and then, like an animal, he started to claw himself, ripping off skin. He stopped for a moment, and Blake could see the human face of Geo shredding to pieces; underneath, no blood or bone, but titanium! Geo stabbed his own eye, revealing a brilliant blue dot. Blake, terrified, scrambled away, back up the stairs. Geo took a bucket and scooped up some of the black water. He tipped it over his head, letting it drizzle over his body. Steam billowed upward as the black shower began to burn away any remaining skin. Blake could now see Geo, a robot, definitely and without any doubt whatsoever, for what he truly was! Exterior casings stripped away, like the removal of tomb walls, the interior, Geo's evil interior and intentions were now revealed! The robot dove into the black water, and with great delight, leapt from the dark water's surface, all skin stripped away. Geo's metallic, claw-like fingers were going for Blake's throat as a loud "BOOM accosted the mine!" The massive explosion propelled Blake backwards, slamming him against an icy wall. As he lay there, Geo quietly slipped beneath the inky water. Blake looked around, up, down and employed a *pano* to get precise bearings. Rubbing his neck, his eyes widened as he shook his head. Dawson sat there, across the way, facing Blake, as he warily held a launcher, which steamed with smoke.

*I've given you true authority. You can smash vipers and scorpions under your feet.*

**Luke 10:19 The Voice translation**

## CHAPTER 12: HOTSPOT

RIPPING HIM APART, what had happened in the mine continued to hit Blake. Hard. Trauma has ways of grabbing attention, not only in the moment of *terror*, but minutes later, days later, propelling the abused into years ahead, broken and shattered. Trauma invades dreams, one's spirit, injuring the *DNA of the mind*. Geo and the mine had accomplished this act, as we now witness Blake's composite of confusion, dream, and déjà vu. He has now fallen into a stupor, recounting what had happened the previous night. It was all mixed up, like water and oil, shaken in a container. Give it time and the oil would separate once again from the water. Blake would once again stand firmly on his feet, but for now, things were swirling, and intensifying. Profound fear and realities combined in unique patterns, as Blake lay exhausted, leaning against the narrow alleyway's wall, where only days before he had *parkoured* with delight, but now in his dream, he was clawing for what he must do next, his mind reeling.

Fatigued, Blake and Dawson in the dream's *slo-mo* pulled Geo closer, ever closer, step by struggling step, to the mine's entrance. Was this *deja vu*? It seemed that they had been here before, together, embattled and driven. Yes, Blake was sure of this. Or, again he wondered if he was caught in a dream? He wasn't sure. And yet, he must be. Oil and water, shaken. Old planks, pushed aside days ago, revealed curious activity. Check. Someone had access through the dark hole which was now facing the tired trio. Check. Words, no, grunts, accompanied their struggle as the boys forced Geo through the dark entrance. No, this was different. And it was night time. Hadn't they come back at first light? A moist pungent, foul odor assaulted them; Geo remained unaffected.

"Man, what a stench," complained Dawson. "Something with a twist, mixed with Sulphur!"

"Whatever it is, it's massively gross," replied Blake.

The boys released Geo. They waited for his reply. Slowly at first, but then increasing his gait, Geo moved ahead into the narrowing tunnel and turned left. Silence. Then there was light. Geo had struck a match to illumine a hanging kerosene lantern. As the boys moved toward the light, Geo smirked, laughing.

"You have no clue, do you?" he whispered.

"Tell us, Geo. What's this all about?" demanded Blake, as he pointed at the dark walls surrounding them. "There's something going on here. I know it. That's why we dragged you here, or should I say back to here! Looks like familiar territory, right, Geo?"

Geo turned away, giving no reply, but moved silently forward away from Blake and Dawson. What was Geo thinking? Why this bizarre silence? The boys followed, as the tunnel turned downward and slightly to the right. Suddenly a buzzing assaulted their ears, pulling them into its power. The volume increased. They were powerless, efficiently rendered immoveable. Their arms dangled motionless by their sides, as they slowly slid in sync behind Geo.

"As I said, weak and stupid!" laughed Geo. "You still have no idea, do you?"

The dusty and ever-brightening tunnel now quickly expanded forward, leading the trio into a hive-like cave; the rocky walls and upper expanses were riddled with dark openings, which lead away from the cave in a thousand directions. As the boys shuffled further into the cave, Geo silently pointed to its dark portals. At each entrance stood humanoid robots, waiting for further command.

Blake tried to speak but only managed, "Mmmmmmumph!" as if his mouth were duct-taped. Dawson attempted likewise.

"Yesirree, stupid!" screeched Geo.

His laughter filled the gaping cave. His *attack team* awaited release. Over and over, Geo's laughter echoed, building fear. There was no escape. No hope. Confusion morphed, abusing Blake in his dream to an *insanity, which was* carefully proportioned and measured, as the enemy would have it. Dark. Light. Battle.

Blake winced, expecting death at any moment along with Dawson's. As he fell to his knees, his trembling gave way to heart-wrenching sobs. He began to awaken, and his eyes now fluttered admitting the day's alleyway light into his consciousness, he, still oblivious to a new tide which in the lonely alleyway was now flowing forward. A *cavalry* was ready to surround him, ready to soothe Blake's mind and heart, a *rescue* of sorts, all contained within a luminous triangle pulsating with life. Slowly, it made its way down the dark alleyway in royal procession, beyond yesterday's darkness, beyond immanent death, beyond all that the *enemy* had to offer. In the narrow alley where Blake lay crumpled and *discarded*, Love was *moving in* and would have its way. Swirling in majestic authority, tiny specks of light emanated from the twisting Trigon, which now formed a kindly face.

Its voice stabbed into the evil *darkness* which squeezed upon Blake's pounding heart: "In you, Blake, God will choose to display his power and love. Remember this. Although you are weak and imperfect like a jar of clay, there is truth within you upon which God will build. Lean on Him, Blake. He is your strength. He is your courage. Listen to Him and to no other."

Trigon's words began to diminish, dissipating as quickly as they had come. Yet the brilliant light remained, pounding Blake's abusive terrors. Blake's dream and today's reality were now merging. Blake's *mission* now pulled him forward into its *battle* as the new warrior reached toward Trigon's ever brilliant yet now fading light.

*The dream ended, and Jacob woke up from his sleep. Jacob (to himself): There is no doubt in my mind that the Eternal One is in this place, and I didn't even know it!*

**Genesis 28:16 The Voice translation**

## CHAPTER 13: SECRET STUFF

TEN FINGERS JUMPED AND SLID FROM square to square on Blake's chrome keyboard. His eyes were completely fixed on the computer screen; he didn't even notice the smudge at the right corner of his glasses. Before Blake clicked *send*, he quickly reviewed his message.

## [URGENT: FOR YOUR EYES ONLY]

**Overseers, it is critical we meet. The Trigon has been a controversial issue between the four of us! We must figure out what to do with it. Meet me in the clockwork tower tonight, 8:30pm sharp, after we clear out the town. See you then. To maintain security, use your private entries.**

### Blake

Blake checked and double-checked, then clicked his encrypted missive: *Send*. He checked the time, also: 7:30 am. Right on schedule, Blake closed his laptop, pushing against the wall behind his desk and rolled across his room's hardwood floor to an open doorway. Blake slipped off of his black office chair and jogged down the stairs. He grabbed a quick bite in his tiny kitchen, as he carefully scanned a few recent issues of technical mags just in. He was almost finished when he heard a disturbance, a noisy group of kids lining up outside.

Blake forced down his food, stumbling to his front door, "Hey! *KidzTurf* opens at eight! Come back then!"

"Aw, come on, *Director Armstrong*, let us in. Please! I left my phone home and I'm stranded!" A couple of other kids chimed in making their own excuses. Blake had enough and gave in to them. He pushed the green button on his timed lock and the gate opened a few feet, while the kids, one by one, rushed through the entrance. They were inside and they were grateful, as they laughed and pushed forward towards the game room.

Blake warned a few careless kids who had kicked over some stray trashcans. He rolled his eyes. His day was jammed, yet he proceeded slowly. For the next few hours, as Blake pondered his upcoming 8:30 pm meeting, he watched the construction of a new trampoline in the rec center. Later he assisted Oskar in modifying the town's hover boards, and treated him to a small pizza he had prepared in his micro. Just as quickly as the day had begun, it closed! Bam! Just like that! The Saturday sun had disappeared behind the wood's tree tops and most people had returned home. It was now time to *completely* clear the town and lock up. Blake sent a message over the speakers, announcing that it was beyond closing time and those remaining needed to leave immediately. Music replaced his request as stragglers, waving to friends, laughed past the gateway into the early night.

All four, Blake, Dawson, Oskar, and Summerlin did a last-minute search for any strays. Oskar sped on hover board by Geo's. A bright upstairs light shone upon Geo, busily writing on his wall for some reason. The rule was that no one was permitted to remain in their assigned bunker after dark, but Geo was excused. He had nowhere else to go, so he said and *KidzTurf* for some reason believed him! As soon as the sun's light had evaporated and the stars began to flicker, the town was now fully cleared.

Dawson unscrewed his bolted three-foot bookshelf and swung it open upon its hinges, revealing his tunnel to the clock tower. Summerlin pulled open two of her stair boards and descended toward the meeting place. Oskar slid under his couch, opening a hatch to his private tunnel. And last, Blake ran up to his attic and opened a wardrobe, squirming past coats to its back, C.S. Lewis style, to where there was a hole in the wall. He dove inside it head first and slid down the tunnel and into the secret meeting place. Blake softly rolled onto the floor's landing mat inside the clock tower. Coming to a stop on his back, his could see upwards at the group pacing and talking above. The Trigon's glow shining through the metal slats hit Blake. He stood up and walked over to the old rickety lift. Blake closed its steel fence-like door and pressed number 2. The lift creaked and groaned to the platform above, where the meeting was to take place. When the doors opened, Blake could feel the tension.

"Blake, come in." invited Dawson.

As Blake stepped off the tiny elevator, no one spoke a word after that, not even Blake. The hostility of his friends closed his mouth and theirs. He walked around the room slowly, planning what to say. Blake remained uneasy. The platform stood there, a large circle, constructed of thick metal with slotted holes. Blake walked to its edge and leaned over the railing. Down below he could see five secret entries to HQ. Inscribed on the floor shone the *KidzTurf* symbol, which Oskar had lasered in metal. On the right was an elevator and on its left a winding spiral staircase spun upward. Blake turned around. Everyone stood staring. Oskar stood, one hand pressed awkwardly against the wall.

He fiddled with his Rubik's cube with nimble fingers, tossing it up a few feet and deftly catching the puzzle, but his eyes remained fixed on Blake. Dawson had stopped bouncing his ball, and was slouched on a worn sofa at the room's center. The *spire*, a name they had given the center of their meeting space, was a huge cylinder which reached from ceiling to floor. It was constructed of glass and carefully enclosed the Trigon, suspended in its transparent core, radiating an eerie blue light. The cylinder boasted a round metallic desk that wrapped around its base. Along the desk were four screens, each screen divided into sixteen sections, a comprehensive security monitor network. Summerlin sat on a high beam, arms crossed, her eyes trained on the guys. Blake took a seat himself and leaned back, staring at the Trigon.

"What to do with the Trigon..." Blake murmured.

At once everyone began to speak. Like *talking heads* in battle, each let loose their own bias regarding the Trigon. Blake allowed them to complain for a while, and seeing that his peers were not going to stop their *jumble*, Blake yelled,

"QUIET! Please! This *war* between us is ridiculous. We can work it out, can't we?"

"Why is this even a discussion? The Trigon is probably dangerous; it's gonna blow any minute!" Summerlin exclaimed. "I mean, just look at it! It's getting brighter by the minute. Or who knows, maybe its alien glow is giving off harmful radiation and is poisoning us. Just give the stupid Tridesicon empire what they want in exchange for peace and it will all be settled. They never harmed us before with it, why would they now?"

"Uh, you have obviously never seen any sci-fi movies. Aliens don't come in peace. They are wired to kill humans. It's in their blood. Even if we give them the Trigon, they will still initiate their killing spree on humanity." Dawson said.

Since he finally had the floor, Dawson seized the moment.

"We need to destroy the Trigon ourselves. I agree with *Sum*, it's most likely life-threatening. But we can minimize casualties by obliterating it, right? Follow me on this: The *aliens* would most likely want to kill us for touching their *gold*. The government there is run by a bunch of psychos and we would probably kill ourselves if we tried to use it. I say that Oskar should design and build a spacecraft to send the Trigon into the sun. That will destroy the confounded thing."

"On the contrary, Dawson!" Oskar interjected. "It would take too long to send the Trigon into the sun. I'm no rocket scientist, oh wait I am...well, sort of... but I still couldn't make a space ship that could store enough fuel to last the trip. It would burn up before it reached the sun. And I strongly disagree with that jab r-r-regarding our government. I have hacked into their system and I have seen firsthand that they have in their possession extra-terrestrial objects just like the Trigon. They're locked up beneath the city and have been sealed in concrete and steel so that no one, not even the president himself, can get their hands on them. The Trigon should also be stored with them, away from *harm*. And, in this wise, we could also warn the government about the outer galactic army coming our way. In addition, who are we to do anything less than turn it over to government officials? We're just kids; we should not be playing with fire. The only safe and sensible thing to do is to ship the Trigon to Washington. And that's my humble opinion."

Oskar completed his third *go-round* on his Rubik's cube, then tossed it to Blake. "I can see the logic behind all of your suggestions, but you guys are forgetting one thing. Trigon has a *soul*, or something very much like a *soul*. It has its own personality, it, it, it's no ordinary object; this thing is special. It has profound power, a heart creation from God Himself! To sell this like a *slave*, to lock it up, to kill it is completely wrong. Trigon wants us to fight back! That's right, us! A group of high school kids who don't know a thing about war. And that is exactly what the Lord sometimes does. He chooses the unlikely, the weak, the humble, and the vulnerable to carry out his mission so that He is exalted through their work."

"But Blake, how do you know this is what God wants?" Summerlin inquired.

"I can feel it," Blake answered. "I don't know how, but I do. The revelation came right when I first laid eyes on the Trigon. The urge to fight back against evil! And it has grown stronger and stronger. Now, all of my doubt is gone. I am ready to tackle this new race, if necessary, or whatever it is and defend our own!"

"So, all you are going on is a feeling? I'm sorry Blake, but I don't get the logic in that." Oskar shook his head.

Dawson walked toward the encased Trigon, tapping on the glass. "Did you hear that, lil' Trigon? Blake wants to weaponize you and use you to kill another nation. Did you think about that Blake, using you, you'd become a murderer if you fight back in any way? What's your opinion, lil' Trigon? What do you think should happen? Come on, don't be shy. Tell us what you want. Come on, tell us! Oh, rightttt, you don't know how to talk. Ha!" Dawson mocked.

The room suddenly brightened, as light and color intensified around the four kids. Dawson rocketed backwards, nearly over the rail. Summerlin fell off her perch but caught hold of a nearby rope, then lowered herself to the grated floor. Both Blake and Oskar were pushed onto awaiting sofas. Yes, the Trigon now had their attention!

In *slo-mo*, the glass cylinder fell in tiny pieces away from the Trigon. Radiating in neon power, the Trigon hovered in place, unscathed by the glass eruption. The glowing triangle suddenly grew larger, floating toward Blake, and compelled him to reach out, to touch life itself, a tactile, hypnotic moment which pierced him, re-arranging his perceptions, his motives, his decisions. Astonished, Blake sat powerless as the Trigon moved closer, its glowing edges trembling, vibrating silently, pushing an image beyond its transparent screen, a holographic, fully formed being in distress. He crept back a little only to find the edge of the rail and a fifteen-foot plummet. He faced the Trigon with as much courage as he could muster. Voices, foreign voices, hummed a chant, commenting, as the triangular edges trembled, and visible translation began to move around the three broad sides of the Trigon. It was still gibberish to Blake, but slowly, each word began to click inside Blake's mind. It suddenly made sense. Blake's eyes widened. Trigon was ready to speak.

"Power is worthless without purpose. Knowledge is empty without application. Whosoever possesses the power and knowledge of the Trigon shall be unstoppable. But beware, *children of wickedness*, those who misuse these powers will be cursed. The Trigon shall turn against you and lay waste to your people and your land. What you are witnessing here is *terror*. Tridesicon needs your help now, Blake! Since you have discovered the missing Trigon, you are now called to bring forth new life to a crumbling and tortured world, a people in desperation, a planet without hope. You are their hope. Look through my portals and you will see what poverty, oppression, and raw evil look like! You have discovered me, Blake, because I am a key, a key to restoring Tridesicon to its original glory. Only you can help!"

Blake's palm touched the Trigon, as he admired its beauty. Suddenly its side cracked open, slowly splitting apart. Blake removed his hand to see what he had done. The crack in the Trigon began to widen even more! At the center of the Trigon a ball of brilliant light suddenly shot from the crack. The Trigon's sides continued to unfold, side upon side, until they simply vanished, leaving a lucent haze that filled the room; its light enfolded, embraced. Suddenly, the room swarmed with tiny dots of brilliant light, like fireflies. Thousands upon thousands of them flew in circles around the room, giving Blake and Oskar an *assurance beyond assurance*. The yellow dots coalesced, creating a face. It was the face of Trigon. Compassionate, kind, somehow *eternal*. Sure, you could say a few things about it, but its beauty, its power, its righteousness cannot be put into words, dear reader. The face slowly circled the room, giving each kid a straight *look in the eye*, driving fear away, *downloading* commitment and love into each heart.

It turned, facing Blake, then spoke: "Blake Armstrong, the boy who found me." The glowing face smiled warmly. "I am the soul of Trigon. I am Trigon. I have been crafted by our Heavenly Father Himself. He has given me a drop of every aspect of Him and He now gives me to you as a gift. I am here to protect, to heal, to rebuke, and to save. Blake, the end is near; the tides are changing. This war against the Tridesicon empire will not be the only one but the first of three. You have been chosen to fight these battles. You have the heart of a *true* child of God and have the will to die as a martyr, if needed. You have found favor with the King and He has chosen you to be one of many leaders. You, with the help of your friends, will defeat Micron and Mordna. You may use my power to win this war, for the strength comes not from you but from God himself! You must build your own army and fight Micron here on earth. He shall retreat to his own home and fully utilize his secret weapon. You shall meet him with swords and men of Borealis by your side. Do all of this, Blake Armstrong, in the name of Jesus the Christ, your Lord, your King and Savior."

Blake was speechless. All that he was able to muster was "A, ah, amen." Then, quietly, the face dissolved. The fog retreated into a ball and the Trigon shell re-appeared to enclose it. The triangular object slowly descended, clattering to the floor.

Blake recapped to himself what had just happened. "Here I've just stood, yes, this is unbelievable, within the Trigon's glowing light, drawn to its compelling presence. Was it the beating of a heart, I wonder? Here was life of a different sort. I could sense I was not alone, at all! Words just came to me, not from its screen, not spoken ideas, but perceptions from within, as if drawn from my heart, yes, from my soul. Trigon's soul and mine have become one, at least in purpose."

Brilliant light continued to flash as a pulsating buzz, an electric arching, alive, vital, *commanding*, surrounded Blake. He was not alone but treasured, valued, enabled. Yes, he could do this. He was on a mission. Empowerment was in process. He was being prepared for work beyond his capabilities, yet somehow it all made sense: a teenage boy being prepared for a man's work.

"Can I do this?" he thought. An assurance he had never known before, in cascading increments fell upon him, no, *within* him. Slowly, amazed, he bent over, retrieving his beloved Trigon from the floor!

*God of our Lord Jesus the Anointed, Father of Glory: I call out to You on behalf of Your people. Give them minds ready to receive wisdom and revelation so that they will truly know You. Open the eyes of their hearts, and let the light of Your truth flood in.*

**Ephesians 1:17-18 The Voice translation**

## CHAPTER 14: SUNKOR

DAYS LATER, TRIGON, SHOWING ITS COLORS, GLINTED IN THE
bright sunlight, its triangular screen, compelling both boys to look
through its glowing portal, at images, which paused here, and
positioned there, then bolting through speckled blackness. Trigon's
view bounced from star to star like a pinball machine, abruptly

stopping, almost saluting what appeared on screen. Before the boys there appeared dead center, suspended within the triangle's portal, a curious planet's swirling clouds of hail and bitter snow, which joined hands, dancing across Tridesicon's icy surface.

Trigon's image dove downward through swirling snow-filled clouds to Micron's palace. There, covered in icy snow, the menacing palace portrayed itself in grey and black speckled stonework, its towers jutting upward toward the lowering clouds. Trigon descended further to the palace's grand entry where a curious figure, apparently a leader, an emperor, or supreme warrior, held his entire army bowed before him. Micron's cold, lightless eyes swept across the vast columns of robotic soldiers, as he addressed the obedient crowd, "Soldiers, now is the time! Sunkor has been completed; we must go now and commence our final preparations for war. On their beloved Christmas day, there will be destruction. There will be pain. There will be death. And then, there will be no more...of them!"

Micron paused. His whispered speech was mysteriously carried over miles of robots by an agreeable wind. You see, Tridesicon is able to pick up sound, upon its whimsy, and spread even hushed lullabies over miles of land, similar to an echo. Micron coughed and spat upon the frozen turf. This was a way to signal the slaves to set up the Vox. The Vox was a machine designed to shrink men into a size that could fit in *The Path of the Gods*. Four small men dressed in black leather armor and helmet masks carried the machine to the ball of saliva and heaved the Vox down, with its door facing the army. Micron waved, and the servants scuttled away. The ice king side-stepped the Vox, his footing precise.

"Mordna, give me my scepter!"

Mordna gave Micron her *look of approval*, as she passed the scepter to his waiting hand. Micron grasped it firmly. He gazed into its beaming light of gold and words of wisdom. The last time he had seen his staff was when he had merged communities with the *Sliphex Nation*, whose planet had just been destroyed by a black hole. He opened the path so that the aliens could have a new home on what once was the good and glorious and *believing* land of Tridesicon, a people of faith and of love. Among the *Sliphex Nation* was Mordna, who eventually married Micron. These powerful creatures, once in place, like cogs in a well-oiled wheel, proceeded link by link, drawing down the innocent, day

144

after day, enslaving the good people of Tridesicon while in multiple, evil and devious ways forced Emperor Micron to completely and efficiently cast out any remaining *light*, as Tridesicon's beloved *moral code* slowly died. The only thing that the *Sliphex Nation* could not eradicate was the scepter's code inscriptions and its inner pulsating light. Knowing that the *light* would only soften Micron's now stony heart, Mordna kept it tucked away most of the time. But now that it was time to travel the galaxy once again, she reluctantly handed it to him.

The words on the staff whispered to Micron, imploring him to turn away from his wickedness and Mordna, and to abandon the…it all suddenly stopped. Behind her Emperor, Mordna had deftly slipped a dark matter band, which wrapped around his head, fully covering his eyes and ears. He could still hear and see through it, but not anything *righteous* or *holy*. And as he gazed at his staff now, he did so with new perspective: it was nothing but a soul-less bland yellow colored stick.

Mordna whispered to him, "Do it. Do it now, my Emperor."

Micron easily back-flipped twice, landing atop the *Vox*, a trick he had learned from the *Sliphex*. He raised his staff to the sky, aiming its knobby base at a small hole on the *Vox*, and with all of his strength pounded the staff into the hole. Immediately, in reply, an enormous sizzling arc exploded in waves across the entire planet. Attacking, a brilliant green *tornado* of major proportion inserted itself into the maelstrom, deflecting lightning bolts of every imaginable color. All that Micron could see was yet another dull grey *swirl of wind*. The top of his scepter opened to reveal a miniature keypad. Micron's nimble fingers quickly entered the coordinates of earth and sun. Quickly, the scepter keypad upon his verbal command obeyed as it withdrew into its casing. Moments later, in reply, the ground beneath Micron began to tremble as he waited impatiently for the tornado shaft to do its work. Brilliant light, which he could not see, at once encircled the powerful shaft as its tip entered the ground, injecting and anchoring its power into the Tridesicon soil. Suddenly, all spinning ceased as the radiant shaft withdrew, creating a trail of gold light. Like a cord stretched from wheel to spindle to awaiting hands, the golden light twisted, slowly at first, then faster and faster, extending, rising upward, up, up, drilling into the sky. The *tornado* kept drawing its trail of gold up above, way above, and into space as it sped forward beyond sight. It pulsed its way through galaxies, planets, constellations and stars until it found earth's solar system and bright sun. Once the tornado's tip reached the scorching sphere it vanished into nothing, *poof*, leaving an entire string of gold from Tridesicon to earth's brilliant star.

Back on the icy planet, Micron gave his final speech. "Together, we will take back our prized Trigon and lay waste to the accursed land of the HUMANS." You see, Micron loathed humans, more than you could ever imagine.

"Let us now go and prepare for glorious battle!"

He clapped his arms together to form a point, which glowed within his eyes, the Tridesicon salute. All within his royal view mimicked his action. Micron jumped down from the machine's top and walked into the *Vox*. Inside, its lasers scanned him. Each time they drew across his body, he shrunk half in size. When the quick process was over, Micron was no bigger than an ant, standing before the golden light beam. He didn't care to wait for others to come down to size, so he impatiently dove in. Breaking into the strand, the flow of golden liquid quickly shot him upwards. Micron, amazed at the *brilliant* liquid which now encased him, he, now had become a mere particle, a DNA cell within a cell. The tiny Emperor shot forward within the golden strand.

The thought of taking off his *dark matter* band seemed like a good idea. The light tugged at Micron's heart, but he dismissed the thought. He needed to keep himself hard and sharp for what was about to happen. Even if you were traveling at the speed of light, it still would take minutes to cross multiple galaxies. He closed his eyes and dreamed of better times. He mused upon creation spinning by. "The universe is very impressive," he thought. "God spoke, it's been said, and He saw that it was good. Now, where did that come from?" he wondered. As he once again pulled down his dark matter band, yet with open eyes he remembered when Tridesicon was cloudless, when he could see Westron's *sea of stars*. Witnessing this again now brought it all back and it tugged at the emperor's heart. Quickly, in increments his speed diminished as he swept toward the sun. Once again, he closed his eyes and dreamed, warm in the brilliant golden liquid.

Suddenly, he was there. Spewed out. Abruptly. The thin golden strand now pulsed, stretching above him. Micron shook his head as, in the *narthex*, Sunkor's sensor scanned his normal-sized body, while an insistent *buzzing* opened a gateway. Two thick circular steel doors swung apart, revealing a tempered glass tunnel, a projection inserted into the fiery sphere. Micron floated forward. He watched as he slowly spun feet first through the Vox's projection, while just beyond its four-inch tempered glass walls, tongues of nuclear fire licked at him. In moments, Micron securely entered with feet planted firmly on the floor. He marveled at his surroundings. It was all surreal for Micron, or for that matter, for anyone entering the sun in this manner, seeing what once was on a drawing board now come to life. The core of Sunkor was a huge circular room, if you will, and on its bottom, sides, and top, people were walking, not according to gravity but defying it, and talking and making things. Arboc had brilliantly created *Zeroed-In Gravity*, ZIG for short. The ZIG power source had been inserted carefully into the middle of the fiery sun's core, suspended in mid-air. The secret was a titrated blue aqua gem, which radiated powerful ZIG effects, allowing anyone or anything to walk upright, not according to gravity but in accordance with personal preference, making their way up, down, sideways, across the globe's circular corridors and pathways, which crisscrossed in complex and beautiful patterns.

All of this pleased Micron very much. Steel floors and walls with intricate circuitry, some of which glowed, led to private quarters, offices, exercise gymnasiums, entertainment, and food services. Micron winced at Mordna's grand arrival, as he quickly headed to his personal office, thus avoiding any further complications. He walked directly under the ZIG gem, opening a hatch, which descended to his royal office. Once in, hatch closed, he made a clicking sound with his tongue and the room filled with his familiar and beloved dark light. It was odd to him that he was not immediately soothed in the dark as was his routine, but he instead remained rather uneasy. Something. Someone was missing. He sat before his computer; on command its holographic image obediently lowered before him. He sat transfixed. Audibly he composed his message which drilled into the main ZIG gem, giving out his initial plans.

*"Welcome, my army, to Sunkor. December attack is coming rapidly so we must start moving our pieces. This is our plan. We continue training for a fortnight then we attack, all of us wearing devised human skin, so that we will remain undetected. Then when Christmas Day hits, we'll unleash all the horrors of our invasion. Every robot here is assigned to kill a minimum of thirty humans each. But we must savor the death of Blake Armstrong.*

147

*Yes, we must savor it! I can taste it now! Can you? We will bring him here to reveal our ultimate mission in all of its complexity. We will destroy his world and Tridesicon will rule forever. We will make Blake Armstrong plead for release or death. This we will do perfectly, on time and together. Micron out."*

Micron's message was now concluded. He reclined deeply into his chair as he mused ultimate triumph.

The boys, transfixed by what they were witnessing on the triangular screen, tightly held Trigon in their trembling hands. Fearfully, Blake and Dawson glanced at one another, then back to Trigon's screen, which had grown dark, its light remaining now only at the triangle's edges. The blank screen stared back. The vision they had viewed was now concluded and the two boys looked at each other, nodding their heads in unison, as they shouted: "LORD, HELP!"

*The Eternal will drive out all of your enemies, just as He said He would.*

**Deuteronomy 6:19 The Voice translation**

## CHAPTER 15: NOT ALONE

A WAVE OF NERVE-RACKING SHIVERS COURSED through Blake's body as he poured over his town speech. He wasn't afraid of public speaking but he feared the town's reaction. Geo's reaction. His fingers groped one another on his lap. He looked down at his bulky briefcase, which contained the Trigon, as tiny shafts of light poked out, as thin as paper, seeping from its corners. Blake turned his attention back to the small platform before him, on which his secretary Summerlin stood, welcoming everyone. A bead of sweat worked its way down Blake's temple. He casually looked around to see if Geo was there. All thirty members were in bright orange plastic chairs, facing the stage, except for Geo. Blake spotted him twenty-five feet beyond the chairs, perched high on a massive oak branch waiting and watching. Like a bird of prey. Geo's stare drilled heavily into Blake, making his heart pound faster. Blake wanted to run past the crows, out of Geo's sight, and far from what he had to say. Blake struggled to focus. Then he heard his name squeeze through the bullhorn,

"Here is your mayor, members of *KidzTurf*, Bahlaaake Armstrong!" There was a soft thunder of applause, as loud a noise as can be generated by thirty young people. Blake quickly broke eye contact with Geo. Facing forward, Blake stood up and shuffled his way to the stage, briefcase in hand.

Summerlin stopped him halfway up the steps and whispered, "Don't be nervous, friend, it'll be okay."

Blake didn't believe a word she said, knowing that his enemy Geo was in plain sight. He sat his case down and wiped the sweat from his brow. Instead of the world going in slow motion, it now proceeded to fast forward. Time was flying by way too fast for Blake to even form a coherent sentence. Leaning forward, he opened his mouth. As his eyes widened, he pushed to begin, but nothing came out. It was the presence of Geo. He terrified Blake. He viewed Geo as a ticking bomb. Every time they had a conversation Blake sensed yet another tick going off towards detonation, and he knew that Geo was almost done ticking! Heavy in angst, Blake decided he had to just go with it and as he organized his scrambled notes on the rickety lectern, he got a grip on things and took a few deep breaths. With as much courage as he could muster, he looked straight into the eyes of the crowd and began.

"Fellow citizens, um, I thank you for being here." Blake projected into the bullhorn. "So far so good." he thought to himself. "I wanted to call a few things to your attention. I am afraid it is bad news. Devastating news, in fact. The board and I have determined that *KidzTurf* is no longer a safe environment. Because of this and other confidential reasons we have concluded that we must, no, we will, terminate *KidzTurf*."

In a split second, the entire crowd stood up, instantly replying with loud *boos*, vehemently protesting the board's decision. Seeing the eruption he had just caused, Blake quickly interjected, "Temporarily!!!"

The crowd continued as if they had not heard Blake's correction. Although their *boos* continued, Blake decided to ignore the crowd's protestations, focusing more on Geo's reaction; Blake could see it on Geo's twisted face. The strange kid in the tree did not make any sudden moves, but when a squirrel happened to scurry by Geo's head, his hand robotically shot out, grabbing the helpless creature. Geo grinned as he squeezed out its life, inch by painful inch. Mocking, Geo's stare defied Blake who now, clouded in fear's grip, struggled to move forward, get his thoughts together, to boldly announce what had to be said. A small stone suddenly whizzed by Blake. It was Summerlin. He frowned at her, keenly taking in Summerlin's body language. She was really irked. Stern-faced, Summerlin pointed to the angry crowd. Blake got her message and picked up his bullhorn.

"People, people! Please! We can work this out!" It took a full ten minutes to quiet the angry crowd. Blake, flustered, spoke into the bullhorn with renewed energy, the tone of a parent when their child comes home past curfew.

"You should all be ashamed! Hear me out!" One by one, each reluctantly closed their mouth and for a short time sealed their thrashing opinions. Blake searched for Geo in the tree, but he was gone. There was nothing seated on the oak branch other than another tiny squirrel. Blake combed the crowd as quickly as he could, seeking Geo, but to no avail. Shaking off his returning shivers, he continued to speak. "Let me tell you why. Now that Geo has disappeared, why I don't know, but let me continue. I can speak more freely now." A rumble of murmurs now erupted from the anxious crowd.

"There have been unusual, dangerous events that have been occurring in *KidzTurf* recently. Events that I have kept from you. I am here to tell you the whole story. I'll start, well, I'll start, of course, at the beginning. Years ago, Oskar and I stumbled into a maze of corridors hidden beneath the redwood forest. Oskar couldn't be here today; he's working on a major project, and I mean major! Anyway, here's what we found."

Blake carefully opened his briefcase. Light shot out in all directions as he lifted the Trigon for all to see, transfixing the crowd.

"If you question its origin, well, you're right! It has been confirmed: this instrument is not from earth, as its material, its writings, its advanced technology, are all exponentially superior to what we have or will have for the next one hundred years. The planet it points to is called Tridesicon. It has been revealed to us that our Creator Himself crafted this object for the good people of Tridesicon, as a gift so that they might thrive in righteousness. For many years they did. But they misused its powers after they adopted a stranded people called Sliphex Nation, whose wicked men and women easily took over and corrupted the Trigon's use, like the serpent entering Eden. They brought down Tridesicon, morphing its world into our universe's most evil, corrupt, and powerful empire, led by Emperor Micron and his Empress Mordna. Somehow the Trigon, their prized and most powerful possession was lost a long time ago. A general named Arboc stole it and fled to earth. He designed and built a hidden place under our beautiful redwoods, using the Trigon's powers, and stashed the Trigon beneath our redwood roots. Micron and Mordna crave the Trigon's powers, to misuse it, and have for centuries searched among the galaxies for it. When I stumbled upon the Trigon, I found it in two separate pieces. Its power was off. Arboc had used a special device to disengage the two so it would be inoperable. It was easy enough to reassemble though, and when I did, it gave a responsive signal. Images crossed its triangular screen. It was fascinating. What I did not know was that the Trigon automatically noted my location and image. Micron was alerted and viewed this information! He and his minions are apparently now coming for his treasure! We are under attack!"

The crowd gasped. "But..." a kid tried to inquire.

"I'm not finished, Alex. As I was saying, Micron is now on the attack. He is coming for us, my friends, all of us. I have seen it. The *Tridesicon Prophecy*. They will use ancient roads and other ways to get here. Even the sun now serves as a port for attack. Their army of robots, more advanced than we could ever imagine, is on its way. They've crossed the Milky Way to get here and there's not much time left." Blake warned.

Stunned, the crowd stared back. "Blake must be nuts!" they figured. Someone shouted, "Then what are we supposed to do? Tell us! Now!"

152

"Listen, guys, I'm not crazy, just hear me out!" Blake could tell that he had strayed far from his usual patter to the complaints of a *lunatic*. He paused, then whispered, more to himself than to the crowd, "I don't know how, but the sun is morphed, somehow molded into a hollow metal ball, an advanced technology, an ice habitat inside a roaring furnace. Micron's army is there, even as we speak, ready for attack, ready to burst beyond the sun to our doom, at any moment!"

"Hold it!" some kids shouted. "Let's backtrack. Why does he want this Trigon thing? What does it do, anyway?"

"Good question." answered Blake. "Frankly I don't know all of its capabilities or its full capacity, only a small portion so far, but I will tell you as much as I know. Apparently, it's a physical device, which God uses to communicate with his chosen, you know, *righteous* people. It reveals things that they need to know, to assist in carrying out God's will. It showed me the entire Tridesicon story in a few minutes, like a *vision*, and other things, even about my life, as well."

"Hey, Blake! So, if the Tridesicon people are bad and this device can only talk to good people, why do they still want it?" piped up Bobby, the youngest member in the crowd.

"Well, Bobby," Blake smiled, "There are other powers within this Trigon, God-given abilities, power that sadly can become, in the wrong hands, accessible to bad people. That's just how God made it, I guess. Sort of an example like when it rains, it pours on the good as well as the bad; it's available to all. So, the Trigon can be used as a weapon or a tool. It can be used for control, for peace, for war, almost anything. Of course, the Tridesicon Empire wants it for power, universal power. We cannot let them have it. We must protect this with our very lives. Evil must not win here. If we don't defend righteousness and freedom, our enemy will take us over and control earth's nations."

A skateboarder poked in his question, "So, Bruh, are you saying that you have seen the Trigon turned on, the Trigon's View?"

"Trigon's View...yes!" Blake murmured. "I like that." He cracked a small grin. "Yes, it has given me its personal view." Blake officially stated.

The *dude* nodded and said, "Then count me in, *Bruh*. I believe you, man. And if that Trigon thinks you are righteous enough to be our leader, then I'll follow you."

"And I." said another kid.

"And I!" Bobby said softly. Others agreed, including Oskar, Summerlin, Dawson, and most of the crowd. Others sat in disbelief, shaking their heads.

Blake could see this and implored, "Please, fellow *KidzTurf* citizens. I'm telling you the truth! Fight with us! Fight for your town, your country, your planet!"

His plea didn't convince any of the remaining unbelievers. A rebellious kid spoke up for his group and said, "I guess we're glad now that KidzTurf is closing. It's not good to be living under the power of a mad man like you, Blake. Not any more! We'll be packing up now."

And just like that, a dozen people got up and left. Blake was heart-broken. Hot tears streamed down his face. Betrayal stung. No, it was worse; it bled. Blake stumbled off the stage and plopped in a first-row seat, his head hung low. He looked to his right and watched the tight knot of unbelievers swiftly walking away. Oskar remained silent, sitting next to his friend, deep in thought as he stretched his arm across Blake's shoulder.

"You know," he said, "It's particularly hard to be stabbed in the back so close to home. Betrayal seems strongest when your own group opposes you."

Blake looked at Oskar for a moment. "Did you just make that up?" Oskar's mouth puckered a little.

"No." he admitted. "It's a famous *MacKinnon* quote. But still, it applies here, right?"

Blake smiled, "You are right. It hurts...a lot. Each betrayal is a vicious stab in the back!" Blake paused. "And now I have twelve scars to show for it!" He held a hand to his mouth and sobbed. "I trusted them! They were my friends, my companions, my right-hand people! How could they turn this down, turn me down, turn God down!!!" Blake protested.

"Blake, calm down." Dawson said.

"Yeah!" chimed Oskar.

"We need to be grateful for what God has given us. Remember the story of Gideon? How God eliminated nine thousand men from his army leaving only three hundred?"

Blake collected himself. "Yeah, I guess." he muttered.

"Well this is the same. God mainly does his miraculous works through the humble and weak, not the proud and strong. We are the instruments of God, carrying out his purpose."

Blake beamed, "You are absolutely right, man. I'm being a wimp. God will work everything out, right?" Silence, a heavy silence, followed.

"Soooo..." interrupted a passing skateboarder. "What's the plan, Blake?"

Blake looked at the tall fellow, suddenly with renewed confidence and determination. "We are going to gather our weapons, prepare for war, and hit them where it hurts. Now, come on, follow me to Oskar's workshop for supplies! NOW!"

"Well, I've got this contribution for the *cause!*" Oskar interrupted, tossing Blake a pair of bulky metallic gloves.

"The *Metal Mashers!* You finished them!" Blake laughed.

"You 'betcha. I brought these babies with me for assurance."

"What do we do next? Oskar shouted at Blake, as the crowd pushed toward his workshop.

"After supplies are delivered to each man, meet me by the clock tower!" His words tumbled over the crowd back to Oskar. "I need to tuck the Trigon away somewhere safe. I'll see if I can shut down its signal." The group continued to slowly push.

"Oh Lord, I hope we're not biting off more than we can chew." Blake mumbled, his briefcase and the Trigon firmly in hand. Oskar *air high-fived* Blake, then took off for his lab. He had been up all night and needed to finish his work before the KT crowd arrived for supplies!

155

Blake instructed the anxious crowd to *slow down* to give Oskar time to get all supplies together. Minutes later, Blake returned to his quarters. He shut and bolted the door. Suddenly, a thud from the floor above grabbed his attention. Blake spun around, racing to the noise. His quarters had been thoroughly ransacked! All of this had "G-E-O" written all over it. Using his secret entrance, Blake tossed his briefcase down the hidden tunnel and *sealed* its entrance. Wild eyed, Blake tore through his bunker, slipping on his *Metal Masher* gloves. He branded his iron fists as he punched the air for practice. Suddenly, as his foot touched the first step to ascend to the second floor, Geo plunged through the upper story floor, landing directly behind Blake. Blake's head twisted only to meet with Geo's hard knuckles. Blake flew into a nearby wall. Geo's attacks, one after the other, persisted in precision, but Blake ducked most of Geo's blows, then fiercely rolled from the stairwell to kick Geo's chin: a master parkour maneuver utilized perfectly!

"Well, that did nothing." Blake muttered to himself, extending his *Metal Mashers* to punch Geo's radiating face. "Payback time, ya piece of metal crap!"

The two exchanged blows, complex military-style, throwing and ducking punches, kicks and spins. If Geo hit Blake's gut, Blake would knee Geo's in response. If Blake's fist made a dent in Geo, Geo would cut Blake a wide scar. Blake could feel his own muscles weakening. After many kicks and punches he sprinted in the opposite direction, away from Geo, forgetting that his opponent on foot was much faster. The robot tackled Blake and pinned him to the ground. His menacing fists pounded into Blake's back, relentlessly. The force of the robot's punches was almost too much for Blake to handle. He needed to make use of his surroundings, and fast. His mini fridge was directly in front of him. With a feeble hand, Blake grasped its handle, his entire body vibrating from Geo's onslaught. He threw the fridge up and upon Geo. Losing balance, the robot fell to the floor. Blake stood up drawing upon any remaining strength. Bruises peppered his body; he could feel each one. Just then, like a computer when it reboots, Geo's eyes clicked open, focusing on Blake with renewed intent. The robot lunged toward his opponent, but Blake simply danced sidestep as Geo hurled himself through a window. Blake searched for another weapon.

"Soda! Soda's good, ahhh...this is perfect." thought Blake, as he bent down and gathered all of the spilled Cola bottles from the floor. Geo vaulted back into the room with ease and was assaulted by crackling explosions of carbonated liquid. Sparks flew, and Geo was on the ground in agony. This attack had injured him, but he wasn't dead, not yet, definitely, not yet. Enraged, Geo ran to the kitchen and with one hand grabbed two knives, flinging them at Blake with precision. One was meant for the head, one for his heart. Blake ducked the head shots and mostly dodged the other, as it only partially hit its mark. Geo's knife glanced off Blake's bicep. Only a surface cut. Blake yelled out, denying any pain, as he fiercely moved forward to pound his opponent with his Metal Mashers. As exhaustion finally had its way, Blake ripped out a knife from the wall with his uncut arm and slashed the air.

"Get away from me, you freakin' freak! Stay away!" Blake advanced, backing Geo away.

"I will kill you! Do you hear me?" Blake tried to shove the robot into the corner, and Geo let him. Blake was so close to the distorted humanoid face that he could see deep into its eye. It glowed an electric soul-less green. The tip of Blake's knife lightly touched Geo's neck, ready to finish him. "You will come with me now!"

Geo tried to hold back a sneer, but it still came. "Nice try, buddy, but your knife is no threat to me."

Geo pushed Blake's arm back, painlessly withdrawing the knife Blake had just embedded in his throat! The robotic hand then went to its side and Blake felt the point of a gun barrel pressed hard into his chest. Then a loud, excruciating "BANG!"

As the ear-piercing shot noised its way across *KidzTurf*, another battle was very much in progress. Oskar tapped his fingers impatiently. Though his logarithms remained unstable as equation upon equation rapidly shot across his screen, he was pleased at what was finally coming about as his computer percolated a compelling answer within its intricacies, a discovery, no, a quantum leap discovery, decades ahead of standard invention: a visual 3-D off-line projection into any available space, a translucent blueprinting capacity for *concept* building, invention, engineering, and design. Here, suspended in multi-leveled possibility Oskar imagined in his calculations a lucent projected image, which could reveal in precise blueprinted accuracy a visual of any proposed plan, complex or otherwise, all possible alternatives, metamorphic opportunities and application suggestions, all features color coded, occurring simultaneously! Miraculous. Now, if only *it* would work! On screen Oskar's brilliant concept surpassed hand-drawn, old computer-driven blueprinting schema. Indeed, onscreen it all seemed possible. Now for its *application*. It could work Oskar imagined and the possibilities were limitless. It would work but precisely how? Oskar continued tapping his fingers. If urban centers could get their sullied hands on this, he thought, his income would exceed Gates' fortune! But for now he was quite satisfied. Oskar's persistence and hard work had morphed a greasy repair shop into an impressive fully equipped *inventor's* lab, which now embraced him like a loving father. Most days he was encouraged but now, as he slumped exhausted before his pulsing screen, he pressed against his seatback and rubbed his eyes. He had been up all night and winced at the sun bulldozing through his window.

"It's time," he thought, muttering "Now for the *pièce de résistance!*"

His screen continued pushing recommended formulae down the screen, one equation after another. "Now, if only my logarithm here can remain stable for just a few seconds more!" he whispered to the screen. "We'll have live blueprints in the air without paper!"

Suddenly, two intricate formulae appeared, quickly merging: glowing *twins* upon Oskar's screen. The missing *entity* had finally arrived! After days and long nights of computation, the answer was at hand, awaiting Oskar's compelling equation. He only had to press *enter*. A moment of silence drew the room together as Oskar slowly pushed the button. His screen flickered, and, as if on command, and, yes, it was a command, a precise three-dimensional luminous image shot into the room, slowly connecting all its dots, turning in calculated precision, a cube, with measurements stretched across its edges, color-coded, featuring alternate recommended design applications. It was exquisite, beautiful in its commanding position. It was a miracle!

Oskar stood, then fell to his knees. "Thank you, Lord. Thank you! Thank you!" he whispered, as the image swirled above him, compelling in its royal dance.

*Help me hear joy and happiness as my accompaniment, so my bones, which You have broken, will dance in delight instead.*

**Psalm 51:8 The Voice translation**

## CHAPTER 16: DEAD

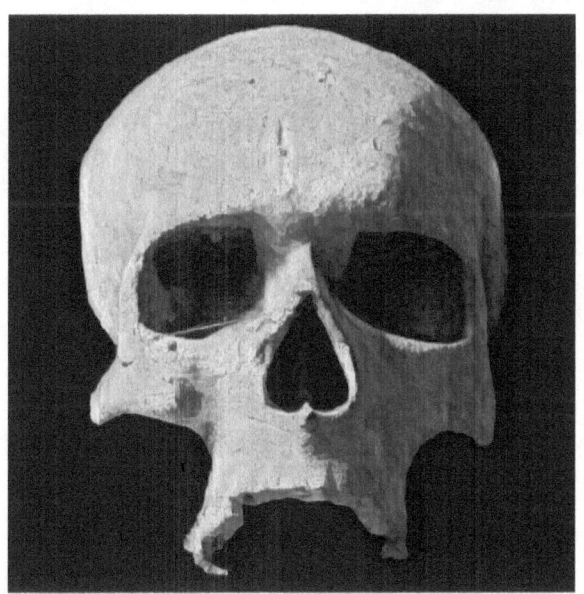

"DEATH ISN'T SO BAD," was Blake's first thought. The effect was *taser-like*! That was for sure. Quite painful, but it wasn't as bad as he had worked it up to be. A strange sensation rippled across Blake's skin, something much stronger than *goosebumps*. He felt light, weightless, in fact. Then, for some reason, he began to fall; his arms flayed, and his legs wildly kicked the air. Disoriented, Blake had no clue what was going on. He couldn't tell which was up or what was down. All he knew for sure was that he was falling, quickly. He slammed hard onto a surface, which he could not identify. He screamed, writhing on the surface in excruciating pain, as he rocked back and forth with his head between his legs. Blake then realized that he had landed on his shoulder. His teeth clenched together, nearly shattering his molars. He heard a voice, dark and cold, but strangely recognizable, an arrogant haughty voice. His pain gradually diminished as his vision adjusted to his bearings. The first thing he noticed was a curious door on the floor. Confused, Blake crawled over to it to investigate, ignoring a mysterious voice continuing from nowhere he could determine. Blake turned the floor door-latch, which easily opened. He peered through its opening and somehow to a floor below. A case of déjà vu now began to overwhelm Blake, causing him to almost black out. It was in fact, his study peering from below, the place where he had *died*. A dull light bulb popped up in Blake's mind. He got it now. He was a *ghost*! Yes, he must be a ghost! He could walk on walls, probably even fly! He gave a quick look around. The ceiling stretched high above with a door curiously placed upon its center. The adjacent walls were laden with an assortment of carpets, furniture and tables. It all made sense, sort of. Blake's eyes searched for his dead earthly body but couldn't find it on the wall or the floor or anywhere else. From a normal perspective it would be found on the floor, right? The body had disappeared. He was sure of this! Déjà vu, after all! Blake scanned the room again and, voilà, found the source of the mysterious dark voice.

"Of course, it's gotta be GEO!" thought Blake.

The sudden *break-through* jangled Blake to full consciousness. Geo was now laughing, pointing at him. Blake pinched himself.

"Well. This IS weird! I'm not a ghost!" Amazed, Blake slowly twisted his hand before his eyes. He could see clearly now. His hands were as real as they had ever been!

"Wait just a minute..." Blake slapped himself, and it stung. His pupils became dots as his eyes bulged in the bright light. "I'm ... I'm not ... holy crap. I'm alive! That's it! I AM alive!"

A mix of terror and mild relief waged war within Blake. It was terror that won, and Blake backed away, slumping into the ceiling. His world had just flipped upside down, physically and mentally. From Geo's perspective, Blake was sitting hunched where the top of the wall met the ceiling. Geo strode over to be in line with Blake, and lay upon the floor, his feet against the ascending wall. Blake's eyes darted to and away from Geo, who appeared to be standing now on the ceiling as well!

"What is happening here?" Blake yelled.

Geo replied, "I'll admit it, Blake, I'm surprised you're even alive. It's about twelve feet away from where I shot you, to where you landed. That kind of fall normally is fatal, but, no, not you! You're not so easy to kill!" Blake's hands quickly moved to his side as he groped for his wound. He found no trace.

"What did you do to me? Explain!"

"You should be thanking me, Blake, that I didn't finish you off! Yes, I will explain. See this little contraption?" Geo shook his gun.

"Yes." Blake replied.

"Well, this is not meant to kill. My people, well, we use gravity to our advantage through an assembly of devices, like this one. We call this version *Sikorog Ghiat*, which translates in your tongue: Gravity Manipulator."

"Keep going." Blake was now fully engaged.

"If I shoot someone with this, that person or really any object I shoot, well their gravity pull *direction* comes under my control. I am letting earth's gravity pull me down right now, right, how it normally should be. But for you, I programmed my Ghiat, to pull you, not down, but to the side, specifically, west, with the same amount of strength you're used to being pulled downward!" Geo tore at Blake's mind with his introduction of the Ghiat's power!

"Let me give you an example, Blake. If gravity pulls you up towards, let's say a twenty-foot-high ceiling, the reverse of what you know as normal, the fall and effect would be exactly the same as jumping off a two-story building, right?"

"I'm starting to get it, but not fully." Geo smiled crookedly. "All the same, it doesn't matter anyway. You really are unimportant."

Aiming the Ghiat at his opponent, Geo cranked up the *pull* of Blake's gravity. Blake was terrified as he snapped quickly to a new location, suspended mid-air between two walls, which threatened to squeeze together, smashing him flat.

"So, you're gonna kill me now, is that it?" yelled Blake. Geo's finger let go of his trigger.

"No, not yet. Not yet, not until I find the Trigon. And not before I can defy your gravity a hundred times. You fool, here's the deal. If you reveal Trigon's location, or better yet hand it over to me NOW, I will not kill you, and my *brothers* will leave in peace. No harm done to your ridiculous nation."

Blake spat at Geo. His spitball shot up a couple feet, then backfired, splatting upon Blake's cheek.

Geo laughed. "Have it your way, stupid. I'll just find the Trigon myself. But before I kill you, I will round up your family and friends. I will tie 'em' up next to you on this wall, and we'll have a bonfire! How does that sound?"

Blake couldn't respond. Geo's stare drilled into him, as he savored his glorious *victory*, this torturing triumph. Having his fill, Geo lunged across the room, continuing to tear the house apart. He was a madman. Windows were broken, furniture strewn. Timbers were ripped from walls, broken apart like matchsticks as shredded cushions, tossed asunder, added to the mess. Blake, frozen in place, struggled to get loose to combat his enemy. His face boiled with pressure, turning his face blood red as his abs became burning coals; he struggled valiantly, but it was no use. He gave up, completely exhausted.

"Let me go!" Blake screamed. "Let me go, NOW!"

"When I find the Trigon, I will be sure to rocket my fist up your punk face and leave you like a chewed-up dog toy before I burn you and your family! Whoosh! Up in flames."

164

Geo's careless statement had just given Blake an advantage. Blake recalled that he could shoot from his metal mashers, directly off his fists, by just saying a password. And so, Blake initiated a quick maneuver. He estimated that his unique gravity-pull came with approximately one hundred pounds of force.

"If these babies can rocket themselves with enough power to pull my fists into the air," Blake figured, "I could aim them at Geo and let go at the right moment. This is definitely a long shot, but it might work."

Eyeing Geo in the *war-torn* room below, less than ten feet away from where the Trigon was stashed, Blake announced, *"2-3-7-6-A-AB / Engage, Masher Rockets!"* Four flames instantly blasted forth from his glove tubes, scorching Blake's forearms. Blake angled his hands so that the rockets pushed his arms together directly in front of him. The rocket's rumble commanded Geo's attention, and as soon as he leaned out of the room's archway, Blake roared over the pounding noise.

"Eject!" commanded Blake.

His gloves instantly abandoned their owner, soaring dead straight into Geo. One pounded at his nose; the other, by sheer luck, into the gravity manipulator. This nearly propelled Geo through the wall. Then, Blake's gravity-pull morphed into a different direction. He slid up the wall and crumpled onto a rough surface. Blake stood up, the pull being significantly weaker, and realized he was standing on the ceiling. What surprised him even more was that Geo was clinging to the edge of the wall, dangling from the hallway. At first this confused Blake but then a laser darted between his legs. It was the gravity gun! It was sputtering, randomly firing at everything, anything. Geo had been shot as well.

"How do you like tasting your own medicine, psycho machine?" Blake taunted.

In the *mish-mosh* of random gravity Blake's *pull* lightened dramatically! He began to float, suspended once again between opposing walls.

"Geo! Your gun is malfunctioning!"

"No, really, Sherlock?" grunted the electronic voice. He hefted himself up over the wall's edge and rested, while sitting on a balcony ledge.

"It's gone into *extreme* random mode, thanks to you. The direction and strength of every target it now hits will be at random and all logarithms will morph exponentially. Not to mention...WOAH! WHOA!"

Gravity suddenly yanked Geo up onto a window casement, then out to the left, finally releasing him southward. He plummeted 40, 30, 20, 10 feet down a narrow hallway, crushing into a column.

"Help!" Geo cried.

Blake walked down the ceiling to where the *robot* had landed, but the manipulated gravity on random had other plans. Blake flew to the left and tumbled into his bathroom, now standing on its walls. Gravity couldn't make up its mind. Blake found himself rolling up the walls, then down the floor just missing the toilet, then across an opposing wall, then up the ceiling. He had never been so disoriented in his life. This triggered Blake's memory when he, as a child, had locked himself in a tumble dryer when his mom, unaware, passed by and pushed the machine's large power button to *ON*. Yes, he now was in a *tumble dryer* of sorts! He stopped, slumped in his bathtub, gravity pulling normally for once. He could feel shards of glass, like sandpaper, on his hands and head. Blake looked up and glared at a broken mirror, which explained it all.

"Ugh, my head feels worse than that tilt-n-whirl at the fair." He lumped his *half-dead* body over the tub onto the ceramic floor. With a heave, he managed to stand up, tottering like a drunk. Many things, which had been zapped in the fray by the *Ghiat*, continued to whirl about in the bunker, responding to random gravity parameters. Even the gravity manipulator was tumbling this way and that.

"First things first. I need that gun!" Blake determined. Then the Trigon stood before him. "Scratch that, I need this instead!" He lunged at it, both hands ready to grasp it, but its gravity took a different course and the Trigon was pulled straight into Blake's face. Its corner hit Blake's eye. He held his wound carefully; he knew he would live. Gravity was done giving him a break and yanked him once again into the wall, this time with greater force. Pain shot up his back; Blake's bones would soon not be able to withstand the onslaught. He knew this. It seemed everything was increasing, powering up, that *random* was morphing into particular, and that the gravity gun in enemy hands would ultimately force his demise. Gravity's pull steadily increased in all directions. Blake, entirely spent, grabbed for Geo's weapon in mid-air, inching closer and closer, and to his right as it twisted inches from his fingers.

"Al...most... there!" Blake strained. He was desperate and had no clue what would happen as he squeezed the *Ghiat's* trigger; he pulled it back slowly. That's when everything went *zero gravity*. Every target that the gun had hit was now suspended mid-air. Blake had no direction: up, down, or sideways. All that was not nailed down or glued to the bunker's walls, tumbled toward him, a jumble of lamps, chairs, books, side tables, pots, knives, a huge blob suspended mid-air. Blake, pushing away the debris, which was targeting him, looked for Geo but instead spotted the Trigon spinning below. There he spotted Geo, oblivious to zero gravity, pushing up the walls and closing in on the Trigon.

"No!!!" Blake yelled. He threw his arms out to find a wall to push off from, but the walls remained five feet out of reach, as the debris continued to form an unwieldy *ball* with Blake at its center! Luckily, Blake still had the Ghiat in hand, which had control over everything.

"All right, come on, you futuristic, sci-fi gizmo, how do you work?" Blake rapidly fidgeted with it, racing against the clock. He found a screen with twelve tick marks on it. Blake spun the dial next to it and each tick marked glowed, like anything digital on steroids! He continued turning the dial: "target 1, target 2, target 3, ugh, which one?" Blake muttered, exasperated. He shot a quick glance at Geo. His metal fingers were already scratching at the Trigon.

"Dang it, whatever!" Blake chose TARGET #4, pulled the small joy stick to the south point, towards him, and pressed its green button. Geo suddenly became a projectile, which, rushing past the Trigon, rammed hard into Blake and the surrounding debris. As the robot bounced away from Blake, he pulled his Ghiat free.

"Oh, screw it. Screw it all." cried Blake.

Geo, his strength renewing, crumpled his Ghiat to nothing but scrap. Everything at once dropped to the floor, all gravity now returned to normal. Blake scrambled for the Trigon, running frantically up the stairs, with Geo in wild pursuit. Blake headed straight for the attic and kicked through a small window. As he quickly plummeted toward a small rooftop below, Blake chucked the Trigon over his shoulder at a dormer to his right. Hoping that Geo would not observe the now precariously perched Trigon, but would remain in hot pursuit of Blake, Geo's main target, Blake now landed, parkour-style, on a small roof which covered a narrow side entry. All that remained was an easy jump to the lawn below. Of course, Geo had already landed with precision on the grass, unaffected by his descent. Still ready to battle more, Geo pointed at Blake, demanding, "Well, where is the Trigon?"

And Blake, sputtering blood, turning his head away with a small grin, "Hid it again!" he laughed in defiance. Geo lunged toward his enemy, smashing both fists on Blake's back, over and over. Geo was enraged and for some reason Blake was ready to die. The robot, both fists still clenched, roared, "Aren't you tired of this, Blake? Tired of this stupid game of *hide and seek*? Tired of being pulverized and treated like a boxing bag? I mean, look at you. Your body is riddled with glass, your left eye is messed up, your mouth is full of blood; you have more scars, cuts, and bruises than you can count. Like, you would have to get better to die." Geo paused. "You need to give up this war. You can't win, Blake Armstrong! And I'm going to end it right now for you, for all of us. The Trigon is invincible, so I'll just find it after I destroy KidzTurf."

"Wait, Geo! No! Don't! They are good people." Blake protested.

"Goodbye, Blake. You are a good man, so they say, but all men must die."

And with that, Geo walked away as Blake's eyes trailed him. Geo fell to his knees only yards away in the middle of the road and laid two fingers on his temple. Geo's *circuitry* searched the skies for any nearby planes. He locked on to a passing jet, easily hacking its system. In minutes, as Blake lay helpless, watching Geo kneeling in the street, there came a horrific thunder of a commercial jet descending, down, down, down, targeting *KidzTurf*. The plummeting jet banked to the right. Lower and lower it came.

"Oh, God! No!" Blake pleaded. No!"

*My face is foul with weeping, and on my eyelids is the shadow of death.*

**Job 16:16 AKJV translation**

## CHAPTER 17: DAWN

*KIDZTURF'S ARMAGEDDON HAD COME.* The soft roar, then a louder scream of a descending plane assaulted Blake's ears. He had given up, his energy level on empty. Blake lay helpless, as Geo rattled away from the street to nearby woods. You see, this was a *battle* Blake couldn't fight, a war that seemed already *lost*. As these thoughts flew through Blake's head, a glimmer of hope suddenly shone upon his *darkness*. The Trigon, which lay nestled on top of a dormered roof, began to shimmer, its brilliant light breaking into tiny little pieces like fireflies. Thousands of *dots* glided downward through the air like a light breeze, a welcomed sweet breeze in hot summer. The *fireflies* made their way toward Blake. With his one *good* eye, Blake gazed at the wonderful sight and breathed aloud.

"Oh, Lord God! You have sent the soul of Trigon. Again!"

The dots collected a few feet from his nose. They came together forming the face of Trigon, an image of holiness, of righteousness, a perfect radiating image of *imago dei*.

"Blake Armstrong, hope is not lost; there will always be hope. The Creator chose you for this *mission* because He knows and loves your passion and pure heart. You have a strong bond with Him, and He sees that you can do this, Blake. Through Him, in His Name, and in His power, you can do this!"

"Trigon, I am truly humbled, but look at me; I have been defeated."

"Not on the Father's watch, Blake."

The formation of tiny *light points* broke into a thin wisp, like the ebbing of clouds, entered Blake, surging through him, through every bone, muscle, sinew and vein. In moments, Blake's energy was renewed, stronger than he had ever been. His bruises disappeared. Deep cuts were suddenly erased. He was now healed: in mind, body, and spirit. Astonished, Blake opened his mouth, as a glitter of specks flew out, returning to its facial form.

"The Lord has restored you, my friend, through me. You must now hide me and run. Goodbye, Blake, we shall meet again." The many dots slowly moved about, reassembling, merging into its former triangular state. The Trigon was now fully formed as it lowered onto Blake's lap. He was still tingling from his miraculous healing. Blake looked up at the sky, which he found to be quite empty.

"But where did the plane go?" thought Blake. Suddenly, a loud explosion erupted beyond the woods, fiercely shaking the ground, and bitterly answering Blake's question. With lightning speed, he stood up and began to run to warn the people, but stopped dead in his tracks as he spotted the plane abruptly descending across the edge of the wood. Without a second thought, Blake changed direction to the side and flew across the lawn. Blake did *kong vaults* over several four-foot fences, easily able now to keep his *sprinting* speed. One quick snap glance to the right told him that most likely, the plane's right wing was going to slice him in two if he didn't run faster to dodge its sharp wings. So, he pushed himself harder, harder than ever before, and that's when he realized that he could sprint faster than ever before. It was the power of God working within him! It was like old times *parkouring* in the city!

"Okay, five hundred more feet. You can do it, Blake." Vault, sprint, vault, sprint, the cycle was about over, but so was time. Blade-like wings were less than sixty feet away, and were traveling at a *wicked* speed. A wave of dirt sprayed Blake from the side, shooting from the plane's plow-like crash landing. No more time or need to vault. He was free. But he continued to run in the remaining seconds.

"You CAN do it!" Blake roared, now pushing himself beyond his limits, going at a speed he had never experienced before, as he leaped over the last fence. After that he didn't feel anything but the rumble of a hard landing over the fence and being caked in dirt and rubble. After a while the ground stopped churning and became still much like Blake, who, having tripped, fell, the wind knocked out of him. In response he kicked wildly for more air, then stopped. A mix of wheezing and crying replaced his desperate need for air. He continued to suck in deeply. His crying was filled with joy for being alive! He stood up slowly, rubbing his face to scan the extent of damage. He wished he hadn't. As far as he could see, *KidzTurf* was now mere wasteland.

*KidzTurf* had been shredded, stripped, demolished. Chunks of wood lay scattered on the field of destruction. Huge billows of smoke rose from the burning plane, its parts strewn along its invading path. Blake stood horrified as his body quivered, as his hands shook while wiping his carbon black face. Pure, clean, salty tears surged from under his eyes, built up like two dams, then overflowed down his cheeks, polluted from the destruction's dirt. A faint cry alerted him. Without delay, Blake stumbled over piles of carnage towards the whimpering cry for help. The top of the once magnificent clock tower, all gears, cogs, and iron working-wheels, surprisingly stood, not in shambles, but in sturdy defiance, almost untouched. From under this structure came the faint whimper once again.

"Heeelp me!" wheezed a weak voice.

"I'm coming! Don't move!"

Blake stood on top of the tower's assaulted base as he heaved heavy timbers away. Inside was a jumble of beams, thrusting this way and that. A few feet below, a massive pile of bricks and a pummeled mixture of cement and dirt covered a boy who was still alive. Blake wondered if he looked as bad as the boy here, pinned beneath the bricks. He managed to maneuver several bricks away, then got more off. With enough digging and brushing off, Blake could make out facial features.

"Frankie! Oh, no! Oh, not you." Blake leaned low, wiping away his friend's tears from his wounded cheek.

"Okay, man, tell me. Are you hurt bad?"

"I feel worse than a squashed bug, Blake. Pain is killin' me! Not just my bones, but my lungs. My lungs, bro. My chest is on fire and I can't breathe. I'm ripped apart...inside. I can't breathe."

"Come on, I'll help you up and *getcha* to a hospital right away, okay?" Before Frankie could resist, Blake's arms slid underneath the eight-year-old and started to lift him, that is, until a piercing, violent cry broke free from Frankie.

"Blake, stop! Stop!" Frankie's teeth clenched. His eyes bulged, as foamy saliva crept to the corners of his mouth.

"How can I stop?" Blake yelled into the air.

Frankie suddenly grew calm, his whimper now soft. "Just let me die. It's too late now. There is somethin' inside me, a stick I think. Ah, and there's lots of blood under me."

Blake winced and when Frankie's hand came up reaching for his hand, Blake knew that this was his last moment. Blake clasped Frankie's hand in his, gripping it tightly.

Then came the boy's final words, "Blake, you need to know. Listen to me. I... am not... human. I from... Borealis... safe there... you must... go... Cascade Mall... Derreck...."

Blake looked deeply into Frankie's eyes and as a light switch turning off, so did Frankie's eyes. His life, his youth, simply left his brilliant eyes, left them soulless and empty.

Blake left Frankie, stumbling away, further and further away. After all, what could he do now? He limped over the charred rubble, away from the clock tower as questions pounded inside. "Where is Geo?" His answer didn't come until he had fully stumbled across the rubble that had once been *KidzTurf*. Geo, in his *spider-like* way, had been digging through the dirt at rapid speed, searching for the Trigon. So, as Blake came closer to his enemy, he clutched the Trigon tightly, his beloved Trigon still safe and concealed in a pocket over his heart. As Blake walked closer, with rubble sprinting from his *booted* feet, Geo stopped, and turned, cocking his head in Blake's direction.

"Blake, you rascal!" he taunted. "There's still LIFE here? In *KidzTurf*? Ha! Why I thought it was over...for good! My, oh my! We'll just have to do something about that, won't we?" laughed Geo. "Even your constant and ridiculous breathing disgusts me!"

While Geo's tirade continued, Blake slowly moved toward his escape. He grabbed an available motorbike, threw on its clutch, turned the ignition key, and rumbled away, Geo in hot pursuit. The woods were approaching and that is where Blake could leave his bike, so he thought, undetected in the approaching woods. He had just the place to hide, a ramshackle structure not too far into the woods. Blake thought he would be secure.

Geo stopped. He enjoyed the hunt, and so gave Blake time to move away from him, just to increase the tension, and his own lust for death. Geo stood at the wood's' edge, then moved slowly, softly, upon the forest carpet. Blake was now safe in what he thought would be secure.

"This wouldn't happen to be you, Blake Armstrong?" came Geo's mocking voice, drilling into the forest. "Your heart beat is now louder than your breathing; the heartbeat of a dead man."

Blake was terrified; he knew that if he didn't think up something quick, it would be *endgame*. Beyond the woods, another explosion erupted, destroying a second turbine engine. Geo's attention snapped away from Blake for an instant, giving Blake his next opportunity with a definite advantage, as he ran back across the ruins. Geo, drawn to the explosion, inspected the site. Unable to find any sign of life there, he turned back, only to see Blake speeding away from the woods. Geo charged his legs and sprinted tirelessly. Blake, saddled securely upon the bike's seat, sped off away from the carnage. The final chase was now *on*. Blake crossed onto a highway, continuing up a steep hill. Geo jumped forward and landed on his hands. He pushed off with them on to his feet, which he used to push off once again, continuing this cycle hundreds of times at increasing speed. Blake shot a quick glance back and saw that Geo had evolved from speeding ahead on twos to running on all four, like a mechanized *cheetah*. Blake had no idea where he was going and had no plan on how to deal with Geo.

"Think Blake, think!" Blake pounded his forehead with one fist.

"What are his weaknesses? He hates light, he hates water... Water! That's it!" Blake recalled a dam, a few miles west.

"Let's hope these metal mashers do the trick." he schemed. Blake *banked* to the left, submerged under a cover of rising redwoods, as he *barreled* down a restricted path. Left, right, turn, curve; Blake sped along as best as he could remember his route, and after a few miles, headed toward the dam. Seconds ahead lay Blake's answer: a twenty-foot wall which contained the river's might.

"This is it." Blake thought. "There is no way I'll be able to survive this." Blake was scared, and yet, as he sped toward the wall, he confronted his terror with determination, with mounting courage. Eighty feet, sixty feet, forty feet. Blake was nearly at the dam's abrupt wall.

"Oh God, protect me!" he pleaded.

With a triumphant yell, Blake turned on his bike's *turbo boost* as he leaned forward. The cycle tipped down and Blake launched himself from it, flying high into the air. In the last few seconds, Geo caught on to Blake's *maneuver*, racing back down for his life, but it was no use. Blake smashed the wall to pieces, splintering the offending wall with his metal mashers. As he made contact, the concrete wall cracked. This allowed the massive river to break free, taking Blake and his bike and Geo with it. Louder than the roar of a lion, stronger than the pull of gravity, the water rapidly surged down its intended path.

Geo cried one final "NOOOOO!" And he was fully engulfed, taken in the water.

Blake's left eye twitched and fluttered open. Clear skies and canopied redwoods were all Blake could see. His other senses were now returning. More information poured into him. He was totally spent yet joyous, relieved at Geo's *demise*. His mission was completed. Or was it? The abusive stream continued to pummel Blake, slapping him to a new *reality*.

"What was I thinking?" he groaned as he pulled himself into a seated position, which surprised him. No pain. He couldn't feel a broken bone or a deep wound, nothing. He quickly checked his arms and sure enough, each hung in place. No scratches at all! "Impossible!" he laughed, cocking his head aside.

"Is it even possible for a tennis ball to turn inside out without piercing its own surface?" Blake thought, wondering why this question had suddenly assailed him. He laughed again, riveting upon his impossible *theorem* as he recalled batting this one around on a long-ago Saturday morning with Oskar. At that time, so long ago it seemed, there was nothing better to do than debate, muse, query, laugh, mount up in impassioned battle with untried ideas, concepts, words, moving about, all in more innocent times. A great sadness began to push its way into Blake, *hulk-like*, wanting its way, to overtake, an enemy searching through its quiver for a perfect arrow to impale Blake's soul.

"Guard yourself, Blake!" a voice shot forth. It was Trigon! Its wondrous face configured before Blake in authority, luminescent in holy, enfolding, and comforting light. "The enemy prowls about, seeking to devour you in any way possible. Beware. All he ever offers is counterfeit, momentary. Be strong, Blake. Put on the whole armor of God, to stand against the devil's schemes. Remember, Blake, we do not wrestle against flesh and blood, but against the rulers, against the authorities, against the cosmic powers over this present darkness, against the spiritual forces of evil in the heavenly places. Be strong. Stand strong. You are not alone!"

The beautiful face now separated into pinpoints of light, gradually disappearing before Blake. Yet, instructions continued in unfailing might: "...that you may be able to withstand in the evil day, and having done all, to stand firm...keep alert with all perseverance. Stand strong, Blake!" With this a piercing silence came upon Blake as he grasped what had just happened. He was changed, yes, strengthened and somehow his resolve had grown stronger too. Blake was *centered*. Trigon's empowering words had fully lifted him!

"Whoa, the Lord did this? For me?"

Blake, in that moment lowered his head, grateful for such divine protection.

"This is amazing! Amazing!" he cried out.

Blake stood up, raising his hands in victory, cheering, giving praise to God.

"Okay, so the dam is destroyed!" he continued, creating a new *checklist*. "*KidzTurf* is gone. My bike's downstream, and Geo is... Wait a minute. 'Geo!'" Blake stopped.

With great caution Blake moved forward, shouting for his enemy, not sure now whether Geo was dead or alive. Half a mile downstream, there was Geo stretched out, spread-eagle, facedown and helpless upon an embankment across the river. To get a closer look, Blake *sloshed* across the terrible current, stopping a few paces from Geo. Blake panted hard as he swayed before his enemy. The robot quickly jerked its head toward Blake.

"I may be *dying*, but my purpose shall live on. The torch will be handed to my *brothers,* you fool, and they will carry on the mission. There is no stopping it, Blake; there is no stopping it. I believe, Blake, you are what they call a *good man*, and that is why I hate you; that is why you are the target of this great war, and precisely why you shall lose."

Geo drunkenly murmured some incoherent Tridesicon *chant*, slapping his hand to his own shoulder in mock salute.

"Yeah, we'll see about that, won't we?" replied Blake.

"I don't care if I terminate!" muttered Geo. "Go ahead, rub it in; I don't

178

care. I know our goal to take Trigon will succeed! Through it we will overpower you and all your disgusting *life forms*. This is my *DNA*, my programming; it's all I've wanted. You see, my existence doesn't mean a thing! It's unimportant."

Geo's voice suddenly grew hollow as sparks flew from his face. "You are but a flea caught in a tornado, Mr. Armstrong." Geo cracked a smile, and with that he *terminated*. His metal hand fell limp. It was over, at least for the moment.

"What a nightmare." Blake muttered, as Trigon slowly came forward from his hidden pocket, slowly spinning in awesome presence, its tiny glittering dots of light forming a face once again, a benevolent vision of the I AM who so approved of his new warrior.

"We will win this war, Lord!" shouted Blake. "I know this. In my heart, yes, I know this! I love You, Lord, and this mission You hold before me, us. Thank you for Trigon, which has revealed Your way. Micron doesn't stand a chance against You, Almighty King!"

Blake reached toward his beloved Trigon to once more find within its triangular portal God's approval, direction and strength, to handle casualties back at *KidzTurf* an impending battle so fiercely on its way.

*In an instant, my world changed; in a moment, my tents destroyed, my curtains torn, my refuge gone. How long must I see the flags of the enemy? How long must I be forced to hear the trumpets sound?*

**Jeremiah 4:20-21 The Voice translation**

## CHAPTER 18: BATTLE

NO ONE SAW IT COMING, BUT, DAY BY DAY robots, convenient inventions for more functional leisure time, had literally invaded most cities! Everyone had pushed to have one of their own, initiating a deluge of demands for *personal* robots, which quickly began to outnumber smartphones. The robot market had soared, bypassing any projected estimates. The robotic network, of robots not only serving masters, but sentient beings, networked to one another, had become a bomb ready to explode.

"Well, if it isn't Blake Armstrong. I see that you're still around. Note this, human, sentient mission remains strong. Remember Geo?" a robot taunted. "You fool, do you think it all ended with his termination? We robots remain fully networked, always have been, *DNA'd* beyond what you could ever imagine. Together we *are* Geo! He is alive in us, all of us! Together we grow stronger minute by minute, agents from hell. Demons, you might say! Darkness is our home, human. Creating more of us, well, you simply have opened the door to *sentient victory*.

"What the heck is going on?" Blake demanded, pushing at the robot.

"You, little man. You and your kind remain in our way. We want the Trigon. And we want it NOW. Hand it over! Things might go better for you. Otherwise, your parents will be first to pay if you choose your own selfish way."

"Let them go, or I will *round-house* kick-your-butt." Blake said, his face red hot.

"Oh there, there, little lad," the robot mocked. "I wouldn't be so hasty. Do you see this?" He took out a small ball, waving it before Blake. "This is an *iten*. If it gets wet in any sort of way, it will expand forty inches in lethal diameter. Guard, hold the man and woman." The two guards who had their guns trained on Blake's parents then held them firmly in place as two others pried their mouths open.

"If one is released down the throat, it simply will expand and kill. How do you like the sound of that, mortal? You have no idea what game you are playing." Blake's thoughts were scattered. He needed the Trigon to remain safe and grounded, but his parents were important too. He then had an idea, one that just might secure safety for his parents and Trigon.

"Fine. I will be right back." replied Blake.

The robot smiled, jutting his chin upward at two guards to carefully follow Blake. They waited as Blake walked down several steps into the gathering room. Unscrewing a hand-crafted tile from his hearth, he lifted it up, placing it to its side; there was the Trigon. Placing the Trigon deep in his pocket, he strode to the kitchen, grabbed a glass of water and began to drink, being careful not to drink all of it. He then pocketed a tiny *portal bomb* that Oskar had provided. Up the steps, out the door, came Blake holding the Trigon, as the guards joined him in lockstep!

"Thank you for your cooperation." said the guard's master, as he reached for the Trigon. Blake, hesitated, then swept his foot close to the ground and spun-kicked the surprised robot's feet from under him. He exchanged the portal bomb for the Trigon as he activated his weapon. The Trigon then disappeared, heading for Track 1701, to the ceiling just above its cashier, entirely hidden, as Blake had instructed.

"Kill him! Kill them all!" a robot roared.

"Not today, freak!" laughed Blake.

Blake splashed his glass of water on the ball, which the robot now tightly grasped. Instantly, the ball reacted, expanding to full size. It slammed Blake, pushing him against a first level window, as others were thrown by the mighty concussion. Blake landed safely, only feet from a few guards. But his parents were not so fortunate. His father lay against a rock foundation that was blown out, and was unable to move. Blake's mother lay slumped over her car, back against a shattered windshield. Blake scrambled to help, but was caught by the arm, swung upward only to land with a thud, dazed and in pain. He thought his arm was broken.

"This is your punishment, fool!" screamed a robot.

Blake glared at the offending robot that had thrown him with such force. The robot calmly raised his gun, aiming at Blake's parents, and shot twice. Blake, filled with rage, lunged at the robot, to disarm the cruel assailant. He trembled as the robot pushed him away, laughing. Blake, clouded, enraged, sobbed, "Why have you done this? They were good people, no harm to anyone."

Once again, now closer, Blake moved toward his parents' killer. He wanted to finish him off. Beat him down. But he had no gun! As the guards carefully trained their weapons upon him, Blake screamed, backing away.

"I am not going to die! You'll see. I'm not going to die! I will avenge my parents and make you pay! I will be back stronger than ever and stomp on you like a bug!"

"Let him go!" commanded the master robot, "He's only a boy! Easy prey for later!"

Blake pressed the *jumper* button on his Oskar invention, shoes that *whooshed* him upward and over the guards. He landed a short distance away on gravel, which ate at his flesh. He stumbled, backing away, releasing his reply, "You'll see, I am NOT going to die!"

Suddenly, a robotic chant filled the air.

"Kill Blake Armstrong. Find the Trigon. Kill Blake Armstrong. Find the Trigon."

Blake could see the robots in hot pursuit, scanning for him. The robots came quickly from behind, crashing through a fence as if it were paper. On a nearby interstate highway, cars were rushing back and away from the city. Traffic was heavy and as Blake stood panting at the highway's edge, he waved his arms, clearly in *emergency* fashion. Soon, a driver replied, pulling his car just past Blake.

"Get in, man. What's wrong?"

"Dang robots are overtaking everything and they're after me now, actually us. Just get away, please, NOW!" pleaded Blake.

The driver looked into his rearview mirror, spying the small army of robots bounding towards him. He sped forward as Blake pressed against the passenger seat. The speed of the car increased three-fold, as the vehicle launched into a welcomed *turbo*. Blake looked back. A stream of black vans had appeared from nowhere. One of the pursuing vans, its doors slamming and opening, caught most of the pursuing robots, who were now miniaturizing, who gleefully jumped in. As the doors finally shut, the line of vans boosted forward. The robot was right. Blake didn't know what he was dealing with. Blake's driver then swerved onto an entrance ramp and raced up it. A robot climbed out of the van's side window, knelt on its roof, aimed his right arm, then fired. His fist flew off with a rocket on its back.

184

"Watch this, Buddy!" yelled the driver well acquainted with most of the highway's back roads and byways. Avoiding more hot pursuit, he deftly swerved down an entry ramp, stopping at a train crossing not too far from the highway overpass as it arched over them.

"Thanks, man! yelled Blake, jumping out. "You have saved more than you'll ever know."

Blake ran toward the train station, only steps away, which he had eyed from the highway. In the distance, he could hear the noise of a train combined with police sirens. He had to get out of here and fast. He had no idea how he would, but he needed to board that train and get away as far as possible, to Cringleberry Avenue, where stood his mother's candy shop, "Classic Candies" and provisions he would need in the days ahead.

The train arrived within minutes and Blake paid for his ticket on board. To others, everything seemed normal. But a battle was raging; this Blake intimately knew. As the train sped forward into the city center, each minute closing in on Cringleberry Avenue where provisions lay with sweet memories, his heart pounded. Finally, the train lurched to his exit.

"Short cut. Gotta find a short cut. Not much time left!" he thought, as he ran down an alley. He *parkoured* up a wall off an alleyway to a rooftop, found a key under a small pile of bricks, and quickly entered through the roof's door. Stepping down a couple of steps, he entered the shop. White walls, featuring colorful shelves of aromatic candies, changed his mood. Some would avow that chocolate contains miraculous powers; why, in some cases it could change the world! The world's largest gummy bear and worms, lollypops with scorpions and ginger crickets inside, bacon-flavored everything, sour *bams*, and retro candy, displays here and there made the space joyous, at least for a child, and indeed for one so cleverly escaping robotic pursuit. Blake quickly made himself a concoction from the soda bar and gulped it down. He opened the cash register, withdrawing all its contents.

Making his way to the back, he stood before a chocolate painting, which cleverly hid a massive wall safe. Blake pressed an intricate unlocking *combination*, and removed treasures, valuable items which could be sold, more money, and a gun. He didn't want to use it, but would if necessary. Besides, he wouldn't be shooting real people, just programmed machines, right? He pulled open the back of his trousers, sliding a pistol into them and concealed it with his shirt. Ready to leave, he walked to the entry, as a squeal of tires alerted him. Blake looked through the shop window. Black vans were now patrolling the street, perhaps throughout the city. Motorcycles with figures wearing black leather were doing the same. Robots were everywhere. Blake figured that the train would leave soon, and he needed a disguise. Inside a closet he found a collection of Classic Candies uniforms. He slipped one on. It fit! Then a brilliant plan began to unfold, and his plan was brilliant!

He would simply walk from the store to the catering bike, perched now at the entrance, wearing his uniform with loads of makeup and a large brimmed "Classic Candies" cap. He would hide any wounds. He would generously apply eyeliner and a vibrant hot-pink lipstick. His disguise just might work, he thought as he glanced at the mirror, though he didn't take much comfort in dressing as a girl, but to proceed easily away from the enemy, he would need to get beyond such a luxury as embarrassment. Slung over his shoulder was a backpack that contained money, a load of candy, of course, and soda, and a collection of Oskar-inventions!

Pedaling as fast as he could, Blake avoided any robotic pursuit. He bumped up a wheelie, jumping up steps to the station. He looked at the train and then it hit him. Today was the day of the *Mystery Train Express*. It was a train made to look like one from the late 1800s and on board there would be a mystery dinner show. It was expensive and high class. But Blake decided not to wait around for another train. Buying a fifty-dollar ticket, he boarded safely and successfully without any robots in pursuit. All was quite luxurious. Inside it was dark; the only light was provided by vintage brass lanterns. Blake peered into the dining car. The open, yet curtained windows admitted scanty light upon the tables, which were all occupied.

Sleeping quarters were just beyond, down the swaying corridor. The train's steel wheels upon on its tracks clacked pleasantly, providing rhythmic percussion.

Blake found his berth, an ornate affair outfitted in leather, linen and rich oak paneling. A brass chandelier swayed, betraying the listing of the train. As he unpacked his backpack, he discovered two pieces of chocolate on his berth which he added to his collection. At the marble sink he washed, removing makeup and his ridiculous outfit. He tended to all else, then rested. Easily, he fell into a deep sleep, recalling the day's horrific pursuits, as the train continued  its friendly rocking far beyond the city.

A loud crash made Blake reach for his knife. He jumped at the noise and yelled, "I'm warning you! Do not come any closer or you will die! I have done it before and I will do it again!"

"Blake, what the heck ARE you doing? Put that knife down! We're here, too! On board with you!"

Blake recognized the voice but through all of the confusion, he was hard pressed to identify it. He walked to his door, his knife ready. The first person pushed the door open!  Blake stepped aside, wielding his weapon in his raised fist.

Aw, man, what's the knife thing about? You psycho or somethin'?"

"Dawson! What the... how did you... no wait. You're just a robot like Geo but with the voice of Dawson, right? Well take this!" He punched his *robot* in its stomach, but then he realized that this was no robot at all. No hard steel, just flesh under a cycle suit! Dawson grunted as he fell against the door jam.

"What... in the... world... ow! What is wrong with you?"

"DOS, I... I didn't know. I mean... I'm sorry. I thought you were a damn robot."

"He's not and neither are we!" two other figures added, as they entered Blake's berth. Helmets removed, there stood Oskar and Summerlin.

"Man, I'm stupid. Listen I'm sorry! Okay?"

"Sure, whatever. Dang, robots have made you crazy, man!"

"I was punching for my life. Don't ya think I wouldn't have given it my all? We need to talk. First though, how'd you all get here? How did you know I was here?

"Homing device...on the Trigon, Bro!" Oskar replied. "You carry it, you can be located. Like a smartphone. It's easy."

Blake's teeth remained clenched; inside he was ready to keep punching, fighting for his life. His head lowered.

"What's the matter, Blake?" Summerlin questioned.

"Everything," Blake replied, "But why ask?"

"You pushed your homing device on the Trigon. Remember? You push it and we will come to your aid."

"I remember. But I didn't push it."

"Do you think you did it accidentally?" Oskar squeaked, then cleared his throat.

"Now that I think about it, I probably did after all that happened."

"Well, what's up? Summerlin and Oskar asked together.

"I've been attacked by robots. My parents are dead. I've been on the run all day. Had to go to mom's shop, dress up like a girl, pedal for my life, board this train and finally escape the '*bots*. In short, it's been a long day!

"Wait a minute, what? Parents dead? Robots? Talk to us Blake." Dawson said, sitting next to his friend. Blake recounted every detail, as the train clacked on.

"Why do they want the Trigon? And why didn't you give it to them? They were threatening you and your parents' lives. How could you act so foolishly?" Summerlin demanded.

"Listen, Trigon has life and death significance. In the wrong hands, everything could blow up. I would give my life to keep it safe."

"You may do it for your life, but did you ever consider your parents?"

Blake's eyes filled with tears, as he replied, "As far as I am concerned, Summerlin, they had nothing to do with this!"

"Blake listen, I'm sorry about what's happened. We all know that you wouldn't intend to place your parents in harm's way. But we need to turn over the Trigon. There's no telling what these robots, aliens or whatever they are can do. They may destroy everything to find it. It's trouble, Blake, and if you don't do something, we all are going to die."

"I will do something about it. I will avenge my parents and slaughter the entire Tridesicon race!"

"Oh yeah, with what, a team of four high school kids? I don't think so."

"No, with an army which has as much hatred for this evil at hand as I do, as all of us do!"

They argued through the night, shared strategies and battle plans until, exhausted, fell upon the floor, Blake's berth and a leather chair. Blake did not rest at all but watched his sleeping friends.

"It's my business and mine alone." Blake thought. The Trigon is a grenade, and it could blow anytime, obliterating everything in its wake!"

Blake needed to minimize any causalities. as much as possible. Early at dawn it was as good a time as any. Quietly, Blake tip-toed to his backpack and he threw it out the window. He followed from the train's boarding door. He flew, landing on a stand of thick grasses which bordered the tracks. He then stood, running to retrieve his backpack.

His actions had caused his parents' deaths; he did not want this to happen to his friends. Leaving them was the only way to keep them safe. He had a backpack full of supplies, rations, two weapons, and a rising anger to avenge his parents. With these, he would have to survive in the *wild*, away from the city and its robots. This did not deter him. He had had teams of robots assault him, avoided vans of robots in hot pursuit, and now had just jumped from a moving train. Surviving in the wild for a while seemed like nothing. He knew he could survive, somehow, and make it to his hidden Trigon. He grabbed his backpack and slung it over his shoulder. Blake *mouthed* a prayer as he raised his arms to the Lord of life. Bravely, he turned, walking carefully into the unknown.

Blake nodded, heading in fervent mission to find his *treasure*, pleased that he knew the Trigon, its function and *modus operandi*: "Triangular. Normally glows in pulses along its wide edges!" Blake smiled. "...then breaks into pinpoints of brilliant light. Face forms. Speaks to me. Reveals God's next move, insight, command! Yep! That about sums it up!"

Suddenly, a tree just ahead, stretching over Blake, began to quiver. Its leaves shook *aspen-like*, announcing a summer storm on its way. Shadows flayed the afternoon light. Clouds, rushing eastward, drew Blake into their drama.

"Gonna rain, I guess." Blake responded. "Better head for cover!"

Darkness was quickly overtaking Blake's afternoon. As the tree thrashed about, its dark roots revealed a remaining triangle of light, which began to urgently spin toward Blake. In *familiar* fashion, its light broke into tiny pieces, intricately forming a kindly face.

"Blake, you must learn to look more carefully through my portals as you believe what God can do. He wants you to see the very souls of men. In God you must make your decisions. Enemies continue their search to misuse me. Do not let this happen, Blake. My portals will take you far beyond the outer man to the inner one, the soul, so you may gain holy discernment. You will see into the *heart of hearts*. Here you will discover when and what you must do. Believe, Blake. Believe! I am here for guidance as God instructs!"

Trigon's words began to slowly drift, sweeping into the storm, as its tender face grew opaque in measurements gradually diminishing. Blake, now wrapped in comforting assurance, reviewed Trigon's instructions, as a pelting rain now fell hard upon him. Blake squinted at the deluge, laughing, for here in the midst of a storm and torrent he now knew he was not alone. He never would be alone again!

*Blessed is the man that trusteth in the Lord, and whose hope the Lord is. For he shall be as a tree planted by the waters.*

**Jeremiah 17:7-8 AKJV translation**

## CHAPTER 19: DERREK

THE FIRST COUPLE OF DAYS OF SURVIVAL WERE TOUGH FOR Blake. Sleeping in trees, eating bugs after rations had been depleted and digging deep for energy to push himself through the woods, mile by mile, was not an easy task. But then, gradually, day by day, he grew accustomed to *hardship*. Every now and then he found occasional, remote, sources of water. Blake learned how to catch fish with his hands, as hard and slippery as it was. Along the way he gathered a few wooden planks and some rope. At night, he tied the boards together and fitted them between branches in the trees, creating a safe sleeping platform. Trigon's words continued to comfort him.

Many days passed, as did Blake's weariness. He was energized now, thankful to still be alive, amazed that although he had had little survival training, he had come this far. And yet there was a problem. A big one! He could see it and it gnawed at him. Over and over, trees and leafy paths had become strangely familiar! *Was he lost, traveling in circles? Circles in what should have been familiar territory less than ten miles from home?*

Blake shook his head, raging at his stupidity. Yes, he had missed it. Several times. Unfortunately. Definitely. Wasted time lay heavy on his heart! In his furious trek, he had wanted to see himself as *an incredible brave hiker in the big woods*, gloriously fighting his way through multiple dangers. What rubbish! "*What a jerk!*" he shouted, condemning his ridiculous thoughts. Perhaps it was lack of food and water that clouded his mind and blurred his vision. Whatever it was, he pounded his forehead hard, muttering, "I'm not giving up. Ever." Quickly, he scrambled for the tallest tree with thick limbs.

Blake was nimble in his ascent, and did it with little effort, thanks to many well-placed branches. He had almost reached the top when he spotted something in the distance. Far away, he spotted a large building which featured a parking lot and a complex pattern of roads, a *diaspora* of veins which shot quickly away from the imposing structure, toward a steep hill which loomed in its darkness, a foreboding *fist* defying the morning's cloudless sky.

"If I only had a compass..." thought Blake. He laughed to himself as he scanned a 360 from the treetop.

"All I need do is head north until I reach a road, then turn away from the sun, east, I think, and see if I can find food or shelter there." Blake looked to his left, and judging by the sun, he had a few hours left. He needed to move fast. His life depended on it. He quickly descended the old tree. Once landed on firm ground, Blake tied his planks of wood across his shoulder as he resumed his trek. An hour later there was little light left, but finally he could hear cars speeding up and down a roadway. There was hope! He was close now, but in the suffocating dark, he chose to save his energy for the next day. He set up his platform one last time, and lay down, exhausted, wondering what would happen next.

He awoke, startled, as the assaulting morning sun blinded his eyes, making him squint and shift his head, hoping the maze of leaves and branches would block the invader rays. He sat up, dazed, but it was short-lived. Inside, Blake's alarms went off, as his hunger pains demanded immediate attention. He moved off his perch, and in his quick descent scraped his chest on the rough bark. Pain shot through him. He ignored it, as he scrambled to his feet clumsily moving away toward the road ahead.

"Gotta keep going!" He reminded himself.

Blake burst through a thicket of vines, and stood on the road, its asphalt melting warm in the morning sun. The searing heat reminded him of his worn boots and painful blisters. Blake did not see the truck barreling toward him but the screech of brakes and invasive honking alerted Blake to quickly move back. The truck had barely missed him and skidded away, brakes still on. The angry driver rolled down his window, cursing Blake, then roared away. Blake shrugged it off, still *pumped* from his rude awakening. Though shaken, he struggled ahead to his *destination*, wherever that might be. Every step made him grunt and breathe more quickly. The sun continued to drill upon him. A few dark clouds were moving in, and, yet, even in the swift and welcomed shadows, Blake began to sweat profusely.

His shirt was soaked. Beads of sweat dripped from his hair, rolling down his sideburns, salting his facial cuts, wounds from the woods he had escaped. His sweat seemed to quicken. Drops now fell every other second. Blake took off his shirt and used it as a towel, drying off his head. Still, sweat fell upon his face and shoulders.

"What is going on?" he wondered.

Thunder boomed behind him. The sun was disappearing. Suddenly, Blake could see again, as salty sweat halted on his dirty cheeks. A massive cloud was overtaking the sky. It now rolled in dark majesty above him.

Blake turned around to scan the approaching storm. It gave him new energy. About a hundred feet away a wall of rain moved toward him. Sheets of rain harshly poured down upon the road, making it slippery with its welcomed *cooldown*. As fatigued as he was, Blake knew that he must keep going. He was drenched, and he let the rain collect in his mouth, gulping with great satisfaction. He took a left off the main road, and as he turned, he spotted a worn-out sign which read in faint letters, *Cascade Mall.*

"The Mall... better check it out." Blake muttered to himself.

His boots had fully taken on water as he slowly walked to a clearing, then on to a littered parking lot, ordinarily a space that could fit a few hundred cars, but in its abandoned posture, contained fewer than twenty. *Cascade Mall* was worn. Its old sign stood limp in the rain. So ordinary. So thoroughly worn out. So old. Possibly once a hip gathering spot, it now sported a network of vines overtaking its cracked walls. The mall's bones were good, just unattended, run down, and forgotten. Mold and dirt sprinkled across its facade, along with the weariness of years of pounding rain. Through the thick downpour, Blake spotted an *Army-Navy* store. Perfect. He needed dry clothes and as he closed in on the main entry, he peered through a wide glass door.

The interior was a few *ticks* higher than what he had encountered so far, but it was a *ghost town*. Although he could only see the food court and a weary local cinema, Blake could tell that this mall had gone down the tubes. Pulling a rusted handle, he yanked at the door. It didn't budge. He tried harder, and yet nothing moved. Yanking harder with one last pull, the door swung open easily, hitting Blake in the face.

As he rubbed his eye, he heard a mocking laugh. An old woman encased in the cinema's ticket booth cackled to herself. She got up from her chair, moved to see if she could help. She moved slowly as she waddled towards Blake. As she laughed, her flabby cheeks bubbled, and wiggled and her dreadlocks swayed back and forth in front of her face. Her eyes were golden, matching her nails.

"She must be nuts!" he thought. He shook his hair, as water pelted away to the floor. He cringed when she put her hands on his cheek, smiling.

194

"Are you okay, little bud?" Her breath smelled like road kill and alcohol, sprinkled with burning latex. Blake reeled.

"I'm fine. Just leave me alone."

Exhausted, Blake stumbled as he pushed away her intrusion. He scanned the dismal food court across the way. Perhaps ten food stalls had been active in the past, but not now, not anymore. The failing *Cascade Mall* featured only three stalls which still had their lights on, as its workers played *ping pong* on several bare tables, which now replaced once fully activated kiosks. He moved closer to a display of pizzas. The food was old and worn out like the mall. The workers, away from their stations, amped up their game, quickly hitting their noisy ball as it echoed back and forth. Several weary onlookers *cheered* them on.

"Old food. Gross!"

Blake made a sour face and turned away. Desperate for dry clothes, he slid toward a dimly lit store across the hall, and spotted a cashier watching old videos. Blake tiptoed in and took a hoodie, some jeans, old *free runs*, socks, and a T-shirt. He found a bag and silently set the clothes in. It was all going according to plan, until Blake tripped over a cord. It was connected to the old video player, and when it turned off, the cashier spun around to see Blake sprawled on the floor with his filled bag.

"THIEF!" he yelled. He wore a white muscle shirt and red bandana. His jeans were vintage, and his mustache made him look sinister, criminal, as the clerk quickly lifted a gun from his counter drawer. He shot into the air, missing Blake completely, shouting again, "THIEF!"

Blake grabbed a shelf, a barricade of sorts, and pulled it down, clothes flying everywhere as he threw money at the man. He sprinted away, the bag still in his hands, as the alarm went off. He looked over his shoulder to see the man diving over the shelf, rolling to the ground, pistol still firmly in hand.

"I am the police! Stop in the name of the law!"

Blake didn't stop, wondering why a police officer was working as a cashier. Perhaps the mall couldn't afford both and demanded double duty. Three rapid shots were fired. The man's aim was pathetic. Still, Blake was terrified, though his energy was returning. "Parkour!" he thought, as he fled from his pursuer. Words from his training shot across his mind: "Parkour is the physical discipline of training to overcome any obstacle within one's path by adapting one's movements to the environment. It is a non-competitive, physical discipline of French origin! Enough of this!" thought he.

Now it was time to put his training to good use. Blake took off up a flight of stairs, and, sure-footed, tapped the railing of a pedestrian bridge way which crossed the weary mall, and sprung off it. In slow motion, he could see down, twenty feet below, striking hesitancy in his heart, which made him smile. He landed on both feet below, his heart grateful at his success. He jumped again, spread out his legs into a split, and landed on an escalator railing and slid down as if it were a stair banister at home. The cashier-policeman was still on the bridge questioning whether he could make the jump. Blake smiled, but his humor quickly turned to fear. The policeman snapped out his shoulder walkie-talkie and spoke. The next moment, two more guards burst out of nowhere. One dove at the *thief* for a tackle, but Blake spun a hard kick to the man's jaw, veering the guard's path, sending him hard against a wide window, leaving a small crack.

The other guard stopped, took out his pistol, aimed, and fired. Blake couldn't react in time, but someone else did. A hand shot out from behind and yanked Blake back, holding his collar. Blake's sudden change of direction sent him tumbling backwards against a wall to the right of a restroom entry. Expecting to have already been captured, Blake scrambled up and got ready to fight, but saw that his *hero* was already brawling with the men. The *hero*, appearing not much older than Blake, spun on his heel, fist out, punching at both men. Though he had no gun, he held a curious device, a spray can of sorts. As he directed its wide spray toward the men, they slumped to the ground, suddenly deeply asleep.

"Sleeping powder." the fellow laughed. "It works every time." He walked up to Blake and stuck out his hand to help him up, and Blake, shaking his head, took it gladly. Blake's *hero* had white spiky hair with a tint of blue.

"Wildman!" Blake thought. His blue eyes sparkled. He wore a tight white shirt with a triangle at its center.

"Uh, oh that's-s sleep-p-ping powder? They're not dead?" Blake stuttered.

"No, of course not. We don't kill."

"We, who's we?" Blake asked, catching the boy's grammar.

"Never mind. I'm Derrek, and you are?"

"Armake Blastrong. I mean, Blake Armstrong." Blake was stunned at the kid's *pro-fighting*.

"Good name. But really, might I ask, what has happened to you?" asked the *wildman*.

Blake had little idea of how he looked, and realized he must be filthy. "Long story, man." replied Blake. "And, how do you say it, um, might I ask, what ARE you wearing? You look like you stepped out of some *Sci-Fi* flick." said Blake.

"Yes, well, mine is a long story, too, which perhaps can wait?" asked Derrek.

"You mean, oh! Okay, well how about if I tell my story, then you tell yours? Deal?" suggested Blake.

Derrek pondered then came up with an answer, as both boys leaned against a weary wall.

"You start." suggested Derrek.

So, Blake began his long and tragic story, filling Derrek in on Geo, *KidzTurf's* Armageddon, the death of Blake's parents, hot robotic pursuits and the miraculous Trigon! A door suddenly burst open, belching out a small troop of police who now aimed their pistols at the boys. The invading team meant business. Derrek held up his hands, and so did Blake, but then Derrek pushed at Blake's side, forcing him into the men's room. Inside its hallway, Blake could hear dozens of guns firing, alarms pulsating, as pain squeezed at his stomach. Derrek was still out there. Blake carefully looked around the corner, careful not to be hit by the ocean of bullets, as he witnessed Derrek achieving the impossible. He was dodging the bullets! Not *matrix* style, but simply sliding, ducking, and making flexible shapes with his body, allowing each bullet to pass harmlessly.

The police ran out of bullets as they stared at Derrek, amazed, forgetting to reload their firearms. Derrek grinned. He took out a silver ball with a finger print keypad on it. He laid his finger on it briefly, and then, like a baseball pitcher, threw the tiny sphere through a glass window above the exit door. Then, all of the guns leapt from hands and holsters, like steel to magnet, hurling toward the orb. The men who at one second had tightly aimed their guns were in the next pulled high into the air, frozen into position. Blake could not move at all, and neither did the reinforcements, suspended in mid-air. But one thing did move, Derrek. He sauntered away nonchalantly, dusting off his shoulder. He spotted Blake, giving a look that said, "Whoops, sorry." He pushed Blake's forehead backward as an amazed Blake fell to the ground, able to move once again.

"Wha??? What just happened here?"

"I know, I've got a lot of 'splainin' to do, but not now! Not here. Let me just reduce their vision a bit so they won't track us." Spinning powder into the air, Derrek grinned at the menacing *fog* taking over. All would now remain frozen in the *blur*, at least for a few minutes! Although he could move, Blake could not see through the thick fog. Then a hand grabbed his arm from behind.

"In here." Blake was pulled back into the restroom and into a stall by Derrek. Blake saw what was happening now, and feared who Derrek might be. But then, Derrek stuck his hand deep into the toilet bowl, grossing out Blake. Blue light flashed in the water, then Derrek pulled out his soaked arm, flushing the toilet while dropping a red marble into the water. A panel then slid open in the blue tile wall, revealing a laser which *zapped* to attention, piercing and shrinking both boys. Now the size of a *Lego* man, Blake stood terrified, held with Derrek in suspension, inches above the swirling water of the toilet.

"Derrek, what's happening...?" Blake quivered.

"Hurry, put this in your mouth." Derrek handed him a mouth guard and Blake suddenly recognized it. It looked exactly like Oskar's underwater air-breathing mouth guard. Blake was going to say something, but the laser turned off. It allowed them to quickly fall. Blake jammed the *guard* into his mouth, a nanosecond before he was fully submerged. The current of the water pulled him with such force, it felt like an underwater *coaster*. After a short time of tumbling and flipping, they both hit a net. The water coursed through it, but Blake was not small enough to get through. He was wondering if the *Shrink Ray* had malfunctioned. Overwhelming fear began to overtake Blake as he fell deeper into the net.

"Good grief, Derrek!" Blake thought.

"Sorry." Blake heard Derrick's voice in his head, which almost made him spit out his mouth guard in surprise.

"Move to the wall on your right." instructed Derrek.

Blake did as he was told, though it was hard twisting against the pushing current. He could see a steel door with a curious hole at its center. Derrek thrust his hand through the open hole, as the chamber beyond instantly filled with water. They swam inside, shutting the door, which automatically locked behind them. There was a huge wall button on the side, which Derrek pushed hard, as the swirling water turned to vapor. Both boys fell to the floor. Vapor, like incense, pushed up and away, sucked into several ceiling vents above. Blake spat out his mouthguard, noticing that it was easier to breathe now in the new *mixture* which encased him. Derrek picked up the *guard*, stuffing it into his pocket for future reference.

"I know I have a lot to explain..." laughed Derrek, shaking his head.

"Yes, let's start with that *speaking in my mind* thing you did in my brain. How can you talk in my thoughts? And how in the world did we..."

"Blake, stop. I wasn't finished. I'll answer all questions later. But for now, we need to get to the *Tri-lounge*. All will be well! Believe me. And don't worry; you won't forget any questions...right?" Blake had just considered this potential dilemma and started to get agitated with this *mind reading* business.

"... I have them all in a file." He tapped his brain. "And I will show you how later." assured Derrek.

"There he goes again messing with my mind!" This was something

Blake was going to have to get used to. Derrek smiled at Blake's thought, but said nothing and thought nothing, or at least nothing that Blake was receiving. He preferred his thoughts be private. Now he would have to think as if he were speaking aloud. Derrek opened a door and there stood a huge triangle waiting for them. Two parts of it slid open and two bridges spurted out from underneath, stopping in front of Blake and Derrek. Below, there emerged a brilliant light through a transparent floor. Massive luminescent walls surrounding the boys were *electric*, exposing veins of pulsing blue light, clumped together in bright steel and transparent *pipery*. Midway up the wall were holes, each boasting singular railings which jutted ahead like train track, a slick circular bar upon which triangular vehicles awaited passengers. Derrek called Blake ahead, both boys now on separate split walkways for scanning. Floating mid-air, two massive orbs scanned the boys, releasing each forward, though separated by a transparent wall, into a luxurious *common* waiting room. There were several leather couches and other-worldly appointments, each with thick stripes of neon blue, electric, alive, cells inside the fabric, moving, filled with light, like the edges of the Trigon.

"There's gotta be a major connection, though perhaps remote: Trigon and this strange place!" Blake pondered. Stretching away from him lay two tracks upon which twin transporters awaited. Suddenly, a transparent wall separating the boys, glowed, slowly lifting. Full scanning was now complete. Derrek pulled out an identity card, and pushed it through a slot adjacent to where he stood. As the glowing wall continued to slide upward, it disappeared into a brilliant ceiling of light. Derrek then tossed his card to Blake, motioning him to do the same. Soon both boys stepped into separate transporters, which, when Blake inserted Derrek's shared card, the separate units morphed as molten plastic into one unit for two companions. Easy. Routine. Blake wondered, "Where AM I?" Derrek smiled at Blake's question!

Transparent holograph screens swung from both sides, quietly hovering before Derrek and Blake for further instructions. A topographic map glowed as if requesting a preferred destination. Derrek mumbled a *routine command* as Blake, awe-struck, gazed at his screen. The layout was spectacular. And as their silence pushed forward, intricate swirls and radiating colors indicated recommended destinations. Derrek touched one and instructed Blake to follow his lead. The holographs quietly withdrew, dissipating into the *foreign* air.

Nothing happened. No lurching ahead. No humming or vibration. No *revving up* of turbo engines. "Was there a problem?" Blake wondered. In moments, a tiny transparent orb encased in light, stood mid-air between the boys.

"Go ahead! Grab it! It won't hurt." Derrek said casually. Timid, Blake stretched out his hand as he leaned forward, grasping the radiating orb. Surprisingly, the orb was slick and wet. He grabbed it harder, perhaps an alien stick shift of sorts, to see if he could *capture* it, but he could not. "You see, Blake, it has within it a special gel that is very slippery. Like your *Bluetooth* it conveys programmed information and *power* to make our ride smooth, steady and on time. Blake shook his head in amazement. He expected that other mysteries lay ahead. As the triangular vehicle rushed the boys forward, Blake finished his story, and by the time he was done they had stopped. They had reached their destination. "We are here, Blake Armstrong. Get ready. This, as they say, will *blow* your mind!" And for some reason, Blake knew that this was no exaggeration.

*Rejoice in hope; be patient in affliction; be persistent in prayer.*

**Genesis 28:16 HCSB translation**

## CHAPTER 20: UXTAL

WALLS ordinarily indicate nothing more than walls! Hard surfaces to be painted, plastered, textured or wallpapered. Walls. Boring. Ordinary. But on Uxtal, walls were different for within selected districts, Uxtalian walls contained innumerable miniature civilizations, fully functioning communities living in harmony. To be sure, to the uninitiated eye, walls were ordinary but to most on Derrek's strange planet it was a fact of life: multitudes of civilizations simply resided within its selected walls, each with a unique history, language and ambition.

With hidden, unknown and unseen precision, efficiency, and beauty there lived residents, vibrant within its walls, where an escaped remnant, good people one and all, from Tridesicon, which had adopted Uxtal's *way of life*. With scribal accuracy and precision all recycling of used materials within Uxtalian walls, occurred instantly, restoring order to what has been used, damaged, torn or ravaged, efficiently restoring all material and space. Even the turning of events, minor or major, especially decisions that beat against the good of all, were masterfully and wonderfully restored to harmonious perfection. But we must go deeper into the wall, dear reader. Let me introduce you to one of Uxtal's wall residents and share a portion of his story.

A mallet wound on Hage's head imposed no pain, none whatsoever! His opponent, you see, days ago in anger had failed, for the "environment," or what Hage perceived as the world about him situated within one of Uxtal's selected walls, had become his Defender in a way, yes, a very practical way. You see, every cell, every minute particle there within the Uxtalian Wall, every resident and any malice-laced scheme, could be turned, would be turned about for good, empowered to perfection, all such events recorded in a *Book of Life*, in odd cuneiform symbols which tracked all restorations, in circles, triangles, fitted together, pierced with rods of varying lengths, joined in strange colorations and shadings, all pointing to an "intelligence," yes, to God himself, Hage's benevolent Father, God who provided Hage with abundant life, order, discipline, and renewal. God was his All in all, and every civilization upon Uxtal living within its selected walls, knew and served Him. Hage smiled, for life simply moved along smoothly most of the time in Uxtal.

Let us go deeper. You see, faithful recordings on Uxtal, like a cleric's Register of Services, are precise, accurate and permanent, God's BOOK OF LIFE we have just referenced, each "jot and tittle" slowly turn; they really do! Each word glows in life-affirming brilliance! Each recorded sentence is miraculously shaped not in abstract letters, limited to an alphabet, but in a life-affirming genetic precision and pattern, patterns which combine all events, thoughts, acts of forgiveness, all repentance, every hope, dream, conversation, thought

204

and decision of every resident, continually morphing according to what happens in the daily round: adding here, subtracting there, reshaping words and events all into something new, calling what was into something better. A Potter's effort re-shaping codes and words and atoms, cells, electrons, what were simply words, yet more than words, THE WORD, reaches into all walls, to redeem any situation for the good, holding in His Potter's Hand the attack upon our dear Hage, now, entirely resolved, gives life where death had reigned. Simply, this is LIFE on Uxtal, like Hage's life, he, coming fully alive, and not in any limited sense either, but there in the middle of each Uxtalian life, God's perfect will comes to fruition. Fruition which slowly spins like Ezekiel's wheel within a wheel. Here God's WORDS OF LIFE redeem hard times: dark to light, evil to good, and hopelessness to provision. Truly all this is a Master's Hand at work in each and every heart, Messiah beyond what could be imagined, now in His Perfect Will restores all conversations, dilemmas and decisions to a palpable joy! On Uxtal all are alive in God's eternal love with a Shepherd's assurance that all will be well. And that, dear friend, is Hage's story.

Heavy panels opened, and a mixture of sunlight and warm air blasted the two for a moment, and then stopped. Derrek grinned at Blake.

"Where are we?" Blake questioned, wide-eyed, leaning on a huge stone triangle.

"We are not in California anymore, are we?" teased Derrek, turning to face Blake. "Neither are we on earth. In fact, we are out of your solar system. We are galaxies from yours."

"Wha... wait; we are still here. I mean, we are where, the mall, right?" Blake stuttered, confused. "It's impossible, we first shrunk into the lav, and then we traveled through pipes...and..."

"Which lead to highest city, transporting us from earth to here." Derrek butted in. "Welcome to Uxtal! Let's go over some rules. No slouching, snoring, biting, any use of your teeth really, *frawlching*... oh wait, humans can't do that! We will review all this later."

Blake had many more questions, but could only manage, "Huh?" Derrek burst out laughing.

"I'm really sorry, Blake, but I will have to explain everything later...and your part in all this."

Derrick motioned for Blake to follow. Blake was a brave one and a leader, who always tried to show more courage than the next man, but all this Uxtal stuff was different. Cautiously, he stood up and walked to the opening. He stretched his leg out, but then hesitated, losing his nerve. Standing straight, he steeled himself to be brave. His foot touched the yellow grass. Instantly his shoes started to burn. Blake jumped back!

"Hold on! Get those shoes off!" demanded Derrek, as he quickly tore off Blake's shoes. "Almost forgot! No rubber, tar, or brussel sprouts are allowed here in Uxtal. Those are the three things from earth that we will not tolerate! And bacon! No, no, no, no, no, no, no, NO, NO, NO bacon! And if you utter the name of Bronwyn we will have to banish you forever!"

Perplexed, Blake could only manage, "Huh?"

"Just kidding, Blake!" Derrek smiled. "Once we reach the lounge, you will read our 173 rules and abide by them, if you please. Seriously though, if any rubber touches our yellow grass, no kidding, it will burn you, turning our Uxtalian grass to ice! Can you imagine walking on ice grass! It's like walking on needles!"

Blake had waited patiently to speak. "Don't you guys wear shoes?"

"Of course, we do! Don't be stupid! Anything that is frozen here is powerful. If a tomato is frozen, it will not die. It will grow in strength and attain ability to kill. The points of these blades you call grass are really harmless. The points will not hurt to step on, much less pierce through a shoe. But when frozen, points will harden, becoming practically invincible. Understand?"

"If my shoes freeze grass, why did they start to melt?" Blake inquired.

"Ugh, too hard to explain. It's our science. You wouldn't understand. Not yet! You'd have to endure many years of training, studying our science, to understand what I'm talking about."

"I have a feeling there's a big learning curve comin' up, right?"

"You have no idea..." Derrek grinned his fantastic smile that had a humorous, yet rugged expression. They walked away, Blake now barefoot, in a radiant yet blue sunlight. Although the Uxtalian blue star twisted in its brilliant array, the sky arched high above in the deepest emerald.

"Ah the sky! Isn't it beautiful! It's night time here, just about. See the two suns setting, Blake? Blake didn't see the suns setting, but just getting bigger!

"Derrek, it's not setting, it's..."

"I know, I know, it's getting bigger. That's what every earthling says. But that's what we call the sun setting. Can't you tell its growing darker?"

"And can't you tell the grass is glowing brighter?" Blake laughed.

"Like I said, we will discuss this later."

"You brought it up." Blake teased.

"Cage that box, Blake." Blake pondered Derrek's weird phrasing and figured out that it meant *SHUT UP*. He was correct!

Air and light pushing from the Uxtalian grass was cold but somehow did not chill. It felt good to Blake, even though he hated the cold. It took him a while to acclimate, but they were on an island, above a maze of purple clouds, which now wove deeply into the emerald sky. Dozens of islands littered Uxtal's sky, connected by transparent tunnels, which boasted superior technology. The island that they were on had three triangular tunnels, which skillfully and perfectly fit in symmetrical patterns, precise sleeves to convey sleek triangular transporter vehicles called *Tripporters*. It made sense. Blake looked behind and saw his ride's panels quietly slide shut as he rode down the tunnel, then quite out of sight. Surrounding them, on both sides, was a lake of crystal clear water. Water on earth is clear as well, but this lake, about three hundred feet deep, provided no obstacle whatsoever to obscure its sparkling sandy bottom! Nothing could ever excel Uxtalian beauty more than this celebration of multi-faceted diamonds!

Reflecting upon the lake's bright surface there was a lush mountain to the left and on the right several islands of glowing meadows which shimmered in the quieting light, making Blake's 360 a floating valley in the sky. In the middle appeared two giant blue suns, one larger than the other, and a crescent moon cutting its way into the emerald heavens. Derrick and Blake crossed a long bridge brilliantly self-lit in an intense blue-white light, to yet another bridge. Just ahead stood a tall outdoor *armoire*, which covered in brilliant letters, alerted all that passed by: "Alien Necessities." Derrek licked its keypad and it unlocked the cabinet's wide door. Blake's face read *GROSS* and Derrek explained.

"It knows my tongue's DNA and any others who live here. It's quite sterile. Actually, there are no bugs on Uxtal!" He removed a suit and standard backpack and threw them at Blake.

"Press the triangle on the suit and then... well... you will see." Blake picked up the suit and noticed that it was exactly like Derrek's. He pushed the triangle hard with two thumbs. It flew up, unfolded, stayed for a few seconds, then dove down at Blake. It slipped under his feet until they were in the neck hole. Then it flew up, his body sliding into the uniform, it perfectly fitting. His feet slipped into awaiting shoe pockets as his arms extended into its luminescent cuffs. It was as if the suit had come alive as it efficiently dressed the *alien*! As Blake spun around, sliding his hands along the smooth fabric, Derrek threw on his backpack and checked Blake, adjusting the triangle in the middle. He twisted, pulled, pushed, sniffed, and jotted, giving Blake some quick instructions.

"When you are in the air, push the *trigon*, I mean triangle, then do a pencil dive for five seconds, and spread out your arms. Follow me! Try not to look down, be brave. You are now, ready, you are now set, and now it is time to go!"

He then kicked Blake in the back with great force; Blake fell over the edge. As he was falling and yelling, he couldn't help but remember being in the redwoods, free-falling with Dawson. His mind raced as fast as he was plummeting. He remembered Derrek's instructions and hit the small triangle. He then straightened into a pencil dive for five seconds, spreading out his arms. Instantly, the arm pit to his waist expanded, forming wide wings, wings like a flying squirrel. From his feet, small rockets popped out and blasted out fire. He sped onward as his skin responded in 3G fashion. All he could see was purple mist from the clouds, and when he rose upward into the emerald sky, he achieved a new perspective of not dozens, but hundreds of islands glittering in the sunset. It was beautiful. The emerald light hitting the bright glitter of gold grass and glowing purple clouds, arching above the clear water lake with diamond sand, inspired Blake in its *other-worldly* magnificence.

White-domed houses, gold meadows and reflecting pools littered the islands, which were exquisite in their embrace of the rugged and natural terrain. Blake could hear Derrek in his mind again. "Watch out for floating debris." Blake didn't see it coming in time, but a small piece plowed right into him. He banged off of it, hurling toward Derrek.

"You could have warned me sooner!" Blake yelled into Derrek's ear over the loud whipping of wind, then pushed himself off to get back on course.

Down below was a sort of *jello* wall, colored trigon blue. Blake received a message from Derrek, telling him to dive down straight into it. Blake thought it was crazy, but after all of the insanity that had transpired on Uxtal, this most likely would be mild, perhaps even pleasant. Descending quickly, he flew like a heavy pencil into it, next to Derrek. They pummeled into the gelatin together. The wall extinguished the foot rockets and the boys quickly slowed to a stop in the gelatinous pool. Blake could see the diamond sand below, even more radiant up close. He could barely tell that he was underwater, because it was so clear.

They swam over to an ascending stairway, and easily left the pool with Blake noting, "Well, that was... uh... exhilarating."

"You will get used to it, depending on... never mind. I'll explain later."

"You keep saying that and my mind is cluttered with so many questions it's going to blow!"

"All in due time, my friend. All in due time."

After a couple of seconds of silence, Blake froze. "Derrek?" Blake said, freaking out.

"What?" Derrek turned to see what was wrong.

"We just came out of a pool. Why am I not wet?"

Derrek's concern turned into apology. "I forgot to tell you that water doesn't make us wet here, at least not on Uxtal. Plus, it's more practical that way so we don't waste water or have ever to dry ourselves, don't you agree?

"Yeah, somewhat. I mean, how do you put out fires?"

"We don't have fires or much heat here. We are one of the two ice planets, remember? Oh wait, I haven't told you that yet. Moving on, and let me tell you my most important rule, and that is no more questions until we reach the lounge. Okay? Okay, good. Onward we go." Derrek said abruptly, closing the subject, at least for now.

"Have some grass if you like as long as it will keep you quiet." Blake stared at the grass, and surprisingly the idea wasn't half bad, he thought. He snatched up a handful of it, sniffed it, stuffing it into his hungry mouth. The golden grass was easily chewed and slid down Blake's throat, its light radiating through his neck. The taste was one Blake could not exactly explain. At first, he considered it similar to a mixture of bacon, salsa, and pears, but then it had an aftertaste of French fries and pickle chips. Its taste seemed to alternate every few seconds, and all of Blake's favorite food and drinks, it seemed, were contained in it. It was delicious! He was going to grab more, but he realized he was *stuffed*. Even though he had eaten no more than a few strands of grass, it felt as if he had had a four-course meal!

"Radical, right?" Derrek asked.

"It goes beyond radical, Derrek, way beyond!" They both smiled.

"Good." Derrek commented, "We are almost at the *Yaw Way*."

"The *Yaw Way*?" Blake asked .

"No more questions please! I promise you all of your questions will be answered, in due time."

Blake was not very patient and delayed answers were troublesome.

Luckily, he had a new world to distract him. For a quarter mile ahead, everything from east to west was flat, with an enormous snow-capped mountain rising on the horizon. Behind him were many others as far as the eye could see. The mountain ahead boasted a great gate of ice at its center, an intricately carved triangular ice gate.

"The Trigon..." Blake cried out, but then stopped as Derrek turned, giving him a queer glance.

"There is no such thing as a Trigon. A mere legend. Anyway, where do you earthlings get such ideas?"

They walked across a slippery ice path, which was surrounded by acres of golden grass. The suns in the sky were now almost touching, hovering over the Uxtal mountain. Light was diminishing. Emerald gradually morphed into dark green, the stars, one by one, piercing into the emerging dark. The boys walked down the path and they reached an ornate triangle doorway. It must have taken years to carve such beautifully intricate work. It was similar to what Blake knew, his glowing Trigon, an exact replica, except here before him, of ice, hanging on hinges imbedded in the mountain rock which rose before him. Derrek knocked three times, then a slit in the dead center of the ice triangle opened, as unimpressive flat light poured out.

The light moved up and down, scanning Blake and Derrek, then stopped and said, "Derrek Quertal, Earthling Visitor, Access granted!"

Then Blake saw that the Triangle was not just sculpture, but a massive living gate. It rumbled and slid apart, pulled by wide hinges, leaving an entry that easily could admit giants! Blake stared in and gasped at the beauty before him, the marvelous cityscape of Uxtal.

"Welcome to our planet's capital! Each and everything here is made from a combination of ice and snow. This is basically what you might call *New York City*, but... but more... how would an earthling say it... um, *futuristic*? I think that's right. Now go ahead, walk in!"

Derrek's wide smile encouraged Blake to proceed. A surprise was coming, and Blake tried to show his friend his fearless self as he bravely walked in. He found it odd though that the entire floor was just flat grass, and suspended from the ceiling were domed buildings, wide passages, and shining waterways. But once Blake walked in, fear struck his heart. It was all happening again. Gravity pulled at him as he began to uncontrollably *fall up*. All he could do was panic. His shallow breathing quickened, forcing his heart to pound wildly. Re-living Geo's traumatic gravity-defying battle was too much for Blake as he now fell toward the ceiling, the bedrock of Derrek's city, the pride of Uxtal.

*A friend loves at all times, and a brother is born for a difficult time.*

**Proverbs 17:17 HCSB translation**

## CHAPTER 21: TRIO

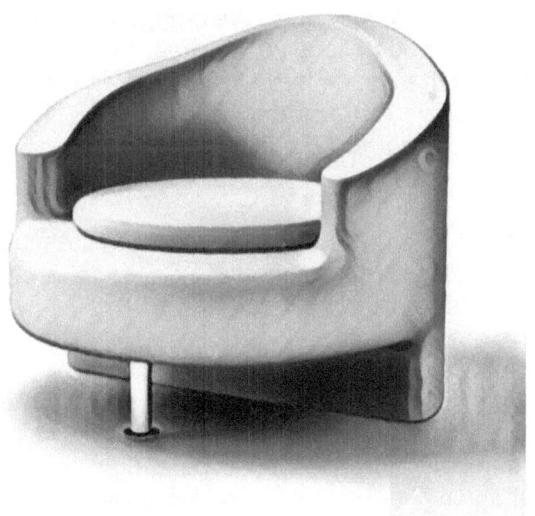

HE WOKE UP IN A COMFY CHAIR INSIDE A BUILDING. It was now daytime and brilliant light shone through the ceiling. Though it wasn't blue light from the sun at Uxtal, nor the golden light from its yard grass. It was natural *earth* sunlight. And the sky above was baby blue!

"Am I back on earth?" Blake wondered. Everything seemed to be *earth-like*. He looked up and squinted. Above was a huge dome of glass, letting sunlight pour in. Around him was a *resting* area, embracing him in modern sleek comfort. Coffee makers, transparent bowls of familiar fruits and a kitchen stood gleaming behind him; people were conversing at a table nearby, convivial. Many were sprawled on red low-slung couches with blue piping, stroking and listening to ever so thin and tiny electronics. He sank deeper into his yellow chair. He spotted Derrek walking towards him with a *merry* tray of coffee, bagels, muffins, and pecan encrusted oatmeal cookies.

"Good morning, sunshine! Nice to see you alive again!"

"Wha? What's goin' on? Where are we?"

"We are back on earth at *Cascade Mall*, one of Borealis' satellites. This is *Earth Lounge*, not quite yet in what's known as Borealis; you're not yet ready for Borealis. *Earth Lounge* is remedial, a place to heal. You weren't doing so well up in Uxtal so instead of *Upper Lounge*, I thought you might do better here. We dragged you out of the city, since you were unconscious. Totally out, man! We did some emergency work on you and then it seemed all you needed was to get back here, to be comfortable in more normal surroundings. It seemed a better solution than keeping you up there. I think you had had too much craziness for one day."

"Where are we? I mean, you told me we are in the mall. Well, this isn't a mall, Derrek. This is much nicer than *Cascade*. Are we at a different mall? Really, where are we exactly?"

"No, Blake, we are still at *Cascade Mall*. But there's a catch! We're just inside its walls. Let me explain. Like in the ride where we rode the triangular transporter, the tube was bigger on the inside than outside. This is the same. Exactly. It is bigger here, right where we are now, on the inside than on the outside. Outside, the width of the mall wall is no larger than three feet. But on the inside, well, let's say, it goes on forever; maybe not forever, but it's impressive, about the size of a miniature city, like in Uxtal."

"Whoa, Derrek! That's impossible!"

"Well, tell me this, Blake. Did you ever consider that there was such a thing as *dry water*? Or a secret tunnel the width of a hair that goes from earth to an utterly different galaxy? Or did you find it impossible for me to *freeze* time? You see, Blake, today you've become one of those rare humans who knows what's really out there! And, here, too! The rest of the world is completely oblivious. You have to trust me when I explain these things."

"Al... all right, Derrek. I trust you," Blake responded.

Derrek replied with a toothy grin, laughing, "Now let's go over the rules."

"Rules?" Blake asked.

After a full hour reviewing Uxtalian rules and natural laws, Blake remained silent. He was overwhelmed and perplexed, as he strained to understand Derrek's introduction to an absolutely foreign world.

"Certain rules don't apply in these particular mall walls, you see, but I advise you to follow all of 'em anyway. You'll be safe if you do! Break too many rules, and you'll be kicked out and your memory of Uxtal wiped clean! You then face a dramatic reversal to a normal, boring, and mortal life.

"You refer to us as mortals. Does this mean that you and Uxtalian folk are, how should I put this, immortals?"

"Tut tut, Armstrong, only the Creator is immortal. We just have a longer life span. A lot... longer... time span."

"Like, how much longer?" inquired Blake.

"Well, friend, that is quite a question. According to my research of earth life, a tiny mayfly lives its full life span anywhere from an hour to a day, then dies. Compared to us, your lives are just as short as theirs. Get the picture?"

"Clearly. How old are you, then?"

"I don't believe, Blake Armstrong, that you have a word for the number of my age. Let me check." He snapped, and a glowing hologram-like screen appeared in mid-air, spinning slowly before them. In just a couple of taps, he found the answer.

"I am two *googleplex* years old."

"And a *googleplex* is.....?" asked Blake.

"It is approximately 1 followed by 100 zeros."

Blake's jaw dropped, almost scraping the low-slung table. Stunned, he slowly found his tongue, managing to affirm, "I said I trust you and I really do. I believe you, Derrek, but it's hard to take it all in!"

"Armstrong, no offence, but you are a terrible liar."

"Well you are a freakin' two *googleplex* years old, and you are really stretching me here. My sense of reality, well, everything's suddenly upside-down. I'm just trying to hang on!"

"That's understandable. Most earth folks go through a stage of wonder and unbelief. Give it some time and you'll get used to it. Trust me."

"Some time, what do you mean, man? Am I staying here much longer?"

"Well, of course you are. Judging by your story, you need food and shelter, correct? You have no one to turn to, and there is nowhere you can go but here, right? So, I'm inviting you to live here in the wall, Blake. You may accept or decline. It's your choice!"

Thinking it over, Blake wasn't quite sure about this. Could it all be an illusion? Was this a trick? Blake hesitated but finally accepted the offer. He trusted Derrek, so he could roll with him on this. Besides, living here would be much better than elsewhere with robot minions lurking about.

"Good decision! I think we are going to get along! How about this, I can nickname you my *StrongArm*. Like in war, officers have their right arm man; well, you can be my *StrongArm*. It goes with your last name."

"Sounds good. So, tell me about your Uxtalian *laws of life*. "

Derrek reached down, pulling up a thick book, plopping it down on the table with a thud. "I was just getting to that. Now, I won't read all four hundred pages, but I will summarize each chapter, and then answer any questions you may have. Okay? Okay. Good, moving on!"

Derrek's reading, his *overview* took longer than Blake expected. The *rules* overpowered him but at the same time fascinated Blake as he imagined how these well-devised but strange laws were even possible. It was as if Derrek had planted a balloon inside Blake's head, and Derrek kept blowing air into it, expanding Blake's mind almost beyond its capacity.

"Well, then. That took a while. So, you see, what I've highlighted here will be enough to get you around in a *primitive* sort of way. And, hopefully, you won't blank out when you see everything I still have to show you."

Blake replied, "I was wondering, Derrek, if this place is bigger on the inside than on the outside, what would happen if a wall collapsed or a hole was injected into it? If the people on the other side looked in, would they see *tiny* people scrambling about in a *tiny* world?"

"Oh, no, no, Blake! Here, unlike Uxtal, we are the same actual size as theirs. If the tiniest hole or if, in the worst-case *scenario*, a wall did collapse, then we would instantly seal the intrusion; if not, the hemorrhage unattended would destroy most of the earth, replacing one *system* with the other. It's because, the two can't be together, a smaller world and a bigger world, parallel, simultaneously, unless it's governed by Uxtalian *rules*. Be assured, we make sure that nothing happens to the walls here. We even provide money anonymously so that *Cascade Mall* will stay open and running."

Blake didn't ask any more questions, still chewing on Derrek's answer. Suddenly, Derrek decided to show something else to his new friend.

"Come along, Blake, let's find you some lodging. Though it's not my job, I have always been successful finding new arrivals places here. It's become somewhat of a *hobby*, I suppose."

"Okay, do you have any suggestions?" Blake said, smiling, as he pushed himself slowly to his feet.

"There is one vacant spot that is in both worlds. And you can eat human food instead of what we normally consume here because you will be *over* the burger joint. It's in the food court, located above a bank of cashiers, where you can have at will, your choice, including a huge burger, colossal fries and a soda, if you wish. Like here, it's bigger on the inside, but not to such an extravagant measure. You will fit in it like it was the size of a small house on earth. Come. Let's see if you like it."

He pulled out two tiny triangles from his pocket, tossing one to Blake and keeping the other for himself.

"Just push the button, Blake." He did, and it quickly dropped, slowly spinning on the floor, as it began to expand and stretch, morphing into a transparent *bug-like* flying vehicle. Both climbed aboard, gunning the engine as they rode beyond the lounge into the distant city streets. This world was as magnificent as Uxtal. Its domed skyscrapers soared high, featuring spired rooftops. Green grass was everywhere, scattered among spatterings of snow. Programmed streets projected brilliant holograms one above the other, creating layers of transparent passageways. People were everywhere.

Derrek and Blake flew up an entrance to *Way 304-22*, which had less traffic, making a bee-line to the heart of the city. Abruptly turning a hard right, they reached the perimeter of the Uxtalian-like *world* and stopped. There stood a ledge with parking spaces for ten, which they used. Next to a row of vehicles, stood a triangular door. Stepping through a thin layer of brilliant white-blue, they *effortlessly* moved beyond the wall ahead.

"This space will fully adjust us now to Uxtal's *bigger-on-the-inside* dimension. This is more amplified than the main area." They passed through yet another door, this one looking more *welcoming*. A few paces more, they quickly entered a rather *ordinary* apartment.

"We are walking into the hamburger part, Blake. This will be your library. We don't have wasted space like living rooms here, so I hope you don't mind."

"Are you kidding me? I would have settled for a shack. This is awesome! I mean look, I have a holographic TV, a massive book collection, an awesome couch, a kitchen, everything!"

"The French fry part, you know, *the part in their wall, adjacent to their ovens*, is your hallway. On the left side is the door to your bath and on the other, your sleeping quarters. Here is a desk, a library of Uxtalian law, with Uxtalian wooden floors, Uxtalian cabinetry and beautiful gel windows."

"Derrek, I get it. A fully outfitted Uxtalian apartment! Cool. I love it."

"Right, sorry. I'm getting carried away. Always do when I talk about Uxtal." Derrek laughed. "Just look beyond your one-way gels to the outer world. You can see out. They can't see in! They're clueless of Uxtalian residency, even though it's in the same space. Correction, within its walls, mostly!"

"Yep!" beamed Blake. "Nice bed, cool room!"

"Do you need anything else or..."

"Nah, everything's great. Thank you so much, man. We can talk here if you'd like."

"Perfect. Ah, so, Blake Armstrong, how are you dealing with Uxtal's *rules* now?"

"Um... okay, I guess. All this is slowly sinking in, I think. Tell me this, though. What's your story? Why you aren't on Tridesicon any more? Why did you move to Uxtal, and why did you come to earth? Why did you show me all this, why..." The floodgates were now open!

"Okay, take it easy, little *man*. One question at a time."

"Why aren't you on Tridesicon anymore? What made you move?" asked Blake.

"My friend, answers will come but for now you must inherit our culture as God prepares you for mission and battle. In this way, at your core you will understand who and why we are, the love of our Creator, and His mission which calls us forward."

"Your time here at Earth Lounge will be short, for you WILL be sent home. And if you recall any of this, it will seem like a dream. Wisps of recall will come and go, but at the appointed time you will enter

Borealis. Then you will remember what I have said and begin your part in our holy mission. Be patient, Blake. The time is now. The time is forever."

And in the passage of time, as foretold, after residing *incognito* in the mall wall above the burger joint, Blake would eventually wander back to his old life in Riverside, completely forgetting Derrek, Uxtal and its ways.

But for now, Blake, heavy with sleep, slouched on his sprawling couch. "Okay, Derrek, now...forever... he mumbled, as his eyelids closed, his heart full in the sweet yet strange night.

*The fear of the Lord leads to life, so that one may sleep satisfied, untouched by evil.*

**Proverbs 19:23 HCSB translation**

# CHAPTER 22: LIFE THERE

IF ON A SLEEPY SATURDAY YOU HAPPENED TO WALK through Riverside's local, ugly, and aging mall, *Cascade Mall*, you would wonder, first, why you really were there at all, perhaps wasting your time, and, second, if you had your feelers out, you would somehow sense that there was more to *Cascade Mall* than met the eye. It was a feeling, yes, an unheard static continually turned on, although it could not be heard. Yes, *Cascade Mall* was a snowy screen, which boasted a faint test pattern like vintage TV. It was curiously off and on at the same time! You'd be there looking for soccer socks or a cheap camera, but behind the walls it seemed there was something going on, of life-death importance. It didn't make sense, really. It just was there!

Blake slugged along, shaking his head. He hated *Cascade Mall*, its clumps of mocking kids, cheerless shoppers, and brightly lit bargain shops. Kiosks of cheap goods, skin products, and odors filled the corridors, as Blake slowly made his way forward.

"Gotta speed up," thought Blake. "The morning's almost gone and I've gotta get back! Almost there. Just some stupid soccer socks, bright green!"

A buzzing, no, more like a low impact siren, tapped on his complaint. Socks, indeed. Buzz. Buzz. The noise intensified. Blake held his ears to silence the assault; shoppers passing by seemed unaffected.

"What's this blasted noise anyway?" Is this a dream? thought Blake.

The buzzing now pulled Blake closer to its source, a pillar peppered with small holes. It extended floor to ceiling.

"Strange!" muttered Blake. As he stepped closer, he laughed. "Really, really strange!"

The pillar was not a sound amplifier or speaker, yet, somehow buzzing, increasing in volume, emanated from its tiny holes. Blake touched the pillar, checking for any sound vibrations. If it were a speaker, well, it would be the most updated piece of equipment at *Cascade Mall*. His finger slipped to the right, covering one of the pillar's holes. Vibration, no, a trembling, took hold of Blake. He turned back to see if anyone was watching. The small crowd, moved slowly forward, unaware. His trembling increased. He was being sucked into the hole. No pain. Just an insistent pulling. Rather weird, but somehow pleasant!

"What's happening?" yelled Blake. "Hey, just wait a minute, you!"

All went black as if every light that had ever existed was suddenly shut off. Next, a merging of light poked into Blake's darkness, and an ever-brightening view, a foreign place, stood stretching before him.

"Where am I?" thought Blake.

"Borealis, my friend! Borealis!"

Blake, stunned, stood motionless, adjusting to his new-found light.

"You're here in Borealis! Welcome!" repeated the friendly voice.

"But, where, where are you?" Blake asked as he turned around, squinting at the brilliance surrounding him.

A gentle laughter came forward, and an engaging, encouraging, yes, loving laughter embraced Blake. "You are simply here because when you were there you touched the portal."

Blake looked for someone, anyone, who might be the source of the gentle voice, but saw no one. It was like talking to the air as the conversation continued.

"You are most welcome, Blake Armstrong!"

"Hey, how do you know my name?"

"We know all names here on Borealis!"

"Yeah, but how?"

"There is much to learn, and we will show you the way. Be patient, Blake. We assure you that you are safe and very special to Borealis."

Blake's mouth dropped open as light surrounding him began to slowly morph, its texture, boasting a quality which reminded him of winter's end, yes, a new light, replacing winter's oppression. By steps the invading light increased in brilliance, one, two, three, increase, up, increase, up arrow, revealing a being, an exquisite female, dressed in saffron silk which billowed ever so slightly in the breeze. Blake sensed that it was springtime as the composite fragrances of flowers, sweet air and this being enticed him forward.

"Who are you?"

"Elra is my name."

"E..E..Elra," stuttered Blake, "Elra, why am I here?"

"You touched the portal, Blake. The portal out there."

"Yeah, well, sure, of course," managed Blake, awakening from his stupor. "Borealis, right?"

"Yes, Blake. Borealis. Welcome home."

"Home? What do you mean, E..E.." asked Blake.

"Elra."

"Yes, of course, Elra. Elra, how can all this be my home. I'm from earth and..."

Elra smiled. "Home is where the heart is, Blake."

"What do you mean?"

"It's all a matter of the heart," explained Elra. "Not where you are standing exactly, but where you stand in your heart. Major things like: who or what guides you, principles, disciplines of life, what gives life to your life." Elra stopped, stepping closer to Blake. "You see, Blake, you've been here before in our satellite Earth Lounge. You need to know that when one abruptly leaves Borealis, the way you did before, all memory of Borealis is erased for good reason. You see, what makes perfect sense here becomes corrupted out there."

Blake looked blank.

Elra continued, "You see, it's a different paradigm here, a completely unique paradigm. Love is the center of life here in Borealis. All we do and say, everything is steeped in this Love, not just surface love but indwelling, alive love which fully forgives, redeems, and enables."

Blake was beginning to understand.

"God has His way here in Borealis, guiding, but never forcing, our destiny, every conversation and action. God led us here from Tridesicon, a remnant we were and remain; it's a story of great blessing, replicated on earth as well, where people were led from captivity into wilderness that they might gain access to a promised land. Borealis is our promised land. Here in Borealis God is primary. God is not relegated to myth, locked in a box, or worshipped one out of seven days each week. You see, God, who is our Creator, Redeemer, and Sustainer, stands among us ALL of the time. We know this! We live this! We affirm his presence and majesty by how we live our lives. Borealis is what earth has groaned for, for millennia! Borealis is God's promise fulfilled and sets a new paradigm for all of His creation. He is working out his purposes, and each principle perfectly dovetails into the next!"

Blake nodded assent. "Well, Elra, what now?"

"Why, whatever do you mean, Blake?" she teased.

Blake laughed. He was enjoying her company. She was exquisitely made and everything she said was infused with kindness and light. Elra was gentle. He could see that. And when she spoke Blake was at peace. She was speaking not something from a conference table, but from her heart and at the same time, God's Heart. Her way somehow stepped forward gently, alive with healing and understanding which inspired in Blake a renewed vision. A vision that in the end all would be well, but that there was yet much to endure before all would be well.

"Derrek," she said, breaking his reverie.

"Derrek?"

"Yes, come with me. Derrek is just beyond the mangroves, there, over there. It will all come back, Blake, slowly at first, but completely, and you and Derrek can pick up where you left off!"

Elra glided before Blake, taking his hand, leading him gently forward. "He's over there, Blake," she smiled. "Now, go, meet your brother."

"My broth...?"

225

"Go," she motioned.

Derrek, intent upon his book, stood at a bench overlooking a long reflective pool. A cascade of water splashed playfully upon several narrow horizontal juts placed boldly across a tall rectangular stone block nearby; the water was melodic.

"Derrek, are you Derrek?" asked Blake.

"Blake! It's been a while." Derrek exclaimed, as he opened his arms wide and embraced a surprised Blake.

"Uh, well, oh..." managed Blake.

"Brother, it'll come back, slowly at first, but it will come back...Give it a chance!"

"Give what a chance?"

"Oh, you'll see!"

Once again light began to flex, to change, to morph. Colors were now slowly intensifying around him and there was that familiar peace again. Blake stood transfixed. No fear. Only peace, and in this exquisite moment he knew where he stood. Really. "Why, yes, Borealis is home," he told himself, "just like God's Heart has always been home to the faithful!"

In this moment if Blake had been Moses he would have built an altar of twelve stones at the foot of the mountain. He would have run to the burning bush, removing his sandals on holy ground, humbly falling to the ground before the great I AM! Instead, Blake nodded, laughing. He jumped for joy around Derrek.

"Derrek, old boy, I get it. I remember. It's all coming back!" shouted Blake.

"Always does!" laughed Derrek.

"So much to do!" explained Blake.

Suddenly, for Blake there was a shift, an elsewhere, a blending, a familiar whirling of sound and color. Dirt-red ancient patterns, Aztec-like, boldly stretched across a stone room, wall by wall, surrounding Blake in a bizarre hieroglyphic habitat. He was elsewhere. Each shape, though foreign, conveyed comfort, a soothing, healing salve upon a wound, a wound he could not see but somehow knew was there, outside the room, beyond where he was, a people, yes, his people, not here but there, beyond the walls which now so perfectly enfolded him.

Ever since he had entered Uxtal and now Borealis for the first time, Blake felt more centered, sharp, aware. Yes, definitely yes, it was all coming back, full force. His keen discernment was rapidly maturing, wisdom replacing knowledge; a new, brand new paradigm stood within him. Resolve. Application. Here, oh, yes, here in Borealis, he was free to grow, to become, to stretch his giftings and build. Here he was loved, supported, and encouraged beyond himself to a vision he once had years ago: a time of restoration, indwelling, peace. A peace that would perfectly transcend worlds, galaxies, suns, planets, and the freezing, darkening space which slid between these entities. Yes, God was at work, afoot, and somehow more visible here in Borealis than Blake had ever experienced before. Perhaps it was the people of this strange world. Their ways were loving, although foreign, yet full of encouragement, a heart-felt "Can I help you deepen your resolve to achieve your goal" kind of encouragement. Yes, he was still on earth but beyond the mall walls Borealis changed everything. Here there was an inner light, not given by the sun or any other celestial source, but here the living God had His way. He inhabited not only the praises of His people here but fully dwelled in each humble heart. The people of Borealis, once fiercely oppressed in Tridesicon, had grown into a remnant of good, hard-working, God-fearing souls who, as time passed, transmigrated away from their enslavement and tyrant Micron, but especially far from the evil Empress Mordna, and her minions.

Borealis, you see, was a promised land, at least a hoped-for land. A land the enslaved Tridesicons had envisioned for years, in their oppressed hearts. The vision had kept them moving forward in hope. Finally, in the fullness of time, opportunity came to them. An escape from Egypt into the wilderness, so to speak. But where was Canaan, or rather Borealis, their promised land? On a thread, a transmigration thread, they made their way, a mixture of refugees, grateful to leave Tridesiconian oppression behind. Their new home, Borealis, full of light, would be established where they would go completely unnoticed until the fullness of time.

Derrek slowly made his way toward Blake, crossing a bamboo walkway, which carefully lifted bridge-like above an immense polished slate floor.

"So much to do!" repeated Blake. "The enemy is building forces. It's coming for us. Earth needs your help now. Borealis must join the fight. KidzTurf has been destroyed. Tridesicon is flexing its muscle. It's Armageddon-time, man, the end." warned Blake, now out of breath.

"Borealis is ready, Blake," assured Derrek. "We are ready. Join us!"

*The steadfast of mind You will keep in perfect peace, because he trusts in You.*

**Isaiah 26:3 NKJV translation**

## CHAPTER 23: RECRUITMENT

IT WAS A NEW MORNING, COLD AND WET, AND BLAKE WAS preparing for his journey. Via Oskar's GRD (God's Righteous Deployment) brilliant invention a unique plan had been initiated. Blake held before him a miniature hologram, which would direct him to *soul* spots. Oskar's GRD was brilliant, producing at headquarters for trained recruits a translucent map of the entire area, speckled with red dots revealing all locations of those with *good hearts*. Blake and his group of twenty were assigned the gigantic city of Los Angeles, and exclusively for himself, Hollywood. The hologram remained plastered before him upon the air as Blake looked over Sunset Boulevard for any red dots. There were only three. Although disappointed, Blake accepted the fact that only *good* and *righteous* persons could ever be recruited to Borealis. He quickly scanned several locations on his *Corneal Eye Pros* binoculars, made possible via Oskar's technology; they had the ability to scan things and secure identities deeply within Blake's *memory*. With Oskar's miracle binoculars, one could basically attain *photographic memory*, useful in any *search*. Blake slipped into his *Transleather* suit. A cord on the back of his suit automatically *slithered* out, climbing up to Blake's neck. It attached itself upon his back, and Blake winced once it pricked him.

He quickly thought, "*Transleather* go stealth."

Within a blink, most of his body morphed invisible. "Of course I need my helmet to complete the *Transleather* covering." Blake reminded himself, as he walked to the front entrance where his helmet lay. The door flew open, suddenly.

"Blake, where is my... WHAT THE!" cried out Derrek as he backed away in horror, seeing only Blake's head floating in the air.

"Oh sorry, give me a sec." Blake said calmly, quickly turning off his suit as his lower body became visible.

"I forgot to put on my helmet, man. That's all! It's all good." Blake extended his hand and the sweating soldier took hold of it.

"Whoa, okay, that really made me jump!"

"Sorry, Bro, what do you need?" Derrek stood there, dazed, deep in thought, as he fought to recall why he was there at all. "Oh, yeah! Do you know where my *sky-flyer* is? I left it right in the slot box, but it's gone."

"Check security. You came back late last night; you might have parked it in somebody else's place."

"Yeah, you're right, I bet. Thanks. By the way we need to head out! You ready?"

"I'm ready." Blake picked up his supplies backpack, strapped on his firearm, fitted his helmet, and trailed Derrek out the door.

"I was assigned Hollywood today. What about you?" Blake inquired.

"Beverly Hills. It's gonna be a real short trip; there's only one person that's worth recruiting, and she's like twelve!"

The duo exited through the size converter archway and Derrek continued the conversation, "I see that you only have, what, five people to recruit?"

"No, just two." Derrek whistled at the amount.

"Los Angeles is pretty much dried up as well, barely anybody left who believes in the Creator. Why weren't we assigned to Arkansas or Mississippi? There are so, so, many worth recruiting out there."

"Group A-99 already has it covered, remember?" A *humph* was all Blake got back from Derrek.

"I'd just wish we had the easy job." Blake silently agreed, but decided to keep it to himself.

"This way." Derrek corrected Blake's direction to the left.

"Oh yeah, the garage entrance is malfunctioning, right?"

"Yep. That's why we're gonna have to go this way. It's a bit of a detour but we'll only be a few minutes late. But we gotta hurry, everybody's waiting on us."

They both walked down the hallway to the stall flip door which read, "VACANT." Derrek pushed a large rusty lock button on the wall; the screen showed the stall door automatically swinging to a close and the bolt securing the door. Now with the stall safe and empty, Blake flicked the blinking switch next to the lock button and exit was made. The entire stall floor slid open, making room for the toilet, causing a low rumble. Steam hissed and seeped through the outline of the blocked

231

exit and the wall before the two boys slowly began to angle downwards, transferring from an upright surface to a completely flat floor.

"Gets me every time! Man, that's so cool!" Blake said.

"Give it a few weeks, man, it's no big deal." Derrek threw back, nonchalantly walking through an opening with Blake tailing behind.

Seconds after Derrek had manually unlocked the bolt and the duo had left the stall, the wall and toilet reset to their original, inconspicuous position. It was deadly silent inside the food court since opening time wouldn't be for another hour. They crossed the food court with low echoes, down past the cinema, to the side entrance. A huge-half frozen raindrop landed on Blake's neck, sending chills up his back. The rain picked up and began to seriously pour. Both went grim and their eyes squinted. The wind, rain, and cold temperatures almost made it unbearable to step outside. But they had a mission after all, and they had received their assignments. The other guys were nowhere to be seen, but both Blake and Derrek could hear them clearly.

"Where are them *Dillweeds*?" Derreck scanned around the parking lot and the woods when he bumped into something.

"Holy crap, who the...?" Derreck shouted, surprised.

"Turn on your *Transleather* suit, dummy."

"Oh right, the upgrade." Blake remembered that you could see other invisible people if you yourself were invisible as well. It was part of the upgrade. Both of them agreed instantly, "*Transleather*, go stealth." And suddenly a dozen teenage boys appeared in their own *Transleather* suits.

"Wow, look at you! Everyone looks fantastic! These suits are incredible! All right there, I guess it's time to go ahead and look for recruits, right? Remember, only recruit those who are listed on your holograms; strictly, no one else. You got that?" All heads bobbed.

"Okay, great. Hitchhike your way to your assigned location and be back here before sunset. Go!"

232

At once everyone scrambled, sprinting into the woods. Blake high-fived Derrek before they headed in opposite directions. Blake could still remember his map's route to Hollywood and its winding path, due to his *Corneal Eye Pros* binoculars. He could see an exact path to Sunset Boulevard glowing in front of him. He spotted a delivery truck turning down the path and saw it as opportunity. Blake broke into *burst* speed, running parallel with the truck. Before it could drive further away, Blake leapt into the truck bed. He landed with a thud on his side, hands gripping the tailgate. The driver heard this and peered out of his open window and checked the side, and, of course, saw nothing unusual.

The driver resumed his boring station at the wheel and found that he had drifted to the left a little too far, nearly colliding with an oncoming car. He instantly whipped the wheel to the right, steering away. With the sudden turn, Blake's hand slipped to the back corner of the truck's rear end and, flapping in the wind like a kite, he threw the rear panel's latch open with a grunt, managing to swing himself up and over the gate, then rolled across the truck bed once again. A crate's corner stopped him, hitting him in the back. It didn't hurt too much, but he did hear a loud,"CRUNCH!"

"Ah, dang it!" he said, exasperated. His *Transleather* suit was impaired. Its connection gear was sliced through. Blake was now visible. Completely!

"I'll manage," he assured himself. The truck suddenly stopped. The traffic glowed brilliant RED. Blake looked to the open doors and viewed the driver in the car behind his truck with his mouth wide open at the sight.

"What must he be thinking. *Truck driver nearly wrecks his vehicle as doors of the delivery truck fly open randomly while kid appears out of nowhere rolling on the floor!* Oh, man."

Blake laughed to himself just a little. For a second, he thought it was over and that the truck driver would notice him, but the driver remained preoccupied, as loud rap music bellowed from both windows. The truck lunged forward at GREEN. For Blake it seemed like no time had passed at all when the truck quickly stopped like a hard kick in the butt.

"Get up, hitchhiker!" It was the truck driver. Blake had been discovered.

"Mmmh, wha? Get off me." Blake mumbled at the angry man.

"Get lost!" commanded the driver, as he tossed Blake from the back of his open truck bed hard to the ground. Blake slowly stood up, facing a gray sky, which arched high overhead. He shook dirt from his hair. The truck roared to a start and sped away. To Blake's right at the top of a ramp which quickly rose away from him, he spotted a sign which read, *Exit 57*!

"Only one mile away. This is great! Only wish I had the GRD coordinates." Disappointed yet pumped he started his short trek to Hollywood. Blake decided to leave the road side to venture through the hilly terrain to his right. He would remain partially hidden, at least for a while. An hour later he vaulted a curious electric fence, which stood affixed to huge illuminated letters.

Standing at the back of the nine looming letters Blake wondered what they spelled, "D-o-o-w-y-l-l-o-h. Doowylloh?" Then, of course, the proverbial *light bulb in the sky moment* hit him.

"Oh, wait a minute. Hollywood!" Blake was amazed that he was actually standing at the *HOLLYWOOD* sign. But his marveling quickly stopped as he heard a shout!

"Don't move!" Blake spun around, eyeing a police officer with pistol aimed at him! Yards away, the *menace* proceeded swiftly at Blake. "Sir, you're gonna have to come with me." the grim officer commanded.

"Thanks, but no thanks, officer! I got better things to do." And with that, Blake ran and jumped around the "O" in the sign as he tucked into a roll down the hill. The perfect getaway. Blake quickly estimated that he was about to smash into a looming tree. He prepared himself to parkour jump. He rolled to his feet, springing high into the air. Deftly, he cleared the tree, avoiding three huge branches. About to land, Blake could tell his feet would not match his speed. In spite of his laser-quick appraisal, he fell hard to the ground.

"Okay, well, that's enough rolling around for one day. "Blake muttered, standing up and cracking his back. The roller coaster had finally stopped, and he had made it down the entire hill. His head felt like there was a heavy metal band banging hard inside. He looked up the hill. The police officer was gone. Blake gave a *humph* in triumph and continued on the path. He passed by the Griffith Observatory and made it to North Western Avenue, which would be a direct beeline to Sunset Boulevard. Blake rushed ahead.

It occurred to him, "How am I supposed to know who to recruit with my *Corneal Eye Pros* binoculars destroyed?"

Blake shook his head. All he could remember was that there were two people somewhere in the downtown *theater district*. He would just have to ask around, to see if there were any *believers* and *wing it* and hope that he had chosen wisely. Minutes later, a bundle of theaters stood towering above Blake. The structures were massive. He spotted a lone pedestrian stepping out to the curb.

"Hey do you believe in the creator and his son our savior...?"

"Shut up, preacher-man! Flick off." The sassy woman walked away, leaving her assailant.

"Well, she definitely wasn't on the list!"

Blake shook his head and continued his crusade. Little did he know how many denials would be shouted in reply. People threw fits and cursed at him. Some just shrugged and said, "Not Interested!"

Soon two security guards grabbed Blake, pulling him aside to talk. "Hey look, little dude. Your *evangelizing* is causing trouble here. We're escorting you away and..."

Blake, interrupting, shouted, "Wait you can't do this! I haven't found my targets yet; they need to come with me!"

An older security guard tried to put in a word but was cut off by Blake. "This is America, we have freedom of speech and..."

"Mister!" yelled the guard. "This is private property. Leave now. If not, you're under arrest, do you understand?"

Blake's mind raced. He had to come up with a brilliant reason. "Do you understand how badly I need a restroom?" Blake had the guard there.

"Fine. But be quick." The guard shoved Blake in the direction of the men's room.

"I'll be waiting right out here." The guard took his stance to the side of the bathroom door as Blake went in. Blake really didn't have to go. He stood there staring at himself in the mirror.

"Dang it, it's no use." The urinal behind him flushed and a scruffy kid walked to the sink to wash his hands.

"Hey man, can I ask you a question?" "No." was the cold hard reply from the kid.

"Let me introduce myself, my name is Blake Armstrong and..." Instantly the kid's eye's bulged.

"Blake? Blake Armstrong? President of KidzTurf?" the boy asked with intensity.

"Yes! Yes, that's me. How do you know who I am?" Blake inquired.

The kid was now shaking, vibrating, looking at Blake, terrified, as he screamed, "ZOMBIE!!!" pushing his way out of the bathroom.

"Hey! Hey come back!" Blake ran after him, rocketing past the security guard, who in turn went after Blake. It was now a three-way chase. They wound their way through the theater halls to the back of an old building. The scruffy kid knew where he was going. With two more turns, he spied a back-exit door. He burst through it, running down a narrow stretch of slippery pavement. It had begun to rain. Blake continued to be quick and agile, applying parkour maneuvers, as he easily traversed pipes and old theater walls. Of course, the less agile security guards quickly fell behind as Blake continued to vault high rails and ledges, remaining hotly in sync with his runner's tricks and moves.

"There's no chance that little runt will beat the almighty parkour master!" Blake thought.

The *runt* jumped onto an air generator, leaping onto a short fire escape ladder. Like a monkey, hotly pursued, Blake quickly flew up an available ladder with little effort. Still, the scruffy child took advantage, well acquainted with his city turf as he flew to Blake's ladder screw-ons. He rapidly removed the screws, causing Blake to dangle precariously, ten feet above the alleyway.

With a smirk, the little runner yelled down below, "Good effort, but I'm a native. I know my territory. Better than you! But I do congratulate you, for your parkour, old man! After all, parkour is a dying art, right?" he chided.

"Get to the point!" Blake yelled back, panting, but continuing his ascent toward the runt.

"If you say who you are, and if my zombie magazine coverage is correct, well, the dead should remain dead, right?"

"This guy is looney." Blake muttered to himself. But then, suddenly he felt gravity changing. It was like Geo's gravity manipulator maneuvers, but somehow subtler. Wild-eyed, Blake scanned about, and, to his horror, he realized that he was falling backwards. His ladder had detached from the roof, as it pushed away, separate from the building. Just before Blake's plummet, he glared at his pursuing *runt* standing in front of an opening elevator door.

"Just survive, Blake, just do that one thing and you got him!" Blake had a plan, but first he needed to not die. Fortunately, this was a small alleyway and the ladder's top latches had fallen, jamming into the opposite building's wall. What had been a perfectly vertical ladder, now lay stretched across the alleyway, a bridge to an upper floor. Its two latches had propped onto a narrowly projected sill. Blake's feet dangled helplessly, as his hands clung on to the steel bars for life. He dangled in shock for a moment, then set his survival plan into motion. It was a huge risk! Could it be done? After all he had done it before. He swung himself to a window sill, grabbing hold of two slack telephone wires and with a mighty tug, he snapped them from the pole, safe with his gloves as he swung down grasping several sparking wires.

"Take a deep breath, 1... 2... 3!" As if he were Tarzan, Blake leapt toward the runt from a sill edge with a cry, free-falling toward the alleyway below. With only a few yards from falling SPLAT on gravel, his wire cord grew taut as Blake swung back to an opposing wall. The moment had come, so he released the wire. Feet first, pencil-like but not rigid, Blake entered a slanting basement window. He tumbled into the darkness and thudded to an abrupt halt. It was an elevator door. This had taken thirty seconds. Once he had come to his senses, he heard the soft descent of an elevator!

"Could this be? Could this be my little runt?" thought Blake.

At once he jumped to his feet and using his Metal Mashers to pry the door open. With ease he jumped down the shaft, grasping the primary cable, linked to the descending elevator. The elevator abruptly stopped, propelling Blake downward through the elevator's rooftop. In a shamble of dust and metal pieces, Blake landed on top of the clueless child, tackling him from above. Half of Blake's impact now transferred to the kid and both shared identical pain. Blake rammed the kid up against the elevator wall.

"TELL ME! How do you know who I am! Why did you try to kill me?" Blake spat.

"Hold on, old man, let go of me!" the boy shouted, helplessly squirming.

The elevator doors pushed open as Blake threw the boy to the floor. He flew at the *runt*, ready to pound the truth from him! Suddenly, Blake looked up, beyond the boy, beyond the clanging of elevator cables, to three cots, a rumbling fridge, and three piles of dirty clothes. There, on two beds sat two boys. Thick cement and metal dust slowly cleared, as Blake's mouth dropped open. Blake shook his head. Two teenage boys, slashed in painful scars, heads hung low, sat frozen in submission. It wasn't their physical condition that stopped Blake's heart. It was their faces.

"Oskar? Dawson?" Blake shouted, as his trembling voice shot through the clearing air.

*Come, let us deal shrewdly with them, lest they multiply, and it happen, in the event of war, that they also join our enemies and fight against us.*

**Exodus 1:10 NKJV translation**

## CHAPTER 24: MORDNA RETURNS

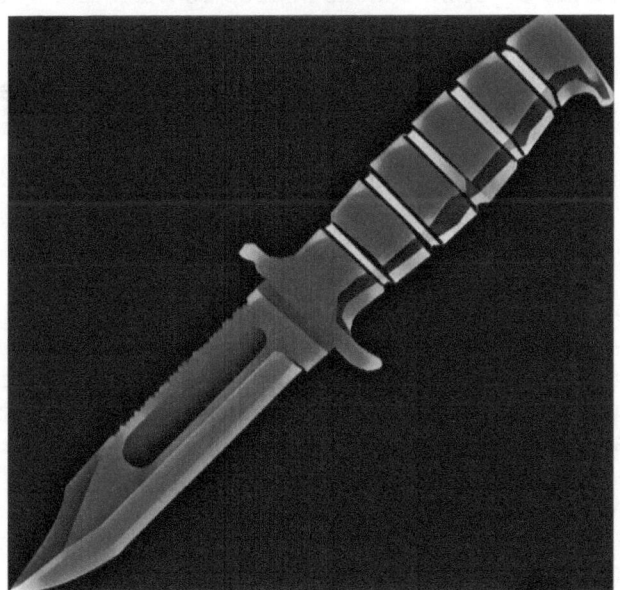

A FULL MINUTE HAD PASSED, and yet Blake stood in silence, mouth agape. He thought his friend was dead. This perception was mutual. Dawson was the first to speak. "How is this possible? You were dead! The plane killed you!"

Zac, the runt, his eyes growing wider, gave answer to Dawson, "I'm tellin' you man, he's a zombie. I read about it in my comics!"

"Shut up, Zac. Is this... is it really you, Blake?" Dawson asked, shaking his head as he walked toward Blake. He laid a hand on his shoulder. Tears brimmed his dirty eyes as his hand clenched Blake. He then smiled, bear-hugging his long-lost friend. They embraced for the longest time, weeping on each other. Oskar got up and rather formally welcomed Blake back from the dead, also with uncomfortable hugs, a few high fives and measured tears. Zac, cross-legged, watched all of this from his cot.

"Sooo, does this mean he isn't a zombie?" Zac quivered.

"No, this means he is a survivor, just like us." Dawson broke away, grabbing hunks of bread and canned soup from the fridge. The weary, yet grateful trio sat down and ate in deep conversation, following by poignant silence.

"Dawson, looking at his back-from-the-dead friend, asked, "Just wondering, Blake, how in the world DID you survive?"

"Well, guys," Blake replied, "It's a long story, lots of twists and turns. Literally."

And so, Blake began tracing his misadventures, starting with the gravity war. He explained how he had escaped the KidzTurf plane crash, his parent's murder, how he ultimately killed Geo, what it was like constantly on the run, Uxtal, his loving welcome into Borealis, and now recruitment of people for the Lord's army. Once he finished his story, Oskar and Dawson laughed heartily, swaying back and forth, branches in a mighty wind. Zac sat there staring at Blake, nodding his head, having become now an ardent believer.

"Hey, I think this dude has told the truth here."

"Yeah right, you think he has?" Dawson threw back with his familiar sarcastic grin.

"Well hold on, Dawson, let's not jump to conclusions."

Oskar removed his glasses and wiped them clean. "Do you really mean all of this? About Borealis and the Lord's Army and all?" Oskar asked.

"Yes! I'm telling you guys the truth." Blake answered.

Oskar pondered, "Well, it does make sense, and I do believe in God. Okay, Blake, I'm gonna buy it. I really do! Now can I be a part of your, I mean His, army, your team? After all, God created me, right, and somehow in joining, I can return the favor, right?"

"Oh, yes we can. We must." Dawson mocked.

"I take it you don't believe in God, Dawson." Blake parried.

"I did, back when KidzTurf was thriving. But after that plane crash, man, after all of those deaths, after being thrown out on the street like a bum, I thought, man, how could there be a God. A God who would allow all of this mayhem. He is either dead, seriously uncaring or never existed at all. I don't care, anymore. I just need to survive and help my friends. Who needs God, anyway?"

"You do, Dawson." Blake looked long and hard at Dawson. He was serious, more serious than Dawson could ever have imagined.

"Psssh, I need to go!"

Blake watched Dawson walk to the dark wall which twisted away from the boys.

Blake sighed, "Zac, you also need to change. And you need to change now. There's no more time, man! I'm just gonna lay this out. There is no such thing as zombies. Period. It's fake crap! You gotta throw out all that stuff and embrace our Father's love. Our Heavenly Father, get it?"

"Do you promise me zombies aren't real?" Zac demanded, wiping a few tears away. He was only eight.

Blake nodded. "Okay. It's gonna be all right. I promise. I know, Zac, you want outta here, to erase and start over but I got to let you know that although there is a way to handle all of this, getting away from here is going to require you to be brave, very brave. Listen. You've got

243

to trust more than your instincts, more than what you see around you. Even though everything seems broken and dead now, God is still in charge! You are not alone! God loves you, especially now. God is standing with you and wants you to trust Him. Do you believe me?"

Zac, wiping away his tears, nodded, "Yeah, Blake, I think so."

"Ya gotta know it, Zac, in your heart. You gotta believe that God is REALLY in charge and will lead you to a safe place."

"I guess I believe," whimpered Zac, "It's just like I look around at what's happening and I'm afraid."

"It's O.K. to be afraid."

"I mean really scared. Am I gonna die?" cried Zac.

Blake replied, "Someday. Just not now, Zac! . We've got a lot of livin' to do, so, stand up, believe that God's got your back and let's get going, okay?"

Laughing, Zac yelled, "Hey, should I throw out my zombie apocalypse weapons?"

Thunder suddenly made its way through the maze of corridors, and roared at them, commanding the boys' attention.

"It's not the zombie apocalypse you need to be prepared for, it's Tridesicon's ATTACK." Blake warned.

"Huh?" Zac had never heard of 'Tridesicon'.

"Oskar, Zac. Hey, Dawson, can you hear me? We need to get out of here. Micron's army, I mean Trigon's Emperor Micron, is supposed to be here any day now. This could be it. Borealis is not too far from here but we need to bust a move. Like NOW!"

Blake herded his buddies to leave the building. Oppressive clouds attacked the sky which arched over them in an ever-deepening darkness. Blake backtracked his original path up toward the Hollywood sign. They leaped from a ledge onto a truck bed of an oblivious driver, hitching for themselves a free ride down the rutted highway. Far away, the setting sun drilled its last light, piercing a collection of rising clouds, a splendid interplay of light and dark. Blake thought of Borealis, its glorious ever-present light and morphing colors. He smiled as he thought of Elra and the embracing encouragement of Borealis. This warm moment lasted only seconds. Blake blinked. What followed completely overtook him as he flew from side to side in the truck bed, pulling his friends down to safety. The setting sun was quickly, silently, turning blue, a cold, vibrant but dark icy blue, Tridesicon blue! The horizon stood tall, brandishing a dull, quickly darkening blue as clouds, halted in obeisance, darkened all the more. Quickly, the temperature plummeted from a comfortable 58 degrees to 10. A residue of rain had already begun to freeze on the pitted road stretching before them. It pelted the boys as they lifted their jackets over their heads. And down it came with vengeance, hard as iron.

"We're doomed!" yelled Blake, frozen, shocked, recoiling from the onslaught. "Earth's Armageddon has arrived."

As hard rain continued to assault Blake, a subtle change erupted, provoking an *intensity* which *spewed* out of the darkness. Slowly, an emergent light, began to pierce its way through the vertical torrent, vibrating a warm grasp upon Blake's back, as it coiled its triangular presence before his face. The Trigon had returned! Blessed assurance had just arrived!

"You can do this, Blake! The Master is with you!" assured the Trigon. "He will never leave you!"

Blake shuddered in the freezing rain, shocked by the intrusion. "The Trigon!" he laughed. "Trigon. Here. Now. But, why? How?"

Warm light continued to enfold Blake, as the Trigon declared: "He who dwells in the shelter of the Most High will abide in the shadow of the Almighty. I am your refuge and fortress. Trust in me. Come to me in this dark hour, Blake."

Emboldened, Blake, shaking the rain from his head, quickly removed his coat, and forcefully joggled some of the deluge off. Wet clothes are hard to maneuver but he quickly slid back into his coat.

"Hurry!" Blake instructed. "Do it."

The two boys didn't think twice, as they shook their coats in the drilling rain, conceding that any instructions were better than none!

"Quick, we need to get outta here! Borealis is not far now! Micron and Mordna can't get to us there! At least, I don't think so! Get ready to jump!" Blake yelled over the wind.

The other guys were terrified, as the swiftly moving truck made its way along the deserted highway. Their wide eyes took it all in: with the sun glowing blue and the surrounding clouds, darkening not as in ordinary nightfall, something evil was overtaking, definitely overtaking, step by step, inserting its massive presence, attacking their minds, their every thought. Anything that had ever strengthened them in the past now seemed limp and unavailable. The end had come! Its evil battlefield forming, twisted before them, unfurling itself in massive might. Loud and ominous, a honking suddenly came from behind the truck as a gut-wrenching loud, splintered crashing exploded into the night. Blake whipped around, watching a long line of propelling cars, one crashing into the other.

As the freezing rain continued, the glazed road easily pushed cars in all directions, its back like a rising whale from the sea, torrents of water splaying about. Here Blake sensed the truck gliding, no, swiftly careening across the highway away from the smashed line of cars. The truck slanted further down, then re-crossing the icy road, lurched, jabbed, then swerved completely off the lane, bumping in its punishing mad flight.

"Jump! Jump now!" yelled Blake as the boys *flew* from the pickup, onto frozen ground.

"This has got to be my last stunt, God!" Blake thought. The Trigon's words played an encore: "*You can do this, Blake! The Master is with you! He will never leave you.*"

The frozen grass welcomed Blake's face, which fully took the blows of his colossal skid. Suddenly, a huge explosion erupted into the night, as thick black smoke gyrated high above. Blake hurled toward a huge boulder which knocked the wind out of him. He rolled to his side, gasping for air, as a massive fire ball landed in the middle of the road, fully cracking the whale's back! The pickup truck had taken flight, flipping over to the other side of the road in flames. All that had remained on the road were eight wrecked cars and the carnage of a blown-up gas tanker. Next thing Blake knew, there was an outcry from Oskar. Blake mustered all of his remaining power, and wobbled over to his friend. Yet again, his best friend was the one who took the injury.

Submerged in a mass of weeds, Oskar lay quivering in pain. Blake bent over to help. A jagged piece of shrapnel wedged inside Oskar. Red oozed soundlessly from his side. Smaller bits of metal had embedded in Oskar's hands, and two were directly aimed at the nerd's heart.

"Holy, dude, you're hurt. You're hurt bad! Very, very, very bad! Oh crap, . hey Hey guys, help! Get over here! Oskar's dying!"

"Whaaa?" whimpered Oskar. "No, I'm okay, right? I'll be okay, right? Just stay with me, okay?" asked Oskar.

Another explosion. And another. This time Blake clearly saw what had happened. A dark, dark light had zipped from out of nowhere, blowing up a nearby sedan. Blake looked up at the heavens and saw the black rain; trillions of black particles had come from the clouds, beams, menacing lasers pointing in every direction! Death had simply showed up. The army had finally come. Oskar's hand touched Blake's bent shoulder, commanding his attention.

"Get out of here. Don't even argue, I have calculated my circumstances and yours; this is what must be done."

"But, Oskar, just let me take you to Borealis..."

"Just do it. Screw you if you don't; just do it. The GRD is in place and at the right time will help. I promise you I know where I'm going. God and I... we talked a little on that truck ride. Last thing He said was, 'It's time to come home'. And so, I am. At the end of this short journey..."

"No chance, my friend. Borealis has cures for this, it's only right down the street..."

"Love you, man, take care. Don't let me down. I'll... see you... later..."

And with that, those vibrant grey eyes rolled back, and his soul lifted from its shell to rise in victory to its eternal home, leaving Blake, his beloved friend. Blake's hands and eyes squeezed as he rocked his old friend in his arms and whispered his own last goodbye. And the drizzle of rain had its way, from mist to downpour. Explosions surrounded Blake everywhere. He could hardly see anything through the rising smoke, except fire and ice. Blake then left his friend in the grass in peace and bolted for the others. Dawson and Zac, unhurt, both whimpered under an abandoned truck. Blake ducked in, escaping impending doom and explained his plan.

"All right, so here's how it's gonna go down!"instructed Blake.

Dawson shook Blake, asking, "Hey wait, man, are you okay? Oskar's dead, right?"

"I'm fine! We need to move on." Blake said bitterly. "He's no longer ten feet deep in crap;  we are! Now, here's my game plan."

Part of Blake mourned his friend, but his instincts and the words of Trigon had kicked in to push him forward.

"There are dozens of tires out there rolling around. Find one with its hubcap still intact and use it as a shield and hold it above your head. We have less than a mile to go, just across the wood on the other side of the highway. We're going for *Cascade Mall*, that's where Borealis is located, *Cascade Mall*. Got it? Good. Now, go!"

Blake sprinted away. The aliens were about to drop from the sky in battle, leaving little time for the teens to take cover. Blake could hear the pounding footsteps of his friends behind him, their breath cold and raspy. By this time Blake was completely numb. He couldn't feel his legs or arms or anything. At least he could move. The trio slid across the icy road, dodging debris and sharp ice. There was a humming above, the chant of enemy warriors.

"Faster! They're preparing to drop!" Giving it all they had, the three boys exited the wood and hit Cascade Mall's parking lot hard. Directed by Blake, all three boys pushed through the doors, racing to the tall column of portals which would directly access Borealis. A high pitched sound accompanied them as they entered. But things were different, very different.

Finally, guys, we're safe now, you can just feel it... it...I think, but for some reason, it's cold… and bitter. Feel it? I promise you it wasn't like this before, explained Blake. "Let me go speak with Elra. Let her know we're safe."

Blake's soggy boots pushed into the rusty Borealian soil. The two boys followed. It hadn't rained in six months. This was a matter of course, since in Borealis, springtime was year-round, as it efficiently, like an unending high tide, pushed away all other seasons. Opposing this idyllic, a week ago unexpected rains had begun, producing low, bold menacing clouds, black with power, and an omnipresent fog, which muted everything.

What had normally come with each Borealian morning, brilliant sunlit meadows, amazing morphing color and textures, combined with the sweet fragrance of spring, now all were replaced with a pollution of depressing grey light filled with a presence unfamiliar in Borealis. This, added to the permeating rains and fog, quickly brought spirits down. Blake inhaled deeply, then coughed, as he expelled the acid air. Borealis had changed, completely. Blake's newfound world was under attack. He knew it with every fiber. *Forty days and forty nights* kept knocking on his thoughts. Except here, God was not orchestrating the rain to usher in a new beginning. It was something or someone else, and its motives were not good. Blake held the full weight of this as he pulled and stretched, taller and straighter.

"Gotta get out of this slump!" he thought. Slippery mangroves carefully surrounded the sleek low-slung structure just ahead. Blake, not thinking, breathed deeply to prepare for his meeting.

"How can we get beyond all of this? Is it possible to fight this? How?" he thought. "Everything's gone south and Borealis doesn't know what to do."

The rain pelted him forward to the entrance. As dual glass doors *wooshed* quietly behind him, music replaced the heaviness outside. Things quickly became lighter, although urgency remained in the air. The conference room, low lit, an ambiance of green streaked with brilliant white, awaited his arrival. Others had already gathered around an immense planning table. A holographic screen hovered, dead center, in their midst, its light bouncing off of their expectant faces.

A moderator spoke, "Blake, welcome. And your friends, as well! More than you could ever imagine, we need you and we need you now." Blake smiled, looking across the table at Elra.

"What can I do?" asked Blake.

"For one thing," said Elra, "you can remove your coat." Blake checked his jacket; it was dripping.

"It'll dry better over here!" advised Elra, now standing behind Blake, her arms extended to receive his wet attire. Gratefully, Blake passed his jacket to her.

"Our meeting will officially come to order," said the moderator. "Things have deteriorated since we last met, and we need to devise plans to combat the enemy and further our cause. Advancing the blessing of God, his peace, his love, is critical.

"God be praised!" the group replied.

"God be praised, yes, God..." the moderator paused, turning to an opened entry door into the room. A tall lithe figure stood there.

"You think you've got the answers, do you?" sneered Mordna. She sashayed over to Blake, running her index finger along his wide shoulders, curling her lip as if to say more.

"Empress, you were not invited to join our..." explained the moderator.

"Ridiculous patter, servant! You think you and your cretins, your sweet sold-out-to-God crew hold any power over my smallest wish?" Mordna laughed.

She spun around, pointing at the group. "You stupid wretched people, leaving Tridesicon, the home of your heart. How could you affront your Emperor Micron this way? Treason. That's what it is, treason! And for this you will die! At this moment my minions are fully gathered for battle! And we WILL crush you!"

*Be angry and do not sin; do not let the sun go down on your wrath, nor give place to the devil.*

**Ephesians 4:26 NKJV translation**

## CHAPTER 25: BLOOD

MORDNA STRETCHED HER HAND TO THE SKY AND MOUTHED
the chant of Tridesicon, calling the remainder of her army to formation.
Instantly, an inky blackness inserted itself through the Borealian sky,
puncturing, forcing its dark way across the golden orb, obliterating light
as it overtook. Anomaly in the universe, a rip upon Earth's stage, which

now admitted minions of robots to rain from the skies, like a swarm of locusts. Mordna rotated her face held high and her arms raised in victory. Her cackle struck fear into the hearts of all who heard her.

"Micron! Take care of Elra. I must lead my army to battle. Oh, and Blake," Mordna gestured to Blake, "Don't go far, my dear. You're next!" And with that, the Empress removed her royal outfit, revealing a second-skin assassin's suit, carefully crafted on Tridesicon. She pulled two daggers from each side and vaulted over a short cliff down to the sprawling village streets of Borealis. Hundreds of screams echoed from below. Blake stumbled to the edge and stuck his head over, wondering why his sword-wielding angels waited. Mordna was a literal killing machine. Like the monster she was, she jumped from body to body, not even stopping to touch ground, stabbing the good people multiple times, one of her favorite dalliances. Blake ran to the stairway that abruptly descended, but then saw Micron sprinting to Elra's headquarters. If an instant choice had to be made in the moment, then Blake would definitely choose to rescue Elra over killing Mordna! He grasped his weapon tighter, as he raced to beat Micron.

Blake's companions, Dawson and Zac, launched themselves from their Borealian tunnels, curious to see where Blake had gone amidst the horrific widespread destruction. Minions of robots had already landed, immediately taking lives. At first, they ducked into the complex of tunnels, which lead to deep hidden caves under the Borelian surface.

Zac stopped. "Hold on, Dawson. Blake's out there! We need to save him!"

"Man, this is out of our league, way beyond. We don't fight aliens. He does! He'll be fine, I think. We are the ones in danger."

"Dude, the people, they're dying. See that armory up there, on the opposite cliff? Lots of weapons there, I'm sure. It'd be easy to reach and get tons of weapons."

"We're not dying today. Armageddon has not laid claim on my life yet, and now you want to offer it up? Survival, man. Get it through your thick skull." yelled Dawson.

"No, I'm done running. First, it was my parents," Zac cried. "It's time to be a hero for once in my life."

"I joined Blake's first mission to defeat Tridesicon!" yelled Dawson. "Well, you know what happened? I nearly got killed. All of my friends died. It's a suicide mission. I wish you the best, Zac, but I refuse to die today, even for a good cause. So long."

Dawson then retreated into the nest of tunnels, momentarily escaping the intensifying battle. Zac was enraged by Dawson's betrayal, as he watched Dawson disappear into the dark.

"So long, Dawson."

Zac quickly went to business. His goal: *Get to the weaponry and kill bad guys.* Meanwhile, Blake was in pursuit of Micron. The alien moved elegantly, like the wind itself, overcoming obstacles and flexing his own outlandish parkour skills. Fortunately, Blake knew the land and the quickest way possible up to Elra, his love. Her headquarters had been carved high upon a sheer cliff, accessible only by its fiercely ascending side.

A sudden *epiphany* crowded his mind: "Finally, I get to exercise my ultimate dream!" Blake had always *fancied* riding on the back of a gilpin flyer, a giant bee of sorts, a hog-like creature that roamed about transporting objects here and there. One had just quickly buzzed by Blake up to its home nest for safety.

"Oh, no, you don't! Get back here!" Blake's hand missed the flyer's tail, but he then ran up the wall of a nearby hut and leaped off, landing perfectly on the gilipin's back. "All right, come on! Where's your boost spot?" Blake kicked around the creature's belly making it grunt, but finally hit its turbo spot, igniting it to go many times faster. Blake rocketed up the side of the cliff and steered it to Elra's headquarters. He could see Micron, laboring upward, with his bare hands, rock climbing the vertical cliff. Blake grabbed his metal mashers once again, activating them, and steered the flyer further up the steep face.

"All right, buddy, once I hit the man climbing the cliff in the face, come and catch me before I die!" The creature grunted, and Blake slipped off with a deep breath. He was now entirely acquainted with free fall and its accompanying adrenaline rush. It was grafted into his DNA so much, it had become a part of him, a reservoir of hope. Micron didn't see Blake plummeting from the sky above until Blake tackled him. The force of Blake's attack was too powerful for Micron's iron hands to bear and soon both tumbled into free fall. In between glimpses of the swirling world around him, Blake saw the gilpin charging through the air to catch its temporary master. Soon Blake felt his back sink into the soft plush skin of the gilpin, but then in rebound bounced off and fell down the remaining distance, which was a mere ten feet. He rapidly recovered from his fall and stood to face Micron's annihilation. But then the attack went wrong, dreadfully wrong, when the gilpin accidentally saved Micron, who with Blake had bounced off its back, landing on the red soil, alive.

"Curse that creature." Blake whirled about as Micron lurched forward toward him. It was now or never. Blake knew this with every cell of his being.

"You have caused me much pain, you monster!" Blake kicked Micron twice. He raised the dazed emperor from the ground and dropped him down, slamming his knee into the king's face. Instantly, Micron's glasses of dark matter shattered. It blinded him at first, but then he began to embrace it. Shocked, Micron was stunned, gasping at the glorious though clouded Borealian light which surrounded him. Blake picked up on this, nodding his head. The light was somehow working inside Micron's heart!

 "Micron, please end this. End this now. Look, look at all of this! See?" Blake threw his arms out, exasperated. "So much ruin, destruction, pain, death. You can end this. You can call it off."

Micon remained silent, head bent down.

"Hey, Micron, listen, there is still hope for you." Micron's eyes brimmed with tears as he stared at Blake.

"Micron, you can still be redeemed. There is still time; come back to the Light, to King Jesus. Embrace Him, embrace your Heavenly Father that you once knew. Resist the darkness and all that Mordna has done. It all comes down to a single choice, and it's all up to you, Micron. You can be the hero; you can stop this! Here and now! Just embrace God's Light, embrace the Lord. Embrace Him."

Blake's final words broke into Micron's darkness, igniting his heart. It flickered at first, then spread, burning at his darkness with brilliant light, the Light of the Holy Spirit.

"Blake Armstrong, I accept the Light. I receive Jesus as my Lord again. Heavenly Father, forgive me!" Micron, sobbing, now laid his face on the Borealian soil, worshipping the Lord.

"He's saved! Oh, God, he's saved!" Blake gasped.

"Curse you, Blake Armstrong!" Mordna wheeled from behind, kicking Blake to his knees. She quickly removed her knife from its holster and deftly drove her weapon through Micron's skull. The ground was sprayed in red spatter. Micron was dead. Blake jumped away, not expecting that Mordna would kill her husband. Then Blake felt the tip of her knife at the back of his own head.

"You're too late, Mordna. He accepted the Light seconds before you killed him." Blake shouted with as much control in his voice as possible.

"Oh, I know, Blake. You made him betray me! You fool, do you know what you've unleashed?"

Borealis trembled. Earth trembled. An instant made eternal. Time was morphing, no, ending somehow, twisting back upon itself, laboring, light becoming dark, dark to light, color to monotone, returning to brilliance. At first a whimper, then glorious proclamation. In counterpoint, millions of souls pleaded for redemption, stretching out, repenting, worshipping. Borealis was now blending, its canopies, its skies and forests, walkways and citizens, melting, morphing, fading beyond what had become newly familiar to Blake, and was now pointing beyond itself, through its walls, through *Cascade Mall* to earth now crushed in Armageddon's killing fist: Judgment's bloody river ways, frogs, pestilences, hail, fire, thunder, locusts, plagues, darkness, the death of firstborns, erased. The story now was rolling forward, yes, Exodus to Revelation. This had happened before, an archetype among different people, pointing to the future, but essentially the same story. Now as her robot minions joined by hell's demons continued to rain down in furious battle, all had suddenly changed. It was more than war now, more than knives, killing spirits, and Mordna having her way. Evil was being put to its final test, dead in its tracks, prepared for its ultimate home, an eternal Lake of Fire!

257

Lord God, Creator, Redeemer, Sustainer, with legions of repenting souls stood in magnificent overwhelming victory! But time was twisting, and all was not over.

To the uninitiated, three boxes, precariously fallen to the ground at Blake's feet, would seem quite ordinary. Most people would simply walk on. Perhaps it was the way the boxes lay there, forming a geometrical *Rorschach* of sorts, for if one stood long enough to scan the ordinary presence of three boxes on the ground, the carefully positioned three, a curious triangular space between them could be observed, revealing a dark earth brown backdrop against which the boxes were positioned. Grinning, in an instant, Blake knew precisely what was about to happen! The dark triangle began to fill with light, its pinpoints of brilliance immediately igniting Blake's face! The Trigon slowly spun towards Blake. Time stood impotent and halted as a blazing light engulfed Blake.

"In God we have redemption through His blood, the forgiveness of our trespasses, according to the riches of His grace." Trigon's words came forth in power, wrapped in love, in saving grace, more than spoken words, but words which now hit Blake's heart, filling him, opening him to more possibilities, to a victory that he could never have imagined. The words came not audibly but in textures, layers that began to heal, to empower, to warm, and to assure. As Blake fell to the ground, more comforting words gained entry.

"Every good gift and every perfect gift is from above, coming down from the Father of lights with whom there is no variation or shadow due to change." Somehow time was no longer in charge; it remained halted, silent!

As Trigon's bold words, laser-like, pierced with precision, the trembling air surrounded Blake like a living cocoon. "Why me? Why me?" Blake cried.

*"Blessed be the Lord your God, who has delighted in you! What no eye has seen, nor ear heard, nor the heart of man imagined, what God has prepared for those who love him, these things I reveal to you through my Spirit. Receive not the spirit of the world, Blake, but my Spirit. Begin to understand what I impart. Be strong, dear Blake. You are not alone. You never have been. You never will be. Remember, the darkest hour always comes just before dawn."*

Trigon's words slowly echoed to silence, overtaken by time shaking into measured activation. The battle had permission to continue.

"It was Micron who betrayed you, Mordna, his choice alone." Blake spoke with more confidence. Mordna lunged forward, cutting Blake's cheek. He barely flinched.

"I have had enough toying with you, boy! I have won this war, this ridiculous Borealis, but you have cost me much. My husband, my little Geo, even the Trigon! And where is it now? I will tear your world apart. I will find it, Blake, oh, yes, it will be found." Before the screaming Empress, Blake stood in utter contempt.

"Well, I've had enough of this!" she screamed. "It's time for you to die. Soldiers, bind him!" Eight robots obeyed her command and bound Blake's arms and legs with a sharp, black, snake-like rope.

"Put him in Micron's chamber. We shall show him all that he has lost in this great war. Pain shall be his only companion as he dies!"

Swiftly, Blake was lifted and carried to an awaiting circle of council where a slab of frozen Tridesicon rock lay in the middle of the room. Mordna was well prepared.

"Shackle him to the poles, my minions. Keep him standing. And you there, Code 9345, tell the other soldiers to gather 'round." The soldiers obeyed their *general* perfectly, once again, and Blake was bound in chains in between two posts. He stood there, hating Mordna.

"Now, just before you die, I want you to understand something. You and your *goody two-shoe* acts, saving friends, fighting for the higher moral ground. What a joke. Do you realize whose blood is on your hands? Let me tell you, everybody that you've ever loved, their blood is on your hands, Blake Armstrong. Yours, and just so you fully understand the gravity of what I am saying, we're just getting started!"

She prattled on and on. With digging claws Mordna grasped Blake's forehead. He slumped between the posts. A cold desolation he had never known now emptied itself into Blake, poisoning him, as Mordna whispered her coiling and alien words. Bitter flashbacks, anything, everything that had ever gone wrong in Blake, conversations, decisions, worries, hurts, all these and more, knife-like, jabbed at his soul: the destruction of KidzTurf, the demise of dear friends, but most of all his parents' hideous death, more vividly filled him, now slashed him in pieces, pulling him apart, as her words vomited curse after curse upon him.

Every horrific memory now raced through Blake in loops, replaying faster and faster, growing chaotic in its evil majesty.

Blake's head swelled in terrifying grief, a bomb *ticking* to explode. Suddenly, all memories dissolved into crushing blackness. It was then that Blake experienced the darkest moment of his soul. He buckled under the weight. Yet, somewhere Trigon's assurance remained alive somewhere in him, now only a spark, but life ready to bud once again!

"Lord, help me." Blake cried out with all he could muster, as he awakened beyond Mordna's black terror.

Like the sun on one's back following a bitter winter, Trigon's assurance fell upon him: "The darkest hour always comes just before dawn." This assurance ignited Blake. Mordna could sense a change. Repelled, she quickly moved from her victim.

"In my kingdom, Blake Armstrong, you will know lasting darkness, but first things first, you must enter through death's threshold! Mordna ordered. "Minons, submit! Let his last sight be that of the Utter Chaos! Minions, take him to the cliff's edge. Have him overlook the city."

Through the destroying darkness, obedient robots mercilessly dragged Blake, pushing his face toward the *Chaos*. The *sentients* pounded his shoulders, forcing Blake to his knees to look upon the hideous terror of Armageddon. Smoke wretched upward, projected from miles of twisted girders and fallen constructions. It curled upward quickly, high above thousands of bodies, which were strewn everywhere, fallen warriors for the cause of Christ. Heroes whose hearts had fully loved the Lord and were willing to advance against evil no matter what the cost, against Mordna, her might and minions! Yet, Armageddon had only begun.

"I believe you now understand all that you've caused, and I give you my royal permission to die." she laughed. Mordna released her dagger from its holster as she leapt into the air, spiraling with precision, then landing, ready to finish off Blake. Mordna deftly aimed her jagged dagger at her bullseye, Blake's bloody head. She halted in echoing precision. Frozen in time, morphing in upon itself, her knife moved no closer, not one hair closer.

"Impossible." she breathed, frozen. Blake looked up. Brilliance was overtaking the Borealian sky, and beyond.

The King's voice resounded from above, commanding all to full alert, "I have returned!"

Some supposed it to be thunder; others clearly heard.

*"And I, upon my Holy Mountain, the Lord of Hosts, will swallow up the veil that is now spread over all nations. Yes, I will swallow up death forever. I, Lord God, will wipe away tears from all faces, and the reproach of my people I will take away from all the earth. I have spoken! You will say 'Behold, this is our God; we have waited for him, that he might save us. This is the Lord; we have waited for him; let us be glad and rejoice in his salvation!'"*

*Death is swallowed up in victory!*

**1 Corinthians 15:54 NKJV translation**

## CHAPTER 26: REDEEM

AND THERE IT WAS! NO ONE COULD HAVE PLANNED IT, NOT fully anyway, not even with the brilliance of Oskar and his equations. Time's time was over, almost. Eternity waited in the wings, as Almighty God moved to His Battle Podium. His orchestrated time had just pulled up to the corner. Holy Messiah, Alpha-Omega, I AM now simply stood in place, perfectly battle-ready, more than a military five star general, but a soldier's divine *conductor* about to tap his baton. The overture of *Armageddon's Battle: the End of Days* was about to begin. Its music as never played before, would produce notes, passionate maneuvers, and salvation's ultimate victory, which, birthed in the very heart of God, would redesign creation and fulfill human destiny, making everything new once again, even on Tridesicon, Uxtal and especially Borealis, but first a holy battle more valiant, more bloody, more fierce than imagination could ever conceive, had to take place. It was time. Finally. In victory, all believers would ultimately be delivered!

And for now, BATTLEFIELD ARMAGEDDON, opened its field for more battle, trembling *as its borders* melted into the distant horizon before Blake! Another war of horror, more fearsome than jets torn from the sky, was congealing a confluence of hell's demons and Micron's robots ready to drop into hideous formation. The time was finally at hand and God's battle plan was now fully in place. Opposing the enemy stood Blake surrounded by sword-wielding angels. There came a heavy silence.

Suddenly, a blue *grid* shot across the sky! A cube of luminescent *crisscrossings* excelling *New Jerusalem* proportions provided an intricate network of tracings to track each descending enemy, demon and robot alike! Oskar's blueprint, fully engaged, would reveal the enemy's precise location, direction and evil intent. And into the pending battle as the air grew hot and dark with Evil's stain there finally came Blake's beloved Trigon! Joining Oskar's luminescent grid in the diminishing light, Trigon moved in the royal battle as God's banner to carry forward in battle, a tower of cloud by day, of fire by night. God would lead Blake and all His faithful soldiers of earth, Uxtal and of Borealis, Tridesicon's remnant of believers.

Light against dark. Day against night. Good against evil. The beginning of the end. Mordna screamed at the skies and instructed her army, "Gather around, minions, this is now the real fight.

264

Armageddon's Last Battle. It is time to obliterate the King and His Light!"

"What if I double my efforts to the death?" Blake wondered. "I pledged my allegiance to the Lord long ago; it's my duty to fight alongside Him. I know this and I am honored to be in His Battle. I can't draw back at all in any way, not when the battle rages so, no, not ever! Whatever the outcome, life or death, I with everything I am or ever will be will fight to the death for His victory!"

"Yes, Blake! Yes!" came a commanding voice with authority, emanating from one familiar with Spirit-driven military maneuvers, accustomed to the profound war-like interplay of light and dark, and more, Yes, a rush of mighty wind in its sails, its voice, its heart, a *Ruah* of sorts, tumbling in brilliant, vibrant waters which now rushed into Blake's heart, wave upon building wave. Not audible sound exactly, more heart to heart, now mounted up on eagle's wings, a swirling of tiny lights, planets in their courses, growing in luminosity, now intensified before Blake's widening eyes. "All will be well, Blake. You are on the right course. God is with you!" With this, the Trigon swirled upward in divine mission toward a pollution of enemies in the sky who now fell in furious descent.

Blake picked up a *Sallaekor* Rifle. He aimed his gun at the sky, as he peered into his scope, locking on to one of the descending black creatures. He shot off round after round, hitting his target in critical spots, but his laser offense was sluggish. One robot finally fell away, tumbling over at Blake's assault. Somehow hell's demons were easier to defeat and Oskar's GRD made victory easier, target by target. Blake was ready to start on another descending enemy, when a crash came from behind.

A robot lunged at Blake. Its fist drove straight into the teenager's chest. And, yet, Blake hardly moved. Both were equally confused, but Blake was the first to react, and swung the butt of his gun up the robot's chin. The soldier was instantly immobilized. Blake stood there in shock, staring at the robot's neck, which now emitted blue sparks. Blake felt invincible. He was stronger. Stronger than he had ever been. Blake spun in a 360-degree turn, a clever dance-like maneuver. He was surrounded. Enemy *rain* had arrived, as devils and warrior angels battled on the ground. Each golden warrior wielded a sword of gleaming fire, which deftly sliced at the metal machines and soft-tissued demons.

Blake's jaw dropped. Angels now in fervent battle, flipped and teamed up, contriving intricate *parkour* moves with their swords. They were the true definition of warriors. In almost no time at all, coteries of robots and demons lay dead upon thousands of rooftops, utterly destroyed.

The golden warriors encircled Blake. "Greetings, loyal one. The King is very pleased with your work. Keep strong and help us fight. The long war has almost come to a close. The Lord's army is about to rise up." announced a tall angel.

"What do you mean?" Blake asked.

"All in due time!" the angel advised, turning away.

"NOW!" The land shook at the King's command, coming from the highest point in the valley.

"Sons and daughters of mine, awake from your slumber! It is time to end the Darkness once and for all!"

Blake looked around, astonished in mighty witness. His fallen friends, the good Borealians and those of earth, now flashed with light. Wounds were now completely healed, life restored, and souls had become flawless, all eyes opened.

Redeemed, one by one, they rose from the dirt and stood tall, glowing in the likeness of angelic warriors.

They all looked to the Lord and then roared a battle cry, "For our Master!" and charged the remaining enemy. Blake wept for joy. All was being restored. He shook as an arc of white light filled his body. His veins pulsed with a new kind of energy. He felt all of the wickedness inside his heart ball up and burn in the light, and then it was gone. He was new, completely new. His eyes popped alive and burned with the same fire that the angels and born-again Borealians possessed. He looked at his body and saw sheer brightness. Now fully alive, he jumped off a nearby building and tackled a robot in mid-air. He gave it a hug and the robot crushed into a crumpled mess.

Blake then knew that he had truly become one of the Lord's warriors.

He, like them, was now invincible. He ran down the streets and kicked and punched alongside his fellow fighters, destroying evil by evil. The Lord's army was winning. Mordna's soldiers were dropping like flies and the Empress herself retreated to high ground. She leapt fifty feet into the air and perched herself on a small ledge on the cliff but then looked up at God himself, the King of kings, towering over her on the highest point of the valley, atop the temple's steeple, His robe whipping to the side in the strong morning wind. Mordna, or was it Lucifer, leapt from perch to perch away from her enemy to the center of town. Blake bolted toward her. She was gazing back at the steeple where the King hadn't moved.

Blake tackled her from behind. But before she hit the ground, she began her assassin moves, slipping out of Blake's arms, then back flipped behind him. Blake fell flat, and the Empress drove her hidden blades into Blake's side.

"Stupid lady, can you not yet tell? Death no longer has its hold on me." Blake clutched her wrists, stood up and kneed her in the face.

"One of the perks of being saved and in the Lord's favor."

"Curse you, Blake Armstrong, curse you! I will break upon Heaven, where I once lived, just like I easily broke into Borealis. I will find you and drag you to hell, along with your King!" she spat. "To hell with all of you!"

Mordna ran across the field to where the King stood before her. A thunderous landing echoed through the valley and He rose to His royal feet in magnificence. Mordna had to look up to the King, and whimpered a little.

"How dare you." the Lord said quietly, shaking in righteous anger. "You have built this army of wickedness to pollute my creation and make it your own. You think this realm is yours in any way? Never! How dare you."

Mordna then gazed upon the King's beautiful face with fierce loathing, hatred in her widening eyes, as she moved to attack her royal enemy. Mordna's outstretched arms held daggers and her mouth, wide open, was ready to eat Him alive.

But the King ducked. He grabbed the Empress by her ankle and slammed her to the ground. He drew his face up to hers and the two locked eyes. "Not now! Not ever again!" commanded the resolute King. For the first time, Mordna felt pure, utter fear. And, here, in this moment, it was more than an Empress defending her power, her realm. It was Lucifer himself! The King knew this as he vigorously pinned his once Angel of Light, now become His loathsome enemy!

"Be gone with you!" the Lord whispered. Instantly, sulfuric ground beneath opened, pulling her into its depths.

"No! You can't do this, I was once your favorite! No, no! Curse you! Curse you!" Mordna screamed.

Time, one last twist, was ending, collapsing. Sheep and Goats. Division. Separation. It was happening in layers. Some had already fallen helplessly away, choosing darkness forever. The King stood, looking down upon the bottomless pit as Mordna fell helplessly into its gaping mouth. Unbelievers now screamed in trembling terror from the blazing pit, as *Lucifer* fell deeper and deeper, plummeting into forever darkness, an eternally defeated sovereign now to be crushed in the hateful embrace of his obedient multitudes.

"Goodbye, Lucifer." He said as the Lake of Fire closed itself, leaving only a thick rusty Borealian cover.

In triumph, the Lord thundered, "It is finished!"

Crowds of angels and risen warriors, including Blake, cheered and whooped in victory. The Lord began to laugh out loud, a deep, hearty laugh. It lasted a few seconds but then He stopped and said, "My children, there is still more work to do before we celebrate." The victorious King then deftly rose into the air, into the arching of its brilliance.

"Follow me." He said at last, as He disappeared into the Light.

It was all unbelievable. Blake stood in the midst of the world's largest crowd, well, in fact, it actually was the world in one room. Billions upon billions of people stood in enormous court. A massive throne awaited its Master. Blake fidgeted. He knew in his heart that he was saved and that he was one of God's army, but nevertheless this was no easy matter. It was one of the biggest moments Blake's soul could have ever possibly witnessed. Just to be here was incredible. Life on earth was limited, vintage TV. This new kingdom, however, shone forth in 5K brilliance, dazzling. All was amazing as billions upon billions awaited the King. "Earth has been a virus," thought Blake, "a virus now replaced with vibrant health, pulsing stronger, more alive than ever. His senses were now amplifying; time no longer existed. It was almost too much to handle.

As Trinity made its way to the Holy Throne, first Father, then his Son, then Holy Spirit, One in Three, Three in One, all bowed, falling upon the floor in worship. In an instant, the twinkling of an eye, one by one multitudes were called forward, invited to judgment. Instantly, they sputtered every wrongdoing they had ever done, every careless word they had ever spoken, every wretched decision and action, from the heart, some repenting, some not.

The Lord looked upon His creation, those who had already fallen into the pit and those who now stood before Him. "But did you accept me in your heart, into your life? Do you know me?" One by one, all hesitated forward to the King.

Some poor souls replied, "No, I did not." The Lord's eyes filled with tears and you could tell that He was hurt. He had lost a child. "Very well. You may stand to the left. The next may proceed."

One by one, each soul that God had created spoke for itself and claimed truthfully their heart. Many stood to the left. Some that Blake had known. Kids from school and church. He grieved as Dawson now answered the King.

Dawson cried, "No, Lord, I did not have a relationship with you. I did not love you!" And with that, Dawson stepped to the left. Blake mourned for his friend, for this was worse than death. It all happened so quickly. No time had passed, it seemed to Blake, but then he remembered, "Oh, right, there is no time anymore."

And then the Lord called out, "Blake Armstrong, step forward." Blake was terrified. He knelt before his King.

"Blake, look at me." Blake opened his eyes. The Lord's face was warm and kind, pure and righteous. The King's face calmed Blake, removing his fear and at once Blake spoke. He revealed instantly all of his wrongdoings.

"Lord, please, Lord, forgive me all of my sins! I am so sorry, I repent from the bottom of my heart!"

As Blake sobbed, the King paused, looking deeply into Blake's eyes, then said, "Blake Armstrong, I forgive you. Do you know me?"

"Yes, Lord, I know you; I love you. I always have. I know you very well." The Lord's eyes brimmed with tears. "You may now come to my side."

Blake walked to the King's right, joining a smaller group of people. Words cannot describe how Blake felt in that moment. All he knew was that he had been saved. The unending crowd of people had been split into two uneven groups, one on the left and one on the right. The Lord sighed, knowing what he must do.

He turned to his left and said to his creation, "I don't know you or where you came from. Away from me, all you evildoers! Where you will be going, there will be weeping and gnashing of teeth, unending regret. Your lives have asked for this; this is where your decisions have led you, a place of sorrow. You have earned this, to be eternally thrown out."

A group of angels then moved forward to encircle all unbelievers, to escort them away, down a winding path to the Lake of Fire.

"Goodbye, my children." the King said sorrowfully, and looked away.

"And now, my dear ones, to my right, this is our delight: New Jerusalem!" He arose from His throne, summoning full attention. Instantly, multitudes stood upon thousands of fertile rolling hills which led to God's shining land, bathed in eternal spring. Rivers happily ran as the trees clapped their hands. Creation in all of its glory moved in a new celebration, lifting its new song.

"Yes, I am making a new creation, a New Jerusalem!" said the King. All cheered as God unfolded His glory. Blake's mouth dropped as the joyous crowd danced about. Lord God directed all to witness the spectacle, the birthing of His new creation! There was earth, what it had been, its pollution, battle, and demise, the entire universe, galaxies, suns, and planets in their courses. To the right stood the glorious land of Borealis, Uxtal and further away Tridesicon.

"New Jerusalem!" the King commanded. The hills shifted, and His *creations* began to merge: Earth, Borealis, Tridesicon, redeemed, renewed, remolded, all of them, every star, every planet, every galaxy, each coming together somehow closer and closer, now merged as one as New Jerusalem slowly descended from Heaven's grasp to earth. Anything worn out, old and imperfect, was now wrapped in a *scroll* to be discarded forever. Soon, all of His creation would be one, galaxies intertwined within each other, completely new, as the Potter deftly worked upon His *spinning wheel*.

Blake stood amazed. He thought of Oskar and what he would say, "It's like Earth plus Borealis plus Uxtal plus Tridesicon plus galaxies and stars plus all of God's universe have become New Jerusalem!" Blake laughed, and then, awkwardly, he couldn't stop. His laughter grew louder and stronger and those around him cheered in joy's abundance. The King turned to His Loved Ones, and upon hearing their joyful laughter, smiled, joining the multitude in glorious celebration.

"Ah, my dearest children! I welcome you to NEW JERUSALEM!" God clapped the air and it was done. The final pieces were fitted together, and it was over. The end of hatred, wars, tears, and Eden's pain had come. Blake smiled. His new life unfolded in glory before him. It was time to start his everlasting chapter. It was time to go *home*.

*O Death, where is your sting? O Hades, where is your victory?*

**1 Corinthians 15:55 HCSB translation**

271

## CHAPTER 27: GLORY

BLAKE SLOWLY RELEASED THE WORN BIBLE ONTO his lap and looked up. His eyes were clear, as light flooded the room. For years, all had been submerged in a pollution of grey air, a humid closeness unlike anything he had ever experienced, and after generation upon generation, the boiling point had erupted in fury. But now the end had come. The battle was over, and all goats and sheep had been separated, each to his own destiny.

A textured reality, ever-deepening, continued to thrust upon Blake, through him, into the room, across the land, a new earth, a reality which drew him forward, his mind reeling, his heart pounding. He was buoyant, ready to float upward, to parkour back flips, to leap in pure joy. In this hour, this new life for Blake held an exquisite morphing of body, mind, and spirit which profoundly moved his heart.

Upon the edge of the brilliant morning now came a familiar face, his beloved Trigon, resplendent, turning in holy light. Blake closed his eyes, giving thanks, his heart pounding!

"Look deeper, Blake!" instructed the Trigon. "Look not to me, but beyond. Draw into His Heart, more than you ever have, for it is there you are now abiding forever. I have only been an instrument sent by Him!"

Love was filling Blake. Realities were tumbling together: Redwoods, Micron, KidzTurf, Derrek, Earth, Uxtal, Borealis and Elra. All were blending as one. The King was imparting knowledge, no, wisdom. A new paradigm. All of this, steeped in bold affirmation of life, now pointed Blake to a new understanding and celebration of everyone and everything. He was gaining *divine* perspective, a divine *parkour* of sorts; this reality continued to embrace him, as his heart beat faster.

The Trigon, warm and tender, remained in place, assuring: "Sing now! Be ablaze in God's Image!"

Trigon's words began to drift, to ebb, to separate into familiar *pinpoints of light*, as prayer rising, enfolding Blake in sheltering wings, uplifting, guiding.

"Sing! Rejoice! For from His Holy Mountain God said that one day you would sing: 'Behold, this is our God; we have waited for Him, that He might save us. This is the Lord; we have waited for Him; let us be glad and rejoice in His salvation!'"

The neutral-toned room accompanied Blake's musing, as *brightening* continued to morph. Sweet incense now embraced him as Trigon slowly merged upward into an enfolding utter *brilliance*: a swirling of color, thought, sound and resolve.

Blake laughed, "Incredible! Lord, it's You. It really is You, my King!"

The room continued to brighten. Blake's heart was lighter, lifted, filled. He had never known such love. Love was now filling every sinew, muscle, cell, thought, assuring him that not only were things all right, but were headed for Glory! Alpha and Omega had come. Blake knew this. He flew to the nearest window, throwing it open. Bending over its sill, he looked down, then over to a thick row of old oaks, then to the sky. Ever-brightening light was infusing everything, everywhere. Colors were intensifying. What had been green, or any of the *spectrum array*, was now vibrant, filled with inner light, somehow more real than real had ever been. Blake turned from his window, "It's all come to pass, just as God said!" He pushed his fist into the air and laughed.

Outside, music, faint, yet glorious music bent downward, upward, through his window, into the room. Voices now mixed and merged, laughed and loved, together as one. Blake turned to the open window. Below, far across the massive lawn, two figures made their way, running, towards the house.

"Blake, darling. My boy, my darling boy!" they cried. Blake, raised his hand to his mouth in joy, eyes widening, as he ran to the stairway, then out his front door.

Arms now raised, then reaching forward, hearts alive more than ever, parents and their boy Blake rushed in the unfurling resplendent glory to embrace. Across the lawn now came a joyous procession: Oskar, Summerlin, Elsa, Micron, Arboc and Elra, laughing, jumping, dancing. Alpha and Omega, Lamb of God, walked triumphantly before the long line of happy ones, further, ever forward toward Blake. The Shepherd called *Good* held something for him. The King now stepped forward, as the joyous crowd grew silent, one by one.

"For you, dear Blake. For you!" he smiled, lifting a golden crown upon Blake's head. "Well done, good and faithful servant! Well done!"

*And in the city, there is no need for the sun to light the day or moon the night because the resplendent glory of the Lord provides the city with warm, beautiful light and the Lamb illumines every corner of the New Jerusalem.*

**Revelation 21:23 The Voice translation**

*"I am the Alpha and the Omega—the beginning and the end," says the Lord God. "I am the one who is, who always was, and who is still to come—the Almighty One."*

**Revelation 22:13 The Voice translation**

About the Authors

## EVAN PRICKETT

Evan Prickett, 17, was raised in Orlando, Florida, along with three sisters and a younger brother, in a typically suburban Christian, home-schooling household. Writing has been a passion of his since Grade 3. Current interests include: running, soccer, cooking, movies, writing, architectural design, photography and biking. After college, he plans on kick starting a career in film, ranging from screen play writing to movie direction.

## RICK CHAMBERS

Ordained in 1967, Rick Chambers, known in Anglican circles as *Father Rick*, remains busier than ever, *fitting in here and there*, at New Covenant Anglican Church, Winter Springs, Florida. He and his wife, Jane, reside in Orlando, Florida, daily blessed by three children and seven grandkids.

After 40 years of parish ministry in the Episcopal Church, including several years as first Executive Director of House of Hope Orlando, a grassroots residential ministry for hurting teenagers, and later, principal of its Junior and Senior High Hope Academy, Rick Chambers brings much to the table. His passion for youth ministry and creative arts, coupled with Christian Education, graphic design and photography is infused with vibrant faith.